FREYA

AND THE

DRAGON EGG

BY
K.W. PENNDORF

Open Door Publications

To Sophia,
May your
adventures
keep you
writing!

KWPenndorf

Freya and the Dragon Egg
By K.W. Penndorf

Copyright © 2015 by K.W. Penndorf
ISBN: 978-0-9960985-4-0

Cover Design by Lisa Amowitz, LisaAmowitz.com

Published by
Open Door Publications
2113 Stackhouse Dr.
Yardley, PA 19067
www.OpenDoorPublications.com

For Jakob, Kim, Katja, Rebecca, and Natasja; thank you for being my real-life Viking inspiration.

And for my loving husband Benjamin who has always been my everlasting support.

Table of Contents

CHAPTER 1

THE OMEN BEGINS

a voice in the dark whispered, "It is time."

Off in the distance, a soft breeze strumming a gentle tune in the grass gasped. It bolted, shrieking and shrilling while dropping in temperature as if from fright.

Then all fell silent, and the heavy curtain of night opened.

Three sparks crept through. Glowing and shimmering like crystals of sea ice, they moved across the blackened sky. Streaks of light trailed behind them, stretching to keep up with the ever increasing speed of the sparks but fading quickly as if swallowed by the thickness of night.

The blue sparks journeyed on.

No stars were out; the sky was void of them. It was a sign—one of many.

Traveling in unison, the sparks hurried across the

darkness, then turned and suddenly descended, landing atop a raised slab of thick slate. The stone held them. Each little spark burned without a wick or wood to fuel their forms. Spitting and shooting the sparks twisted, shrinking in size, then twisted again, expanding and transforming into flames. Ready now, the blue fires flickered wildly.

Their once dim light strengthened with each flicker, allowing the light to crawl up the black veil of moonless sky. In its wake, a large oak tree took shape, its roots intricately weaving in and out of the earthen base.

The flames crackled and popped with intensity.

As the veil of night lifted past the trunk, a branch—weighted with might—slowly emerged. Then another and another.

Sparks flew from the flickering flames, growing the fires in number. The original three burst into six, then a dozen, a score, a hundred; all glowing in the same pale hue of blue arctic ice.

A smoky haze of cool turquoise cloaked the tree, casting light upon its eight massive branches. Time had plagued the limbs, growing them into grotesque forms of heavy twists and bends. The trunk, solid and strong, held the branches with ease as they went reaching outward like the snakes of Medusa's hair.

This was Yggdrasil.

In the grass, a lingering wind struck up with new life,

stirring the flames and rustling Yggdrasil's canopy of leaves.

"It is time," came the voice again. "She senses us now."

Twelve-year-old Freya, slumbering far away in her bed, shuddered, completely aware the voice was addressing her.

This was not the first evening these flames had haunted Freya's sleep. Indeed, they had shown themselves to her for the past several nights. But tonight was different. Tonight they spoke—to her.

As the flames continued to flicker, their tongue-like shapes morphed into the figures of bodiless faces. Noses materialized, sharp and angular. Mouths formed, gaping open and closed. And eyes appeared.

Freya shivered; her body sensed an approaching evil, though she didn't wake. She couldn't. It was as if the blue flames controlled her sleeping state. All she could do was watch.

The wild wind swept through the flames, banging their burning faces into one another but extinguishing none. As it breezed away into the night, the faces quickly turned their brooding eyes to the flame nearest the center.

This fire, in a commanding height taller than the rest, opened its jagged mouth. "The fate of the Nine Realms has been altered," it addressed them, its voice that of the one from earlier.

"Ancestors of the East." The flame speaking turned its eyes to the right side of the slate where several tiny sparks shot up into the sky. "Of the West." Flames now to the left began to flicker, causing their sharp angular features to lose shape. "Of the South." The talking flame spun around 180 degrees just as those of the roll call dipped into a low bow.

There was one remaining group to be announced. *North,* Freya could hear her mind thinking in her slumber even though she didn't know who or what these blue fires were.

Behind the flame that had spoken were a dozen of the fires spanning the length of the slate, not huddled into one unit like the other groups were doing. They didn't flicker, shoot sparks about, or bow. Nor did they wait to be introduced. Each mouth, without a signal or command given, opened in unison and declared as one, "Ancestors of the North."

Yggdrasil shook as if a forceful blast or stormy wind had swept through its branches. Freya's ears filled with a symphony of noises as the tree's mighty limbs creaked and cracked under the movement of its massive weight.

"This gathering has but one meaning."

"Our visions!"

"Each Norn—every Norn's…"

Words rose above the noise of the tree. Voices came from every direction atop the stone, from every group, every corner, East, West, North, and South, and from the flame nearest the center.

"A power is growing," it warned.

"But all too soon." It was a voice from the north.

"Time does not appear to a Norn's visions," clarified an eastern flame.

"Such knowledge, I already possess."

"Ancestral Norns, calm yourselves." Sparks from the west shot across the slate at them. Though all it did was stir up the rest of the blue flames.

"Our visions!"

"Our predictions!"

"The evil we foresaw!"

"She has not a forlansk!"

"The gift of sight…"

"The realms…"

"We must commence the summoning now!"

They all fell silent, and in a wave as one, they each looked up—staring directly into Freya's sleeping eyes.

"Yggdrasil," they said.

Freya shot up in bed, eyes searching her room. The visions replayed themselves, floating in and out of focus, their images burned onto her retinas. A blue light here, a blue light there. One was on her closet door. She turned her head from it. Brightly shining in her dresser mirror, it had followed her path of sight. She blinked it away. She blinked them all away, just as she had done each and every morning for the past several days.

The impression of talking flames weighed heavily on her brain. Any other twelve-year-old might wake and dismiss such vivid and strange dreams, but not Freya—not after the conversations she'd been having with her father.

Conversations, that is to say, that she wanted to have— she longed to have—if only he would invest time in her the way he did her two sisters. They were greedy, those two, bookending her in age and leaving her to never be the cleverest nor the cutest, which in her house were apparently the only characteristics needed to win the attention of her parents.

Well, save for one thing. Her father was the great Dr. Andersen, renowned Viking archaeologist, his passion being "all things Viking." The Aalborg Museum, where he had worked from the time before she was born, housed Denmark's largest collection of Viking Era artifacts and had her father to thank for them all. That is to say except for Yggdrasil. Dubbed "The Tree of Life," this thousand-year-old oak drew visitors from all over the world. Surely her father would find it interesting that night after night its image, though much more full of life than the decrepit version tourists pay to see today, was appearing in cryptic dreams to his middle child. Perhaps he would say, "Why, Freya, your dreams have given me an insight that my years of research never have. This summer I will forgo my annual dig with students and spend time discussing these dreams with you instead."

Or perhaps not.

She rolled over in bed and sighed. School had just let out,

which meant her father would be leaving soon for some remote location where he and his chosen team would unearth and excavate exciting artifacts for the museum. He was never *not* successful in finding something. Other families took trips abroad together; hers, however, took them apart. Freya reached into her nightstand and pulled out her journal, then began to write.

"'Yggdrasil.' Last night's dream was much like the others except this time those little blue flames turned into faces and could talk. 'Yggdrasil.' That's what they said. I don't know why they said it, but they seemed scared. I was scared. Here's the rest of what I remember:"

Freya scribbled on, getting every last vivid detail from her memory into written word. What she couldn't discuss at length with her father could at least be shared with her journal—even if it *was* an inanimate object. She loved her journal and filled it with everything from wishes and dreams to pictures and newspaper clippings. If it was filling up too fast, she'd glue in extra pages until the year came to an end; the year being her birthday year and not a calendar year. Each December 20th, at least for the past five of them, she received a new diary from her parents along with a matching pen, though she'd never managed to tell them she preferred pencil to ink. And each year she put to paper what failed to be put into conversation.

With her thoughts stored safely in her journal, she knew nothing could be forgotten once her father found time to discuss them with her. She opened the nightstand drawer and tucked her journal away underneath a warped scarf, her one and very lousy attempt at learning to crochet. As she closed the drawer a slow creaking noise of dry hinges sounded from across the room; there was no need to look up.

"Charlotte, go away, I'm writing." She could feel her seven-year-old kid sister's eyes prying into her room.

"Not any more you're not." Her voice muffled as she pressed her lips through the cracked opening of the door.

"Well, go away all the same." How Freya wished her parents would put locks on the girls' rooms.

Throwing off her blanket, she checked her alarm clock. It read eight thirty a.m. With a rumble from her stomach, she got up and went to the closet to change out of her pajamas. Her mother insisted pajamas go from body to hamper in order to help keep the house cleaner. It made no sense to Freya, but she wasn't going to bring up that argument again. Taped to the inside of her closet door was a cutout from *The Aalborg Stiftstidende,* an article with the headline, "Dr. Andersen to Take Local Students on Dig."

"If only you would have picked me," she said to it. Softly touching the newspaper's snapshot of her father, she then headed down for breakfast.

Freya made it down the stairs without slipping across

their wooden surface, but managed to knock over a perfectly fluffed and placed throw pillow from the sofa.

Swinging open the kitchen door, she was greeted at the threshold by a mouthwatering host of breakfast aromas. She inhaled the smell of sizzling bacon and the sweet scent of freshly baked carrot rolls.

"Wash your hands before you eat, dear."

The open door self-closed and bumped Freya in the face. No "Good morning," or "Did you sleep well?" Simply "Wash your hands." She wasn't sure what was worse: the greeting in a command-to-do-something form or the feeling of being pushed away—which the door hitting her in the face didn't help to soothe.

"Ahem," sounded in her ear followed by an elbow jab to her side.

Freya turned her head to see her older sister waiting to pass, her arms bent upwards like a doctor ready to be gloved for surgery.

"Could you get the door? I washed mine before coming downstairs." Susanne raised her hands slightly to indicate what it was she had washed as if Freya weren't clever enough to guess.

Rolling her eyes, Freya pushed the door out of her face and headed for the kitchen sink. She turned on the faucet, let it run for three seconds, then shut off the water and grabbed the hand towel.

"There, dear, you see? Washed hands drown germs." Her mother gave her an approving smile, then took a plate of bacon to the table.

The towel was dry, for Freya hadn't washed her hands as assumed. It wasn't an act of defiance; it never was. It was just that being a middle child meant being overlooked. And not getting caught pretending to wash her hands was proof of that.

She tossed the towel on the counter next to where her father's packed lunch bag sat.

"Mother, the summer science fair is August 21st. You signed me up for Discovery Science Camp again this year, didn't you?"

"Of course, Su-su, and your suitcase has already been pulled up from the basement for you."

"I hope this year there'll be an emphasis on botany. They hinted they'd be adding courses in the future, and I found forensics and human anatomy to be such a drag." Susanne helped herself to two slices of bacon and a carrot roll. She held the roll before her mouth, her eyes lost in a daydream. "I want to be the next Anders Dahl, Mother."

Mrs. Andersen bent and gently kissed the top of her eldest daughter's head before seating herself in one of the open chairs next to her. "But why be the next Anders Dahl, dear, when you can be the first Su-su Andersen?"

Susanne's eyes drifted further into dreamland. "Yeah."

"What about me, Mother? What am I going to be?" asked

Charlotte, bouncing into her lap.

Mrs. Andersen snuggled her tight, wrapping herself around her as if she were a giant gift bow and Charlotte a beloved present.

"Why you, my darling Charlotte, will be a princess, ruling over all the pretty ponies in the land."

"A hundred ponies?" the thought filled her eyes with a child's delight.

"A thousand."

Charlotte let out a gleeful giggle and hugged her back. Then she shot up in her arms and declared with excitement, "Do Freya, she's next! What will Freya be?"

The game, albeit a bit childish for Freya's taste, had captured her interest all the same, and she found herself frozen mid-step in anticipation of the response.

Charlotte's infectious smile had their mother grinning from ear to ear as she turned to face her middle daughter.

"Let's see, Freya will be..." but her expression went blank. There was silence. She had nothing.

Freya's heart sank.

"Oh, I know what Freya can be!" Charlotte blurted out, still caught up in the fun of the game. "She can be a storyteller!" From behind her back, she pulled out a book tucked under her shirt that had been held in place by her belt. She flipped open its cover and began to read from one of the pages. "'Yggdrasil.' Last night's dream was much like the others except this time those little blue flames turned into faces and could talk. 'Yggdrasil.' That's what they said."

"How dare you! That's my private journal!" Freya flew at her little sister to stop her from reading any further. She lunged for the book and snapped it from her sister's hands. Gripping it tightly she held it close against her chest. "Don't you ever read my things again! Not out loud, not in your head, not to me! You're nothing but a snoop—a spy! I hope your eyes fall out so you can never read my journal or anything else again!"

"Freya, that's uncalled for," her mother scolded. "Why don't you calm yourself down and run your father's lunch to him at the museum? He forgot it again. Then you can come back and apologize to your sister."

"Apologize?"

"Freya…"

Her mother's tone warned her not to push receiving a bigger punishment than running a lunch bag to her father. Freya took the hint. She grabbed the bag from the counter and stormed out the back door.

She went for her bike, stomping and kicking anything she could along the way. She whacked little twigs, bits of grass, and even the tops of her mother's prized chamomile plants—which surely would land her in even more trouble.

"Who cares," she mouthed off to herself, and kicked at the ground again.

"Ouch!" Something hard struck against the top of her shoe and her toe throbbed. She looked down and saw a rock, a dark grey round rock about the size of her hand and marked by three white stripes. She eyed it, then hobbled away to the shed in pain. She grabbed her bike and headed off for the museum.

Leaning forward in the saddle, her blond hair whipped in the wind as she picked up speed down a sloping hill. Being alone put her in her element, for if no one was there, then she couldn't be overlooked. Her speed increased. She whizzed by tree-lined fields, peddled through lifting fog, flew over Salt Creek's wooden bridge, and zipped by a cluster of old-style thatch-roofed houses. Next would come Dreaded Hill. She knew, as did every kid in town, that once the long stone wall border of the National Viking Graveyard came into view, it was decision time. Making it up Dreaded Hill required precision, exact timing, even mathematical calculations. Freya tossed all that aside and simply went for it. She refused to get halfway up the steep hill and be forced to walk her bike the rest of the way. A field of boulders stood off in the distance—the National Viking Graveyard. This was it. With her fingers on the gears, ready to shift them up, she pumped her legs the length of the stone wall border. Dreaded Hill was upon her. Her knees came closer to her chest.

Click.

One gear up.

The incline taunted her, its shallow slope letting her pick

up speed just before its gradient turned to a five percent rise. Freya forced her legs to pump harder. She peddled further even as gravity worked against her momentum. Halfway up the hill, she could feel the muscles in her thighs burning with exhaustion. The slope slanted steeper. She thought of having to apologize to Charlotte. Her blood boiled. Freya pushed the pedals harder, pretending they housed little images of precious baby Charlotte and her fallen out eyeballs. She grinned in delight at her imaginary backlash. The slow pace of the uphill workout caused her bike to wobble, but Freya didn't care— she had just ascended Dreaded Hill.

The view from the top of the hill had never looked so good. She paused for a moment to catch her breath and take in her accomplishment. The boulders in the graveyard looked so small. Sure, she'd seen them from this angle before, but never as the conqueror of Dreaded Hill. Today the hill, tomorrow who knows what! She could conquer it all! She could even tell her father about her weird dreams.

She set back off for the museum, crossed through the trees lining the parking lot, then, in a flash, her happiness was wiped away. Three police cars were parked askew next to the museum's entrance. Twirling round and round, the lights atop the cars reflected their blue hues off the museum's front doors, bouncing a kaleidoscope of colors into the air. Freya followed the display of lights and noticed her family's car parked nearby.

"Father."

Quickly she peddled for the museum doors.

A police officer stood outside, and waved for her to turn around. "The museum is closed," she heard him say. She ignored him, her sight fixed on the doors, nearing them with lightning speed. She watched the large silver door handles come into focus, then jumped off her bike mid-pedal, letting it crash into the front wall.

The officer wasn't thrilled. "I said the museum is closed today."

Freya puffed, out of breath, "I have to get in. My father's inside. He's Dr. Andersen."

A brow rose at the name, but the officer wouldn't budge. He just crossed his arms and shook his head no.

She tried thinking of a way to get past the policeman, but it involved him getting called away to duty somewhere else, and well, quite frankly, she couldn't think how to make that happen. She had no other ideas. Behind her a car door shut; she turned to look and saw exactly what she needed to get into the museum.

"Mr. Taberlig!"

Her father's partner was advancing in her direction.

Gripping a brown briefcase in one hand, Mr. Taberlig pointed his keys over his shoulder, locking the car behind him. He glanced at Freya, barely acknowledging her call. He was a young man, no more than thirty, and had worked with her father since the first day of his apprenticeship. Mr. Taberlig pulled his I.D. badge from his pants pocket as he approached the officer. "I work here," he explained, holding "here" noticeably longer than his other words.

As her father's colleague, Mr. Taberlig had been introduced to the girls many times. He spoke few words, yet when he did they were almost always connected somehow to Viking history, even more so than her father. Typically such conversations Freya found boring. But Mr. Taberlig had a distinct way of speaking, and Freya rather liked listening to him, making a game out of his trademark speech pattern. Nine times out of ten, whichever word he ended with he would hold the final sound for a considerable amount of time. Once he lingered on the final syllable for a count of eight seconds, his record best.

Today, though, Freya didn't count the seconds. She was more concerned about what the police were doing at the museum and why she couldn't get in to see her father.

The officer inspected the I.D. badge. There was a picture of Mr. Taberlig, wearing the same red and white striped bowtie as he had on now, and under his picture the officer read "Neil Taberlig, Archaeological Scientist of Viking Antiquities, National Museum of Aalborg." He handed the badge back and stepped aside, allowing Mr. Taberlig to enter.

"Wait, Mr. Taberlig," Freya called.

"Hmm?" he asked bending his head in her direction, his

frameless glasses drooping to the tip of his nose as he did so.

"I'm supposed to bring my father's lunch to him." She pointed to her backpack, and then added quietly, "But the officer won't let me in."

"Then neither shall I. I haven't time todaaaaay."

"Two seconds," she felt like snapping in his face for refusing to help her out.

She tried pleading once more. "Then what will Father eat today if I can't deliver his lunch to him?"

He hesitated in response, and at first she thought it meant he had reconsidered her request for help, but then she noticed that his lost-in-thought concentration wasn't meant for her but for her bike, or at least its vicinity. Freya looked over at the fallen bike and checked herself at what she saw. Lying next to the back tire was a dark grey rock with three white stripes. As she stared at it she couldn't help but wonder why Mr. Taberlig was staring at it too. He couldn't have possibly also kicked a similar rock earlier this morning. She looked at him.

Mr. Taberlig readjusted his grip on his briefcase. His eyes shifting slowly from the rock to Freya, then back again. Whatever he was thinking, he didn't share it with her. Instead, he only shot her down for a final time. "Today I have more important concerns to deal with than your father's lunch." He glanced once more at the rock, then turned and headed into the museum without her in tow.

Freya stood there perplexed. Didn't she just conquer

Dreaded Hill? She refused to be defeated in this, but what else was she to do? She turned for her bike and checked herself again. There lay the rock plain as day under her *front* tire. Hadn't the rock been lying next to the rear tire? she questioned her memory. Rocks can't move by themselves, but clearly this one appeared as if it had.

Ridiculous.

She walked over to it, bent down with her hand stretched toward the rock, but just as she went to pick it up, her fingers recoiled. What was she going to look for? she asked herself. Little legs on the underbelly? No thank you, too freaky. Instead, from within the side pocket of her backpack she pulled out a permanent marker, leaned down, and drew a thick magenta line right through the rock's three white stripes, then jabbed the marker into the ground next to the rock. "Try and trick me now," she warned the rock.

"What?" The officer's sharp tone told her he had heard exactly what she said, and of course understood it to mean him. He didn't look like he was willing to hear an explanation either.

Freya grabbed her handle bars and pulled the bike upright while watching the officer nod in agreement of her decision to leave.

BLIP PSSHH

"Officer Fisker. Come in, Officer Fisker," called a voice over a walkie talkie attached to the officer watching her take her leave.

"This is Officer Fisker." He quickly responded, squeezing the receiver at his shoulder.

BLIP PSSHH

"Can you bring in another box for the evidence bags?"

"I'm on it."

Determined to talk to her father now more than ever, she hopped on her bike, but not to head back home. She had an idea.

With his attention turned away from her, Freya bolted for the back of the museum, knowing full well the access code to the employee entrance.

Behind the museum and out of view from the officer was the prized old oak tree. It dated back to the Viking Era, and thus the museum owners affectionately named it "Yggdrasil," or the "Tree of Life" for those tourists not familiar with the mythology of the name. Unfortunately, Freya always felt the poor tree hadn't enough life left in it to warrant calling it Yggdrasil…that is, until today. It was this Yggdrasil that haunted her weird dreams. *Exactly* this one.

For as long as she could remember, the overgrown branches had always been supported by poles to keep the weight of the frail boughs from snapping in two. Once, during a storm four years ago, a pole was knocked away, leaving its branch severely split. The museum staff had been absolutely beside themselves.

"The tree surgeon is doing everything in his power to mend and preserve the branch," her father had rambled on for a week during dinner. "In the meantime new poles have been measured and cut for each bough."

And so they were, fitted, secured, and cradling the eight large decrepit branches.

Yet today, as Freya peddled passed the tree, why then were the branches swaying higher than their supporting poles?

Her bike slowed to a halt; perhaps it too was curious how such an old tree could suddenly bounce back to life.

"I'm worried for it," came a woman's voice.

Freya turned and caught sight of a pile of such bushy blond hair that it seemed to frame the owner's soft round face like a halo.

"Oh, Maren, I…I didn't know anyone was back here." Freya's eyes darted, checking for the possibility of police.

"Just me and my old friend." She motioned with her head toward the tree.

"I'd think you'd be excited to see it growing so strong." Freya knew she was excited to see no police back here. Freya liked Maren; she was nice. She also knew Maren wouldn't prevent her from entering the museum. "Is there a new groundskeeper working on the tree?"

Still gazing at the tree, the young woman took hold of the golden locket around her neck and began to rub it between her first and third fingers. "I fear precisely that."

Her response sent a wave of chills down Freya's spine. "Maren," her voice was full of earnest. "I have to see my father. There's something he must know."

No hesitation was made. Maren turned to the security box and swiped her I.D. badge, unlocking the employee door. Freya walked through and headed straight for her father's office.

It was a short distance to his office, and she found his door to be closed. She lifted her hand to knock, but somehow felt cold in the shadow of the dark wooden door. "Dreaded Hill," she told herself. Taking a deep breath, she forwent knocking and instead grabbed hold of the doorknob, then swung the door open wide.

"Oh, whoa!" Dr. Andersen spun around at the sound of her entrance. "Freya! What on earth are you doing here?" he asked, quickly placing his hands and the object in them behind his back. He ran to her and shut the door.

"You—you forgot your lunch." Fool, she told herself. *Tell him about your dream—about Yggdrasil and the flames.*

Her father said nothing.

She lowered her backpack to the floor, careful not to bump it against the seventh century enameled chest excavated just last summer, where in Norway she had forgotten. It was hard not to notice him staring at her backpack. Freya pushed the bag slightly to the left with her foot hoping he'd see the chest hadn't been harmed. His eyes followed the movement.

Unfortunately, as she did so, she also managed to splash coffee from the cup on his desk, which her hand was quick to wipe the spill away from a leather bound book titled *The Raedslen*. But somehow this he didn't even notice.

"I don't know what else to do. It's got to get out somehow. It can't stay here," she heard him say, more to himself than to her.

"What's got to get out?"

He kept his worried eyes on her bag. "Yggdrasil is changing." Again she felt he was talking more to himself than to her.

"About that. I know, I saw…"

"It's a sign of something bad."

A sign? Her dreams flooded her. She barely trusted herself to ask, "An omen?"

"Exactly."

"Father?" It was now or never. This was her Dreaded Hill chance to tell him about her dreams.

He raised his eyes to hers.

"Last night, well really for the past several nights, I…"

"We don't just believe Yggdrasil is some random ancient tree from the Viking Era; we believe it's *the* Yggdrasil."

"Come again?" He wasn't listening to her at all.

"The Vikings believed in the existence of Yggdrasil and the Nine Realms. They believed those things to be very real indeed. And now *I* have every reason to believe so as well."

22

"What are you talking about?"

"This shouldn't be here; it shouldn't have been found. Something of this magnitude should *never* be found."

"I don't under…"

"It can't be here. Not now."

"What can't?"

"Freya, I need your help."

Freya swallowed hard. He never needed anything from her, especially help.

"Sh…sure, of course. What do you want me to do?"

"Get rid of this." He pulled his hands from behind his back and produced an object no larger than her little pinky. The oval item was pale blue and made her think of the flames. On it were several dark blue patches as well as a solitary brown line zigzagging around one end.

Her eyes widened.

"It must be removed from the museum, and not by the burglars who stole from here last night." He placed the object inside a small box on his desk. "You must hurry. The police are due here any moment to question what I know about the break-in. If they search my office and find this…No! I don't even want to think about that. It must be hidden. Do you understand?"

She nodded yes, though she didn't understand at all.

"Yggdrasil is the link between the Nine Realms. That Yggdrasil, outside my window there, it's growing stronger because someone, or something, has tampered with the realms. Could you imagine if the realms were open in the modern day? If all the creatures, along with their powers, were unleashed…here?"

He was scaring her. "You're not making sense."

There was a knock at the door.

"Quickly, Freya!" He grabbed her backpack and shoved the box within it. "No one is to know you have this. Hide it where no one can find it, and tell no one of its location. Not even me!"

The knock sounded again. "Dr. Andersen? Dr. Andersen, it's the police. We'd like to have a word with you now."

Dr. Andersen raised a finger to his lip, "Tell no one!"

CHAPTER II

INTO THIN AIR

The door flung open and in barged Mrs. Iver, the museum's curator, followed by two tall policemen. Mrs. Iver was a stocky, middle-aged woman with nothing but business on her mind. It was she who kept the newspaper reporters well-fed with the latest information on Dr. Andersen's Viking findings. And it was their write-ups and interviews that kept the public's interest and money flowing into the museum. As she crossed the room to Dr. Andersen, quick to introduce the officers to him, she tossed Freya a look that said "beat it, kid!"

For the first time in her life, Freya was actually grateful for being shoved away. She took her leave promptly without any lip or hesitation. But as she turned to close the door behind her, she glanced over at her father whose eyes locked with hers. *Take care*, they almost seemed to say.

"Why?"

Their gaze broke. Both looked over at the officer who spoke.

"Do you suppose someone would want a, uh, an – oh what's the name of it again?" The lanky policeman flipped through his notepad. "A *ristir*?"

"Yes, you have that correct. R-I-S-T-I-R." There was a sense of urgency in Dr. Andersen's voice. And with that, Freya shut the door.

The corridor leading away from her father's office was dimly lit, not for lack of overhead lighting or bright bulbs, but rather from the magnitude of stacked boxes. Walking through this corridor was like walking through an overstuffed closet in desperate need of being cleaned out. Piled haphazardly upon each other in varying mismatched shapes and sizes were cardboard mailing tubes reaching out at those who attempted to pass, flat shipping containers that caught on unsuspecting ankles, lids that no longer fit the boxes they came with, bubble wrap old and popped, and unhoused artifacts, most likely too many for Freya to count. This was her father's lifework, well, at least what wasn't currently on display. In every box and container, shipped back to the museum from faraway excavation sites, were ornately forged sword hilts, welded iron blades, leather-bound wooden shields, carved steering oars, remnants of clothing, broken pieces of pottery, jewelry, combs, keys, you name it. If it dated from the Viking Era, it was here. Or soon would be. As a result, the newspapers affectionately referred to Dr. Andersen as the "Bloodhound of Archaeology" and once ran a story with the headline, "Nothing to Fear for the Vikings Are Here—Thanks to the Bloodhound of Archaeology." The article was clipped and pasted into Freya's journal.

Freya put her hand on the employee door at the end of the corridor, pushed it open, and entered.

"The Great Hall," she said under her breath, realizing her mistake for not leaving the way she'd come in. Police were everywhere, and they all took notice of Freya's sudden entrance.

Quickly she looked away from the officers' incriminating stares and kept her eyes low. That's when the idea came to her that perhaps looking away might make it more obvious. So she looked up and tried to smile slightly, but only slightly so as not to look too suspicious. She put a hand in her pocket—this had always made criminals in the movies look calm and collected—and wondered to herself if she should pucker her lips together and whistle something to help ward off any impression of thievery, but she couldn't think of any tunes. Then she did the next thing she could think of, which was to try and leave without being stopped or questioned.

Standing tall to build an air of confidence, she stepped

onto the marble floor of the Great Hall and proceeded to clear it as quickly, though not too quickly, as possible. She passed three orange cones, her curious eyes reading numbers eleven, twelve, and thirteen, marking an empty glass display case, a rusted double-edged sword, and a fragmented chain-mail tunic, respectively. To the left of her came a policeman from the Viking Antiquities Wing carrying two plastic evidence bags filled with iron arrowheads. She froze as he bee-lined toward her, her mind racing to find the right response to his forthcoming interrogation. Her father was her obvious alibi, but how to respond should the officer ask to search her bag? Unconsciously, she clenched the shoulder straps of her backpack, bracing herself for what was about to take place. Only what took place was the total disinterest in her or her bag. The officer walked right past her without giving her a second glance. That was her cue to hightail it out of there.

The Great Hall was large, though Freya had never noticed just how large until today. The entryway to the Tapestries Wing alone must have spread on for miles, making each step she strode toward the museum's front doors feel like an eternity. With one of the aisles displaying ancient tapestries finally behind her, her heart sank at the sight that there were still several more ridiculously wide aisles to go.

Nearing the halfway point, Freya overheard Maren discussing a large, dark-colored tapestry with one of the officers.

"This one? It's titled 'The Great War.' No, there are no signs of the intruder having harmed it. Thank goodness."

The officer jotted down her words.

Freya continued on through the Great Hall. Then out of nowhere came the officer who had denied her access into the museum.

"I told you the museum is closed today."

"Just leaving now," she flashed a shaky grin, then dashed for the doors. Slipping outside, she ran for her bike around back, jumped on it, and peddled across the parking lot with a newfound determination to secure a hiding place for the oval object.

Dreaded Hill was much quicker to get down than to get up, letting gravity pull her faster than she could pedal. Her mind raced in search of the perfect hiding place.

Somewhere where even Father couldn't find it.

Her bedroom? Nope. That was out knowing Charlotte was bound to snoop around and find it. The park? Too public. Her school? Same problem.

She pulled her feet up, placing them on the bike frame as she sped down the hill.

Mother's garden?

No. It was sure to get dug up next spring.

I need somewhere where no one can dig.

The hill leveled out, sending her bike to shoot across the

pavement alongside the stone wall border of the National Viking Graveyard.

Freya slammed hard on her hand brakes.

"It's protected." An excitement of inspiration filled her eyes.

Before her stood a hundred or more six-foot-tall boulders. These oversized rocks were not randomly scattered about, her father had taught the tour guides to explain. Rather, they had been placed by the Vikings in oblong formations to represent the shape of a burial boat. For those not honored with a sea burial, this was the next best thing. And today their thousand-year-old graves were protected. Protected against excavation, against research, against being dug up, against her Father finding whatever might be buried there. It was the perfect hiding place. And Freya knew exactly where to put the object.

Hopping off her bike she propped it against the stone wall and began scouring the landscape for the place to dig. The land was hilly, raising and lowering boulders like a carousel ride, but somewhere, just where the land dipped low, was a boulder in particular that Freya was searching for. It was a headstone, marked with an inscription. Although it looked like chicken scratch to her, the inscription's runes, or ancient alphabet of the Vikings as she had read in an interview with her father, were full of shapes similar to the letter B. Hardly any of the other runes bore much resemblance to her modern-day Danish alphabet, which was why she remembered it.

Having often played hide and seek amongst the boulders with her sisters, she'd come across the B-laden boulder several times and thus felt confident she could find it now.

Freya weaved around the grave sites, making sure not to step through any of the oval formations as the idea of walking on someone's grave repulsed her, especially a thousand-year-old someone.

Any boulder sitting on higher ground was ignored. Any boulder lining either side of the formation was also ignored as it was a headstone she was in search of. The first stone she came up to had one B, but no extras. The next had an inscription so severely worn by weather and the ages that Freya knew for certain it wasn't the one she wanted. Off to the next lowland. No Bs there. To the next, then the next. Freya bobbed up and down the hilly landside determined to find her boulder. Three more attempts and she finally found it. Tall, far bumpier than any others she had touched and searched, and in an evenly colored medium shade of grey, was a boulder with eight distinguishably marked B-shaped runes.

Freya grabbed a nearby stick, sturdy enough to dig with, then knelt down and got to work. She thought cleverly to chisel up the grass as one whole piece of sod. The effect she was hoping for was to have the hole go undetected by covering it with the sod instead of freshly dug up dirt. So she laid the grassy sod carefully on the ground next to her for safekeeping until its final use. Now it was time for some elbow grease. Surely the untouched earth, packed tightly over the years by the constant traipsing of tourists' feet, was bound to be more difficult to tunnel through than her mother's vegetable garden. She thought of running home for a shovel, but couldn't bring herself to leave the task she'd already begun.

Every so often she'd lay the stick down and place her hand in the depression, gauging its depth. The hole reached her knuckles; she burrowed on, then her wrist, on she went. With the hole now up to her elbow, she was ready to hide this peculiar oval thing. How she wished she could tell her father. It was a catch-22, really. To earn his praise she'd have to reveal its location for him to understand just how good the hiding place was. But of course if she told him, well, that would defeat the purpose of him asking her to hide it in the first place.

Freya removed her backpack and unfolded its flap. The box with the secret object seemed much too large for the tiny thing it housed. Too large for the hole she dug was more like it. The box had to go. She popped off its lid, and with her hand cupped she gently scooped up the object from within.

Knowing, as this was the best hiding place ever, that today would be the very last time anyone would ever gaze upon the object again, Freya paused. She wanted to remember this moment, to remember what the object looked like, to remember conquering Dreaded Hill, to remember how she had helped her father. She sat back leaning on her heels.

CRACK!

Freya twirled her head around and met Susanne's evil stare.

"I can't believe you dug! A hole! On protected land! Father's going to kill you!"

Fire swelled inside Freya. Her perfect hiding place was ruined.

Charlotte came bouncing into view, skipping over to her sisters from behind a distant boulder.

Oh, it all made sense now! Freya was fuming. That little twerp of a kid sister was always snooping into her business. It was no wonder she was found.

"You've tampered with a national treasure, Freya! Don't you know even Father isn't allowed to dig here?"

"Leave me alone, Susanne. You don't know what you're talking about," were the best fighting words Freya could think of, her mind distracted with having to find a new location for the object. "What are you even doing here anyway?"

"Well, seeing how it was taking you two hours to deliver Father's lunch, Mother sent us to come get you. When we saw your bike against the stone wall I said to Charlotte, 'Charlotte, I bet you she didn't even go see Father.' Somehow, someway I knew you pulled 'another Freya.' And I was right." Susanne glared at the hole, then at Freya.

The fire inside her burned even hotter now. "Stop saying I always pull 'another Freya!' And for your information, I did go see Father. But when he finds out what happened he's going to be angry with *you,* not me." Or so she hoped.

"What's in your hand?" Charlotte's voice was that of an angel's—full of innocence and utter goodness. Blah! A complete charade for time and time again she always drew attention to whatever it was that was going to set Freya off.

Freya didn't even look at Susanne; she already knew her hawk eyes had narrowed in on her hand.

"You're unbelievable, Freya. Whatever you dug up, you'd better give to Father…or else!"

"I didn't dig it up. And besides, he's not supposed to know where it is."

Susanne's eyes widened. "He doesn't know you have it. You little thief. Give it here." Susanne stuck out her arm, palm up, hand open, commanding to be given the item.

"No." Freya slapped away the hand.

"I *said,* give it here." She yanked at her sister's arm, gripping it tight.

Freya wriggled free and held the object high above her own head.

Susanne smiled at the sight. "Oh, please Freya, I'm taller than you."

But before Freya would allow Susanne to swipe at the

object once more, she pulled her hand out of the air and thrust the object into her mouth, swallowing it whole.

A loud rumble roared from Freya's stomach. Freya, Susanne, and Charlotte all froze at the sound.

This was not the noise of hunger; it was like the growling sounds of a beast trying to escape its cage. The sound came again, followed by another and another. As the noises grew so too did the sudden abdominal pain inside Freya.

She let out a scream of agony—her sisters stepped back in fear. Freya cried once more; then with her silhouette straightening just a bit, she looked straight into Susanne's eyes before everything went dark.

It was pitch black, and Freya was falling fast. She couldn't gauge at what speed she was descending, but she knew by the lashing effect of her hair as it whipped her in the face that she was torpedoing toward who knows where at an alarmingly quick rate.

As she fell, a flash of bright white light dazzled her eyes. In its brief second of illumination she thought she caught a glimpse of the smooth grey rock and its three white stripes, decorated with the magenta line she had given it.

The flash of light came again, burning her eyes with its brightness. She blinked hard, closing her eyelids to flush out the stinging sensation. When she opened her eyes again, she could see Yggdrasil and the blue flames. The flames shrunk and grew, blotching out the view of Yggdrasil with a haze of soft pale blue.

Twisting and stretching, the angular faces of the flames came into view. They were bright and clear as day, falling steadily with her in the void. The faces glanced at each other with expressions of worry.

"She has altered her Fate!" one of them shouted.

"It changes nothing!" argued another.

"Her gift of sight..."

"Aye, lo, she no longer acts for her true self alone..."

"She has answered the summoning. Does that not prove her worthy?"

"There is misadventure in her coming. Be it known she has answered a Raedslen!"

Gasps of horror pierced Freya's ears, and before she could blink, the flames extinguished into nothingness. With a sudden hard landing on solid ground, she stopped falling.

Freya rubbed her right thigh and peered above the tall grass she was lying in, the only thing aside from her thigh that helped to cushion her landing.

Above her was the setting sun, streaking shades of crimson all along the horizon and illuminating the land just enough for her to see that in front of her wasn't the Viking Graveyard or her sisters or for that matter anything she recognized. Instead, her eyes met a thick forest of very tall evergreens lining the field she was in. This forest was none

Freya had ever seen before.

Panic set in.

Was this the bad sign her father had mentioned to her?

Nonsense.

Her father wouldn't have given her the object if he knew what it could do to her. Would he?

But if he had known...would he know how to undo whatever it was that got done?

"Ridiculous." Freya stood up, snapping herself out of such wild imaginings. "I passed out from the pain is all. And stupid Su-su and Charlotte carried me off to this field as an evil, cruel joke. Well, they will surely pay for this when I get home." The forest was growing darker under the setting sun. "*When* I get home."

As she looked out across the field, she saw a stack of twigs advancing her way. They came bouncing, up and down, atop the tall grass.

Freya stooped low to the ground, just to be on the safe side, and waited for the stack of wood to pass.

There was movement in the grass below the stack. A rustling sound announcing the approach of the twigs swished faintly. It was coming closer. Freya held her breath. Swish, swish, swish. The faint noise grew louder. Whatever was moving was now very near. It was just upon her when all of a sudden Freya let out a boisterous hiccough.

"What noise is this?" called a voice from behind the stack. The wood fell to the ground, revealing a young girl no taller than Charlotte.

Freya stood up, pretending to have been tying her shoe, all the while feeling foolish for thinking twigs could move on their own. But when she looked again at the girl, she could hardly believe what she saw. Dressed in a long, pale yellow, linen tunic, with two round broaches clasping a brown cape to the girl's shoulders, Freya knew at once this was Viking attire.

The girl stared back in awe. "A warrior spirit," she breathed softly.

"Come again?"

As if Freya were a celebrity and the girl her biggest fan, she declared, "See how you dress—a style not known to me. You are no foe of mine."

"Foe?"

"Nay, the warrior spirits of Valhalla do my clansmen right to come here. Let our plunder be yours for the taking. Lo! I do beseech you, leave but the burnished cuff, as my wrist has *ever* so fancied its plating."

Was this girl insane? Freya wondered. Warrior spirits from Valhalla? Plunder? This was why she hated Viking festivals—they were always full of weirdos. Though she had to hand it to her sisters for finding a festival so early in the summer.

"Look, I'm just trying to get home, and I don't have any

mobile on me. Do you have one I could borrow?"

The girl looked puzzled by the request, as Freya unfortunately thought she would.

"Ok, I get it. Your parents signed you up for this festival so you wouldn't be bored this summer, but honestly I just want to go home. So if you're not willing to step out of character and lend me your phone, then at least point me in the direction out of here."

The girl's celebrity buzz slowly faded. "If not to Valhalla you wish to return, alas, I know not the direction you seek."

Freya rolled her eyes. "The 'direction I seek' is Aalborg. My city is Aalborg. I'm sure you've heard of it—the fourth largest city in Denmark?"

The girl shook her head.

"No, of course not, that would be too easy. I tell you what…is there an adult around I could talk to?" With an adult, she assumed, she'd be able to use the story of being a little lost twelve-year-old in search of her way home. At least adults were responsible enough to step out of character, not like this annoying little Charlotte impersonator who acted like she couldn't help.

"Lo! My father has fared both land and sea. If any, then surely he will know your thorpe. Come away. The honor is given to us to help a warrior spirit of Valhalla."

Freya rolled her eyes again, which was now becoming a

habit the longer she stayed in this girl's presence. "Look, you can drop the act. I'm not a warrior spirit and you know it."

The last lingering ray of excitement faded from her face. "One day then will I meet a warrior spirit come in collection of our offered plunder."

"Sure you will."

Quickly the girl's eyes lit up like a fireworks display. "Do you believe it to be true? Oh, happy a day when I shall don gear of war and raid in valor as those of yore."

"I'm not exactly sure your parents would be proud to have a kid who glorifies battle or stealing."

"Stealing? You do me wrong. Danelaw decrees the victor of battle all the belongings of the loser. Stealing is detestable, fit only for the wretched fool. I am a Viking and gladly take the sword, would I, to secure my place in the great Valhalla with all the warrior spirits."

"Whatever. I believe you said your father was around here somewhere?"

She nodded. "My thorpe is yonder." The girl pointed behind Freya.

Freya turned, and in the distance could make out several large brown mounds. She didn't see any gate or stone wall, or even any lights, but something surrounding the area was producing a golden hue.

The girl gathered up the wood and gestured Freya to follow her into the village.

The golden haze shone brighter the nearer they came, and finally Freya spied its source. Piled in heaps and mounds where the field met a farmed vegetable garden was anything and everything gold, as if someone had laid out all their valuable treasures. There were ornate goblets etched in various patterns, plates and bowls polished fine, pitchers both large and small, and jewelry, lots of it, all reflecting the sun's last rays. She'd never seen this in any other Viking festival before and wasn't quite sure what to make of it. It seemed a rather expensive display for tourists.

Freya followed in the girl's steps and was equally careful not to knock her foot against any of the golden objects as the two crossed over into the thorpe.

"How are you called?" the girl asked from behind the pile of twigs.

"You mean my name? It's Freya."

The girl paused mid-step and in a dramatic fashion much like Charlotte, she moaned, "Oh, many a morning have I lost by dreaming I possessed a strong Viking name such as yours. Nay, alas I wake to the odious name of Grimhild. The shame; how accursed." She picked up her pace and mood adding, "Be it known, I shall toil all my days skilling myself to the level of warrior until I glory in a new name such as Blacktooth or even Grimhild the Red, as befitting, for my red hair."

Freya would have disagreed about the name Grimhild but

that would have only started another conversation, which she wasn't looking to have with the girl, so she kept quiet.

Her silence made no difference though as Grimhild continued to chat on anyway about a new name she wanted to acquire and of her prospects of becoming a warrior.

Freya ignored her—it was easy, her mind now distracted by the authenticity of the thorpe. The smell alone from the livestock would have been distraction enough. She noted how the brown mounds weren't piles of dirt but rather homes made of dried mud and hardened straw. Their roofs were thatched and their walls had no windows, their doors all closed by a large piece of stretched animal hide. The museum had one such hut on display, but only one. Typically the Viking festivals had tents, many made from animal skins, but that's as far as they went. Never any mud huts. She had seen wooden pens for housing pigs and goats, though not this many. Here, each hut displayed two or three at least.

"So where's your father?" Freya asked as they rounded a hut and she had still yet to meet anyone other than Grimhild.

"In the back field *slaughtering* his opponent." Grimhild's eyes twinkled devilishly as she smiled at Freya.

Maybe that was festival talk for "cooking dinner" Freya hoped.

THWAP!

Freya looked in the direction of the noise.

A roar of excited cheers filled the air where she could

only assume was the back field. There was clapping and laughter as loud as thunder itself. The goats in the pen next to her bleated, spooked by the sudden noise. It had even spooked Freya.

"Father." Grimhild said, proudly weaving Freya further through her thorpe. "Always a winner at kubb."

"Kubb? My family plays that game." Of course they did; what a stupid thing for Freya to share. It was a Viking game after all, so naturally it's what her father would have them play. She should have recognized the sound of wooden batons hitting kubb blocks and just kept her mouth shut.

Grimhild led Freya around another hut as the clamor of sportsmanship was calming in the distance. There they came upon the center of the thorpe. Near a small campfire were several wooden tables, adorned with floral arrangements and covered with platters full of cheeses, meats, and breads, all set and ready for the hungry inhabitants of the thorpe to come and feast.

Grimhild dumped the kindling near the campfire. "Speak now of your Aalborg to my Father for this way he comes," she said, turning to Freya and pointing out a man dressed in a grey tunic and baggy burlap pants. He was a tall, burly man with hair as fire red as Grimhild's and whose demeanor was equally as jovial. Lit with the smile of a champion, he welcomed the celebratory claps on his back congratulating him in his kubb domination along with his teammates who all shared a drink with him from a horn-shaped goblet.

Freya scanned the group of Vikings. An uneasiness swept over her. The actors were too good, the food too rustic, and the clothing too primitively made. This was a *reenactment festival*...it had to be.

A young boy ran over to Grimhild's father, tugging on the man's sleeve. "A story, Uncle Harald, a story."

Harald's red-bearded face smiled even wider. "A story?" He ruffled the boy's hair. "Am I to be both skald *and* chieftain of Borg?"

The nephew nodded with an air of a child's command, proclaiming to his elder, "Aye!"

Harald chuckled at the boy. "Then I must oblige. Lo, strength and courage to you, Magnus, for a grimmer tale has not filled your ears."

The boy's eyes widened and remained so when he caught sight of Freya. Harald also took notice of her as did the pan piper who dropped the musical tune he was playing. The kids playing tag, the sword fighting boys, the flower binding girls, and the men and women all took notice of Freya who stood frozen near the fire in their sea of stares.

"Grimhild," Harald addressed his daughter. "You have brought us a guest."

Freya felt herself begin to tremble.

Grimhild wiped her hands of the kindling wood and threw

a hug around her father's waist. "Aye, Father. Here is Freya—lo, be it known she is *not* of Valhalla." She threw her father a look as if he too should be disappointed by the news. "She is of Aalborg and desires to make her return. Lo, she knows not the way. Know you the way, Father, for I have told her you know all the seas and roads of our lands and abroad."

He welcomed his daughter's embrace with a hug in return, but replied to her with an examining eye still on Freya. "Aalborg I confess is not known to me in my travels."

How could he not know of Aalborg? And why wouldn't he just step out of character? This wasn't a game. Freya's hand quivered uncontrollably in her jeans pocket, nervous he honestly wasn't going to help her. "Please. I'm twelve-years-old. My father is Dr. Andersen. I don't know what I'm doing here or how I got here. First I thought my sisters played a joke on me, but now I don't even care—I just want to go home. So if you're in on the joke could you please snap out of it? I'm having a hard time finding this funny."

Harald released Grimhild's embrace and stood tall. "I know of no joke, young Freya, nor of the sisters you speak. Lo, help you I shall."

His voice was earnest, and Freya believed him—that's what frightened her: that he actually didn't know of a joke, her sisters, or Aalborg. "But you can tell me how to get home?"

"Come away. Let us sup on this wondrous of feasts. You

are most welcomed as our guest. Share with me of your Aalborg for your speech and attire lead me to believe it lies indeed in foreign lands." She saw him nod to a man who then tapped two others, and the three of them set off away from the crowd, each in different directions.

Freya quickly picked up the serious tone of this action.

The man next to Harald exchanged glances with him. "The omen?" mouthed the man, but Harald gave no reply.

She fumbled for words, wishing she were dressed like them and spoke like them. Did he see her as a threat? *Was* Aalborg in a foreign land to wherever she was now? If it was, she certainly hoped Aalborg wasn't a rival of any kind to this thorpe.

Harald gestured her to share in the prepared foods, then took a seat himself next to the campfire. "Please, I beseech you, share with us of your Aalborg."

"Um, I—uh—" she faltered. So many people were watching and listening. She only hoped what she had to say would be well received. "Well, I'm from Aalborg. As, um, as I suppose I already said. And it's, well…well it's in Denmark." No one shifted uncomfortably at the mention of her country or gave her an evil glare. But did that mean they'd never heard of it either? "Is *this* Denmark? Here, I mean. Where we are now?" It was an awkward feeling not knowing what country one was in.

Harald smiled politely. "Aye, you are among your

kinfolk, the Danes."

She felt her shoulders relax.

"Uncle, let us hear of her tale after for you have promised us one yourself most grim," Magnus pleaded to Harald, then beckoned Freya and the others to take a seat.

Grimhild squeezed up close to Freya and handed her a pewter cup of something cold to drink as the other children began to gather near at Harald's feet. Then rather excitedly she clinked cups with Freya and said, "Tidings to you; for before we part will your ears merry make in a tale none can word so well as my dearest Father."

Several of the children shushed Grimhild, equally excited to hear Harald's gruesome story.

Harald leaned back, stroked the short braid in his bushy beard, and with narrowed eyes looked over each child. Then he slowly began. "Who among those here dare speak the name of the vilest beast known to Viking kind?"

A few of the older boys took the dare. "Berserk," they answered confidently.

Grimhild squeezed Freya's arm, pretending to be scared by the name. Freya didn't know what a Berserk was or how dangerous one could be, but she did wonder what type of warrior Grimhild would make if ever faced with one.

Harald shook his head, delighting at the boys' incorrect response. Then in one swoop of his mighty arm he pulled the smallest boy up on his lap and hugged him in mock protection. "A good guess was that indeed for a Berserk's bearskin form can slash the lives of an entire thorpe without shedding any blood of its own. Lo, take warning; this beast of which *I* speak harms deeper than a thousand Berserks. And unlike the mortal Berserk, this creature is not born of man."

Now even Freya was curious to learn what could be so horrible.

Grimhild leaned in closer, hanging on every word.

"Its given name…is 'Raedslen.'"

"Raedslen," whispered Grimhild.

"I'd slay one," yelled out one of the boys.

"Aye!" agreed the other boys and Grimhild too.

Harald smiled at the would-be-warriors. "Excellent, for the morrow will offer you the chance."

"Harald," spoke a woman with long blond braids. She placed her hand on his shoulder and said skeptically, "You would send your nephew to do battle against a Raedslen when he has yet to go raiding?"

He shrugged away her hand. "Dragon slaying builds skill necessary for raiding. Or do you desire to raise a hatchling in our thorpe?"

The woman shook her head.

"No. It is agreed. We will destroy the egg in sun's first light and stand guard awaiting the beastly mother come to weep the loss of her young. It is then shall my nephew witness the mastery of dragon slaying for which this clan is known."

Excitement filled the listeners, followed by a clamor of metal sounding in the distance. Immediately came a warning call of a deep-voiced man as he shouted, "BERSERK! Save yourselves!"

In a wave as one, the gathering jumped to their feet. Freya, not knowing what to do, was pushed, shoved, jarred, and shouldered as everyone scampered away in a mad rush for their huts. Freya didn't know where to go, who to follow. Nor had she seen in which direction Grimhild or Harald ran. Searching for a place to hide, a table caught her eye. Quickly, she flew under it and lay as still as she could on the dark ground.

The village was silent, save the crackling of the campfire.

It wasn't long before the figure of something furry came into her view. Against the light of the fire, Freya thought the Berserk to be nothing but a bear. Yet if that were so, then Harald's Vikings wouldn't be so fearful of it. Freya kept low, recalling his words that one Berserk could slay an entire thorpe.

The bear walked steadily, keeping a quick pace as if it was after something. Then it came to a golden bowl atop a neighboring table and paused. Freya shielded the fire from her eyes. Her view was good. She watched the bear reach into the bowl, and pick up a deep blue oval object with patchy light blue spots.

Freya did a double-take.

The bear placed the object in a side pocket of its fur, then turned from the bowl and headed back for the fields—with Freya following quietly behind.

THE BERSERK

The gap between the two of them grew, the bear having almost cleared the length of the field and Freya having only entered it. She managed her way over the ring of golden loot without knocking a single piece, sticking to her plan of going unnoticed.

The bear was less bulky or meaty compared to those she'd seen at the Aalborg Zoo; perhaps it was a cub, she thought. Of course she was no expert on the matter, but how odd that it seemed to move with purpose. Not once did she see it linger in the field, stopping to smell the air or ground. Instead, it headed straight for the forest. Freya stepped forward two paces, not nearly enough to reduce the growing gap between them, then halted. Why would a bear, or Berserk, or whatever this thing was, go specifically for that object? Was it on a mission to hide the object like she had been? A wave of horror struck her as she realized hiding it was *not* what she had done.

"It's going to eat it! It's going to eat my ticket back home!"

Freya broke out into a run and jetted through the tall grass. Halfway through the field she slowed her pace again, knowing full well that if a village of Viking warriors feared this beast, then so too should she—even if she did dare to follow after it.

Very carefully, hoping her movement wouldn't rouse the attention of the Berserk, she continued slowly through the field.

The grass brushed against her jeans and began to rustle noisily as she went. Freya threw the long blades a questioning look, wondering why they hadn't produced any such sound until now, then ducked low just as she saw the Berserk glance over its shoulder. Crouching beneath the height of the grass, Freya waited, holding her breath and hoping the Berserk wouldn't come to investigate the root cause of the rustling noise. With ears perked, she waited. The blades of grass, however, continued to swish and rustle. Freya's eyes darted about. Was there someone or something else causing the grass to move? She licked her forefinger and held it upright to the air. Her fingertip remained warm; no trace of any breeze. And yet the blades continued to slap against one another, bringing on a noise that would surely call the Berserk's attention.

Stop it! She wanted to yell at them.

In an act of desperation, Freya stretched out her arms in

front of her and grabbed ahold of as many blades of grass as she could to help silence their sound.

All fell quiet, save the loud thumping of her racing heart.

She waited there—listening for any approaching sound of the Berserk.

Freya waited a few moments more. Then, when her pulse finally returned to a resting pace, and she deemed the coast to be clear, she finally dared to peer above the grass and check the location of the bear. But before she did, fearing her forehead would be spotted before her eyes had a chance to view the danger, she uprooted a clump of silenced grass and camouflaged her head with it. It was a perfect plan, had the bear actually been looking in her direction. Instead, the bear was pacing back and forth in front of several large trees at the forest's edge. Its head was tilted low, its interest occupied by something on or near the ground. Then suddenly it stopped, stood facing a tree, raised its paws to both sides of the trunk, and slowly entered the forest.

With the sun setting and the evening hours upon her, Freya knew if she didn't follow that bear into the woods she'd risk losing the object for good. With one quick shake of her head, she flung the grass away and bolted toward the tree she'd seen the Berserk put its paws against.

She passed the tree, and with one step into the forest, darkness set in. From behind her came a rushing sound of wood creaking and cracking. She turned with a start to witness her entrance now covered in a thicket of overgrown vines and branches.

Freya did a double-take.

The field she had crossed to get here was blocked from view and completely barricaded. It was impossible to return.

Her hands unconsciously reached for her shoulder straps, as if the knowledge of her backpack was all the confirmation she needed to assure herself that none of this was a dream.

They were there, tightly gripped to the point of wearing thin, but they were indeed there.

Freya turned back around and stared blankly at the forest. She had to retrieve that object. A bit of luck: Everywhere she looked were shimmering streams of moonbeams harpooning down through the treetops. Their dim light helped reveal bits and patches of the forest floor and flora. It was enough. Off in the distance, Freya could just make out the movement of a dark figure.

The Berserk.

Using the moonbeams to guide her, Freya carefully navigated her way under broken branches, over loose stones, past ferns and bushes, and through a patch of something rather sticky that kept catching hold of the soles of her sneakers, all the while hot on the Berserk's trail. The task wasn't easy, keeping one eye on where she was stepping while with the other, searching in the dark for the Berserk. But it was a good plan for she just missed tripping over a fallen log.

When she looked back up, the bear had halted. Freya halted too.

Then, just as it had done before entering the forest, it raised its paws to either side of a tree's trunk. Freya watched in anticipation of its next move. The Berserk leaned back, leaned forward, leaned back again, then embarked further on its journey. Freya followed. As she did, she thought she heard the twisting of wood again. When she turned to look in the direction of the noise, a breeze whistled in her ear.

"Who," it seemed to say. "Whooooooo." Freya brushed her ear and wrestled her foot free for the umpteenth time from whatever kept sticking to the bottom of her shoe.

Another creaking sound came. This time when she looked, she could have sworn she saw a tree branch spring upward, swaying in the moonlight. Yet when she scanned the area for a cause, she found nothing. No squirrel jumping about, no fluttering bird, no anything. She held tight to her backpack strap and quickly stepped away from the area.

The Berserk hadn't gone far. Standing with its paws to either side of a trunk well-lit by moonlight, Freya watched again the leaning back and forth ritual before readying herself to set off again.

Not exactly sure how she would actually retrieve the object from the bear, she hoped for something easy like nabbing it as it slept. She checked the ground and surroundings, as was the custom she had developed during the time it took the Berserk to continue its further path through the forest, and found only a shallow pile of dry leaves in which she knew not to tread. Dry leaves were sure to be crunchy and loud and would most definitely draw attention to her location. Then, with no rhyme or reason that she could figure out, the Berserk was off again. Freya was quick to follow, getting quicker as the night dragged on.

Zigzagging deeper into the forest, Freya was beginning to lose patience with this bear. Where was it going? Or of more interest, when would it stop? She wasn't sure how much longer she could keep after it; it was a tiring task to go undetected through a dimly lit forest full of things to trip over or get stuck in, like whatever was suctioning to her feet again. She pried her shoes free while continuing after the bear. Then finally, in a small clearing filled only by beams of moonlight, the Berserk came to a rest.

Freya stayed hidden behind a tree.

Standing in the clearing with its ears perked and eyes focused in one direction, the Berserk appeared almost as if it were waiting for something to come. Or someone? A sense of uneasiness overcame Freya. She grabbed ahold of a branch to steady herself, though could feel vibrations bouncing through it as her hand began to tremble. Staying hidden, she peered between two branches at the bear. Moonlight shone down on the animal, highlighting its beastly features: the claws, long sharp butcher knives really, its teeth, grinding machines for mass destruction, which could surely tear the limbs and flesh from victims as easily as a baby ripping the head off of a dandelion.

Freya shuddered, then without warning the bear leaned back its head and let out a mighty roar, displaying gruesome teeth blanketed in a pool of saliva. She lost grip of the branch and clambered back. Something earlier had given her hope that she wasn't following an actual bear. But not now. This was real—very, *very* real. One look at the bear's claws told her she was a goner if it decided to turn them on her. She couldn't imagine being slashed to death. For that matter, nor did she care to die by any other means. She was too young! Freya covered her ears to mute out the thunderous growl of the bear. Oh, why hadn't she just hid with the Vikings in one of those muddied huts? She should run. Logic told her not to run from bears, but fleeing in the forest was bound to go undetected as long as the bear kept roaring this loudly. Unless her movements caught the attention of its eye, then she would be as equally doomed as staying here. Or perhaps not. Perhaps bears were like dinosaurs—bad eyesight. If she stayed perfectly still it wouldn't notice her. It hadn't noticed her thus far.

So that was her plan. Freya regained her step and planted

herself firmly behind the protection of the tree from before. Slowly the booming roar finally ceased rumbling. That's when a fearful idea hit her. What if that was some sort of battle cry? Were other bears supposed to answer it? That's why it was just standing there—it was waiting for a whole army of bears to arrive. Once again her instincts told her to run, to save herself and live. But her heart told her to stay. After all, the bear still had the oval object.

Freya didn't turn; she didn't concentrate on the sounds of the forest, the possible advancements of wild bears, or any other thought that might cross her mind. She focused on the one and only sure thing—the bear before her.

The Berserk rubbed its head and face, gave its chin a good scratching, its claws ruffling the fur and leaving lines of skin exposed in the parted coat. Although it didn't yawn, Freya hoped these were signs of sleepiness. She could grab the object as it slept and then be on her way. Easy, especially since no army of bears had arrived. The bear's paws wriggled roughly at its throat. Then to Freya's complete and utter horror it grabbed ahold of the folds in its neck and peeled both fur and the flesh attached to it up over its ears. It was skinning itself alive! She cast her eyes away, doubting she could stomach the sight of blood, gore, and brains. She could hear the movement of the Berserk shuffling its stance as it ripped its coat away from its body, but it wasn't screaming out in pain. The sound of peeling skin suctioning away from its core was absolutely lip curling. She dared to peek at the bear. It couldn't possibly be worse to see than to listen to. As she looked up she noticed no pool of blood or gore soaked into the ground. She shielded her eyes from taking it all in at once. First in view were its legs, still intact and furred. Its waist as well. Perhaps she had been mistaken about it skinning itself. With a newfound trust to prove this correct, she took her hand away, revealing the bear's entirety all at once.

Freya's jaw dropped.

Replacing the head of a bear—its gruesome teeth and large eyes all gone—was the unmistakable head of a young teenage boy. This half-boy half-bear creature had chin-length locks of reddish-brown with bangs worn in a braid running from brow to end of his crown. She'd seen mannequins at the museum fashioned much the same, but none with the body of a bear.

The Berserk tugged at the wad of skinned fur dangling below its neck and proceeded to push and pull it past its shoulders. Out rose two human arms.

Unable to turn her eyes from the scene, Freya watched in disbelief.

Leaving the empty sleeves of fur to fall limp at his sides, the Berserk shoved the remainder of his bearskin coat to his ankles, then stepped effortlessly out of the brown pile. His human form was clothed in a pale grey tunic with trousers cross-gartered from his leather shoe all the way up to his knee.

He bent, picked up the fur coat, folded it to the size of a hand towel, then tucked it under his belt.

"Appear now," he called out into the open.

Freya flung around in a panic, her eyes searching wildly in the dark for whatever should appear. But she could find no movement anywhere.

The boy huffed.

Freya waited.

The boy huffed again.

"Shield your invisibility no longer," he commanded.

Freya glanced quickly from one tree to the next. *Invisibility?* No way was she going to go face to face up against something she couldn't even see. She'd rather take her chances with the Berserk-bear-boy-creature-thing, especially since he was the only one of them who knew it was there.

Leading with her back, she stepped cautiously into the clearing, all the while her eyes scanning the trees. "What is it? What's out there?"

The boy didn't answer.

Surely he was equally scanning the forest.

Freya continued searching for the slightest of movements, not once taking notice the boy had already spied it.

"You are but a maid."

She could hear the surprise in his voice.

"Where? Who is 'but a maid'?" She glanced over her shoulder and found him staring at none other than herself with his head cocked in puzzlement.

"Not a sprite lives which possesses invisibility," he said to her.

"Because I'm not invisible." What an absurd idea. "How could I be if you're able to stare at me?"

He didn't take his gaze away. He didn't even blink. Nor did he speak.

"Ok, which by the way you can stop doing. Staring's rude, don't you know that?"

Rude or not, he continued doing it. "You possess sorcery of another sort if not invisibility. No mere maid at her peril has shadowed a Berserk and lived to speak with him."

Was that a threat? It sounded like one. Freya's heart raced. She'd come this far unharmed, and she wasn't about to let it all end now. Oh, where were those little blue flames when she needed them—hadn't they wanted her here? They seemed to know what was going on; couldn't they appear now and tell her how to get out of this, how to nab the object and get home? Or worst case scenario, how to get to Yggdrasil so they could send her home?

Yggdrasil!

What if she got the boy to Yggdrasil so the flames could get the object from him and not her?

"If not sprite, nor Berserk," he pointed to her waist, suggesting the lack of a bearskin coat on her belt, "then what creature do you fit? Your attire is similar to none of this realm."

She mustered up as much confidence as she could, and spoke with more confidence than she actually felt in order to get what she needed. "Take me to Yggdrasil and I'll tell you all you want to know."

The boy was taken aback. "Yggdrasil?"

"Yes. I'm here on a mission, and I haven't got all day to stand here wasting words with you."

"Well, then forward on." He gestured to her as if he would follow behind. "And be on your way." His voice was not kind, and Freya knew he meant to stay.

Her mustered confidence dashed away. Without a local guide, there's no way she could find the tree.

"You're not going to help me?" Surely he heard the disappointment in her voice, for she certainly did.

"Help?"

Was he laughing or asking for clarification? Freya couldn't tell. She chose the latter.

"I need to get to Yggdrasil because I know what's going on." It was a white lie, no harm done, she assured herself.

"You know of Ragnar?"

Okay, possibly harm was done.

Maybe this boy already knew about what was going on. Maybe there was no Ragnar and he was just trying to trip her up. He glanced over her. Freya knew her modern-day clothes, even if they were Susanne's old hand-me-downs, made her stick out like a sore thumb.

"Yeah, I know I'm not from here." She spat back for staring again, then tugged at the hem of her T-shirt as if it explained where she was from. "Isn't that reason enough to help me? I mean, if someone as far away as where I come from knows about the troubles here, wouldn't that just say to you that you should help? Look, I can't explain everything right now but if you take me to Yggdrasil, then I know who can."

His stare and facial expression softened. "The Norns."

Freya recognized that word. Excitement rose inside her. "The Norns—that's it! They called themselves the ancestral Norns; the North, South, East, and West ancestral Norns."

The boy's jaw dropped as if what she'd said had knocked the wind out of him.

"They're at Yggdrasil. They're why I need to get there."

"Can it be?" His response was barely audible but it was enough for Freya to hear the fright in it.

"Can what be? Do you know them? Why do you look that way?"

A shadow had cast over his face, and Freya got the impression it wasn't from a cloud.

"Ragnar," he spat with distaste. "I would destroy such an enemy with vengeance if I could for he has robbed me of all things dear. He slays at will with a bloodthirsty pleasure for power and control. He will stop at nothing. The Norns must have been given a vision telling of his deeds, for certain they would not have gathered all four directions otherwise."

She almost didn't dare to ask, but she had to know, "Who exactly is Ragnar? Is he…"

"Ragnar must be vanquished. He desires too far: our lands, the Nine Realms, even the worlds of our descendants."

"Impossible." She laughed off the idea. "No one can conquer the future." But as soon as the words escaped her lips she realized how wrong she could be. For, unless this was the best played out festival ever to exist, Freya had already come to the realization that she actually was in the Viking Era. And if she was here in the past, then perhaps it was possible for Ragnar to be in the future. Was he the one who stole from the museum? Was he why her father was so desperate to hide the object? Freya shifted uncomfortably. "How difficult do you think it would be for this Ragnar person to control the future?"

"The degree of difficulty varies not among those who attempt the selfish deed. Lo, the sun shall not set upon the day for me to see Ragnar succeed in this."

"Then you'll help me find the tree?"

"Aye."

"Oh, excellent. I think the first thing I'm going to do before the Norns send me home is ask for a detailed explanation as to why they wanted me here in the first place."

The boy's expression turned to that of shock. "You were summoned by them?"

"I guess you could call it that. I had a dream about them, that they wanted me here. But they never said why."

His face lit up in a rush; he looked like Charlotte on her birthday spying her pile of presents.

"Fire-eyed fury! You are the one! My father spoke this day would come. Lo, never did I envision it of my lifetime. Odious be Ragnar. Lo, Liegeman's joys his powers shall now wane, for you are here."

"Me? Whoa, hold up. Don't go getting all excited. I agree this Ragnar fellow sounds like he's up to no good, but there's no way *I* could put a stop to some archaic creepy Viking. I don't have the brains for it. I can't even get top scores on a science test, with or without cheating."

The boy threw her a weird look. "Is that your magic, this science test?"

"No, that's not my magic. I don't *have* any magic. Don't you get it? I'm just a girl, a maid, from like a thousand years away. I don't know anything about here. My father does. He knows it all. Not me."

"Nay, you speak not the truth. You knew to answer the summoning."

Freya sighed. "Look, I don't mean to disappoint, but I honestly don't know what to do about your Ragnar."

"Our Ragnar."

"Your Ragnar."

"A *thousand* years away is your home?"

"Well, I'd have to check a calendar."

He glared at her.

"Ok, I get it. But what if he isn't here in your time? What if he's gone to where I'm from? I need to go home. I'll tell my father about him. He'll know how to put a stop to him."

"And the others? Will your father put a stop to them as well, when you were the one summoned?"

"What others?"

His look alone was response enough. She knew if Ragnar were as power-hungry as this boy claimed him to be, then he wouldn't be acting without help. "All right. Let's get to Yggdrasil and hope the Norns know in which time Ragnar is." She stretched out her right arm, offering him her hand to shake. "My name is Freya."

The boy stood looking curiously at the gesture before shifting slightly back. Clearly he didn't know what to do with her outstretched arm. Or perhaps Vikings greeted each other differently, she thought, though his hesitation made her wonder if there was another reason.

Then just as she was about to withdraw her hand, she felt his own clasp firmly on hers.

"I am called Erik."

Freya smiled as the two bonded their pact to help one

another.

Now that he agreed to be her guide, she took her hand away and gestured for him to lead the way. "After you."

The two stepped off through the trees, the bright moon from the clearing now blocked by a canopy of leaves. This time there were no sounds of twisting trees, though she did manage to find the sticky ground again. They walked on for some time before Erik interrupted their silence.

"Will you answer me a question?"

"That is a question." Once more, Freya had found a patch of sticky ground, and with her mind focused on freeing her foot she heard Susanne's snobbish remark flow instinctively across her own lips. She couldn't believe she had just used it on Erik, but the sticky ground was really starting to irritate her. "Sorry. Go ahead and ask."

There were no hesitations or hurt feelings from what Freya could detect as he asked her his question without delay. "What purpose served you to follow my path and enter Walden's Forest?"

Ah, the oval object. She couldn't very well spill her plan to steal it from him, not before he took her to Yggdrasil. She had to think quickly of something that would quench his curiosity.

"I, uh, I saw you take something from the villagers."

Erik stifled a laugh into the back of his hand. "You turn soft cheek to do battle with Ragnar, yet you make brave against a Berserk in bear form all for the glory of returning a dragon's egg to their thorpe? You do intrigue me, Summoned One."

Freya faltered in her step, and this time it wasn't due to any sticky ground. "Dragon's egg?"

"Aye. Raedslen to be exact, the most accursed of all dragon races."

A swarm of information started all connecting in her brain. Harald: the egg his thorpe would destroy; the egg the mother dragon would mourn. *Raedslen*, she mouthed too stunned to utter the word she'd once read; the book on her father's desk, the spilt coffee. She thought it had just been some random book. Then her father knew. He must have known. But why not tell her what it was he asked her to hide? She trotted after Erik to catch back up. "The *most* accursed race?"

"Aye. Dark magical powers befall its odious transformations."

"Transformations? What kind of transformations?"

"Eat one and you will learn firsthand."

Freya stopped dead in her tracks. Firsthand? He couldn't possibly mean she was to turn into a dragon!

"Is there a cure?" her heart was racing for him to say yes.

Erik stopped and turned to her. "King Walden guards that knowledge."

"So there *is* a cure?"

"May you need not ever know, Summoned One." He

turned back to continue their journey.

"Just call me Freya." She stomped her foot, more out of agitation over her newfound predicament than at his name-calling. A suctioning noise sounded at her shoe. As she pulled her leg hard, having learned that was the trick to releasing the hold, she stumbled. There was movement on the forest floor. Between the light of the moonbeams Freya could see hundreds of vines spring up from the ground. They crawled up her sneakers, weaving their thin little shoots through her shoelace holes. A wind pushed at her back.

"Whoooo are youuuu?" it asked, rushing past her ears, swirling the question about her head as it engulfed her like a snake. She pulled at her throat, forming empty fists around the cold constricting breeze.

"ERIK!"

More roots were coming. The vines slithered around her ankles. She felt a tug on her jeans, pulling her toward the forest floor.

"My foot, Erik! Something's got it!"

Erik flew at her ankle and worked with all his strength to tear apart the ivy at her feet, all the while more were coming.

"Kick, Freya, kick!" he commanded.

She took ahold of his shoulders to keep her balance, then kicked with all her might. As one foot was freed, Erik lifted it to his bent knee removing its contact with the ground.

Wriggling like a fish caught in a net, Freya kicked and squirmed trying to free her remaining foot. By this time Erik had now removed a small hunting knife from the loop of his belt and slashed at the roots around Freya's left foot. But the vines were not giving up. Freya could hear the forest floor coming to life. The roots slithered all along the bed of the forest, moving in her direction.

He pulled at her, forcing her to run. She ran like her life depended on it. All the while Freya could feel the force of the roots sticking to the soles of her shoes and making clutching attempts to pull her back down. As each foot freed itself from the ivy, she could hear a sloshing sound like someone running through a cola-soaked carpet. Erik ran after her.

It wasn't until the sloshing noise was well long gone that Erik made the decision they could stop running. Freya, although out of breath, was willing to run all the way back home if that were possible, just as long as she was far enough away from the clutching grip of the ivy's vines. Where they stopped she found they had chanced upon a creek that thankfully had no signs of ivy in sight.

Freya collapsed next to the creek. "What was that?"

"Efoi."

The moon was shining brightly high above the trees, and Freya could see Erik's face in the light. He looked very serious.

She lifted her head. "What's efoi?"

His expression grew cautious. "It's a judging plant."

Freya didn't like the way he was looking at her. "What does it judge?"

He looked her straight in the eye, opened his mouth, and said, "Evil."

CHAPTER IV

THE TREE HOME

"Evil?" The accusation was horrifying. She jumped up and paced back and forth along the creek, wringing her hands. "Why would it think I'm evil? *How* could it think I'm evil? It's just a plant; plants can't judge." She didn't need Erik to explain efoi was more than just a plant, she herself having barely escaped from its boa constrictor-like hold. She did an about-face, still pleading her case. "You know, I didn't ask to be here. So where does it get off judging me? Judge the Norns—they summoned me here. Or do you think it makes sense to summon an evil person to put an end to some other evil person?" Erik opened his mouth to respond. "No, of course not," she continued. "It isn't like I've ever physically harmed someone. That would be evil. But that's not me." Though she had once dropped her grandfather's urn, spilling his ashes all over the living room rug. If her mother were to ever find out she vacuumed up his ashes to hide the mess, she'd die. Freya shook off the thought and continued her rant. "I've never even stolen anything before." That wasn't exactly true.

The egg. Her father had her steal the egg right out of the museum. And she did.

Freya fell to her knees. Her heart was heavy as Erik's words rang through her ears: the most accursed dragon race of all. The efoi must have sensed it in her.

"I don't want to be evil," she said half to herself.

Erik turned. "Nor do I," he quietly added.

Hearing his words, Freya's thoughts paused. Did he mean her…or him?

"Let's away," he said. "Seven winters in Walden's Forest have skilled me to many of its secrets. Lo, none enough for me to brave a night unsheltered here. My home is near. We will be safe there."

In complete agreement to get even farther away from any lingering efoi, Freya pulled herself up and fell in line behind Erik, ready to follow him once more. He turned and faced her.

"You misunderstand me. My home is here." Raising his right arm he pointed above his head. A moonbeam shone brightly on his extended forefinger, catching Freya's eyes to follow its direction.

"You live in a tree?" Unable to fathom sleeping like a

leopard on a branch, let alone how to access said branch, Freya panicked she'd roll off and fall straight into a bed of efoi. She shuddered at the thought.

"You needn't fear. Nothing can reach you where I live." He must have read her worried face like an open book. However, his confidence did nothing to calm her.

"That's just it. How will *we* reach where you live? If it's to be anything like the rope climbing course in gym class, I can tell you right now I might as well sleep right here on the forest floor. I failed that test hard." She craned her neck taking in the height of the surrounding trees, her biceps already beginning to wobble as if they were saying don't even bother.

Erik laughed. "Your speech never ends to fill my ears with the oddest of words."

"Make fun all you want, but the joke's on you when you're carrying me up over your shoulder in a fireman's hold."

His laughed deepened.

It was a friendly laugh, the kind that made her feel included rather than the target. And yet, although it didn't come across as sounding forced, like when her mother laughed at her stories, Freya couldn't help but think it sounded, well, surprised. It was a weird thing to notice, she knew, but she couldn't shake the thought now that it was there. Was he surprised to find himself laughing at her, or to find himself…laughing?

Erik regained control of his laughter and stepped under a neighboring tree with long wispy branches. The dim light of night made the tree look as if it was covered in thin braids, the effect created by petal-shaped leaves cascading down each branch. It was a beautiful tree but by no means suitable for climbing. She watched as Erik parted the branches like a swimmer parting water. "Are you looking for something?"

"Aye." He grabbed hold of a single bough and gripped it firmly with both hands. "This."

His chosen branch was bare. Not a single petal grew on it.

He pulled it tautly, extending it to the ground, and just as it reached his feet he released it. The branch sprung back in place and a dull churning noise could be heard coming from the tree's trunk. Instinctively, Freya jumped back. Erik stayed put. The two waited and watched as a side of the trunk rotated outwards, opening a hole large enough to pass through. Erik entered first, ducking his head as he passed through the secret doorway. It was too dark for Freya to see him but she could hear he was grabbing at something.

Click! Click!

Sparks flew from his hands.

Click! Click!

A few more sparks, then a small torch that hung on the inside wall of the trunk took light. He dropped the two flint stones into a basket on the ground and grabbed the lit torch. "This way," he motioned with a nod of his head. Freya followed willingly. They bent low and carefully exited through a hole in the ground where they began climbing down a makeshift ladder of broken branches and dried mud. The descent went quickly and soon Freya found herself having only gone about the height of a tall man before reaching the bottom. There to her amazement were a series of hollowed out passageways—a sort of earthen tunnel system.

"How did you ever find all of this?" Puffs of breath formed in the cool air as she spoke.

"King Walden provided the entrance. All that you see here was labored by myself."

"That's amazing." In admiration, she reached out her hand to touch one of the walls, which bit back at her fingertips with a piercing coldness. Then suddenly the chamber went dark. Darting her eyes this way and that she spied the faintest of light dimming ahead of her. Erik had turned a corner. Not wishing to get lost down here alone, she wasted no time dawdling to catch up with him. As she quickly rounded the corner, shapes most monstrous caught her by surprise; Erik's shadow, brought on by the flickering torch, was dancing about the tunnel walls. Freya calmed herself and stayed as close as possible to him now.

There were two passageways to the left, neither of which Erik turned down. Nor the one to the right. In that tunnel, Freya caught a glimpse of a ladder similar to the one they had descended. This ladder led up, but apparently to a dead end, for Freya couldn't see any opening in the ceiling. They walked on. Next came a left turn down a very long tunnel. A quick, sharp right and she found them in yet a different passageway, this one narrower than all the rest. Freya pulled her arms into the short sleeves of her T-shirt to keep the cold walls off her bare skin.

Finally, after a third sharp turn, the tunnel came to an end. Erik pointed upwards. At about hip level was a fishnet ladder made of ropes patchworked together. Freya groaned; it was gym class all over again. Erik hoisted himself up and managed with ease, even with the torch in one hand, but Freya struggled with the first step alone. She twisted about, angling her foot in every direction while trying her best to place it correctly in the braided squares. Though fumbling with her grip on the rope, she somehow still made her way up, albeit very slowly.

The ladder swayed slightly as they moved higher and higher, its length much longer than the rope they had climbed down. The wobbling only made it more difficult for Freya, and she slipped several times trying to position her footing.

One such sway caught her off guard, and she missed the next square completely, causing the toe of her sneaker to kick against the inside of the tunnel, but instead of a dull thud she expected to hear, there was a hollow ring of a tree trunk. So this was how they were to get up there. Her father had once built a tree house for her and Susanne, just after Charlotte was born, but it was nothing more than a few boards nailed to some branches without so much as a door, let alone an elaborate secret entrance like this tree house had.

As they ascended she could feel the air getting warmer, or perhaps it was perspiration from the workout climb. Not to mention the further up they went the tighter the space grew. With her backpack scraping every so often against the inside of the trunk, it forced her to watch the angle of her elbows so as not to scrape them as well.

Finally Erik halted. "Slow yourself, the end is here."

His words came as welcome relief, for her arm muscles were turning to jelly.

Following him to the final leg of the path, Freya hoisted herself through a small opening in a wooden floor with the last bit of energy she had. She moved to the side, then collapsed. Erik meanwhile slid a large wooden covering over the hole, sealing the tree home's floor.

"It's nice," she offered, her eyes taking in what they could without requiring her head to actually move.

"You have yet to see it."

"True, but the floor is surprisingly comfortable."

"I have other seating should you prefer it." He gestured to a brown wooden bench that looked to be carved directly from the wall itself. Freya sat up, ignoring its inviting pillow and woolen blanket, and instead took notice of a darkly colored tapestry hanging just above the bench.

"It reminds me of home—of the ones at the museum I

mean."

Next to the tapestry was a small torch hanging on the wall by a simple strap of looped leather and an iron nail. Erik lit it. As the light grew the colored depiction in the tapestry became more obvious. In it was a brown bear. Either Erik liked bears or someone had woven this specifically for him, knowing he was a Berserk. There was also a woman in a red tunic with yellow braids, a winged grey dragon, and a white goblet.

"A gift from the Norns," he explained.

She looked at him. "They made this?"

As he nodded yes, Freya looked back at the tapestry in wonderment. "Could you imagine if one of the tapestries at the museum was made by a Norn? Perhaps my father helped excavate it. And to think, now I'm standing here seeing one while it's still new." She took in all the details of the woven scene and noticed something more. Cocking her head, her eyes traced the path of a shiny silver thread. Its pattern didn't make sense. It didn't connect or outline any of the figures, nor did it form a picture itself. Instead, it merely wove aimlessly about the black background.

"So why'd they give it to you? Does it have any meaning?"

With a shrug of his shoulders, he answered, "I do not pretend to comprehend the Norns. Their craft is powerful and lo, they express their visions through such woven tapestries, I have not the gift for interpreting what they show."

"Didn't they tell you anything about it?"

"Nay."

"So they just gave it to you and were on their way? Did you try asking about it? I mean, there's a bear and all in it. Is it supposed to represent you?"

"Alas, I know not."

"Well, do you at least know what sort of dragon this is? Is it a Ray...Ray, oh, how do you say it again?"

"*RAIDS-LEN.* I believe so. Lo, I cannot confirm for I have yet to see one in the flesh."

Hopefully he never would. At least if he did, she hoped it wouldn't be her he was looking at. Freya stared at the grey dragon, desperate for morning to come so the Norns could reverse the transformation and send her home.

She heard Erik step aside and push his arm through what sounded like thick glass clinking together. When she turned, he had reached his arm into a shallow niche and used the lit torch in his hand to light yet another one.

"Watch," he instructed her. With her attention focused on him he released the short curtain of colored glass beads. The strands covered the height of the opening and projected the most beautiful warm shades of reds, oranges, and yellows all about the tree home. Freya followed where they bounced and sparkled. She couldn't help but smile at the display of disco ball colors and movements.

Erik smiled too.

"My mother's creation," he said.

The comment took her aback. She hadn't thought of Berserks as having a family. Well, until today, she hadn't thought of Berserks at all.

The third torch Erik lit hung just above a small round table next to a set of shelves. On the top shelf were a hammer and tools. Below those were a plate, bowl, and cooking utensils. And below them were a bucket and spout.

"You have a faucet and running water?"

"I have a hollow branch outside in which I collect rainwater, aye. Too often I have spilled a bucket brought up the ladder. This solution is far more effective."

They both shared a smile.

"Is that a shower then?" Freya giggled, pointing to a large plug in the ceiling.

"The viewing hole?" Erik stepped onto the chair and popped the wooden plug up out of the ceiling. A sky full of twinkling stars greeted them.

Freya stared in awe. The beautiful display of bright constellations stared back.

"There is yet more to show you." Erik reached his arm through the viewing hole and grabbed the rope attached to the plug. As he pulled it back in, blocking out the stars, little did he know he had also blocked out Freya's family. A silent good night was all she could offer up to them, hoping this very eve they too were gazing upon the same stars as she.

"Here."

She twirled around and caught sight of what looked to be nothing more than a dark crawl space.

"This chamber is for sleeping; I hollowed only half its thickness. The branch is mighty and will hold the weight of a horse I am sure, though I have not tested it. The hay will keep you comfortable."

"Thanks." Freya approached the chamber as she approached everything else in his tree home: in awe. She touched the walls he had carved out for a bed. They were silky and warm. The branch was long and narrow, yet roomy enough for a person to stretch or roll over in sleep without feeling claustrophobic. Lining the bottom of the chamber was the pile of hay as he had mentioned, though she wasn't too sure it would outrank her mattress at home on the comfort scale. Yet lying on top of it was a woolskin that did look ever so comfy.

While she examined the chamber, Erik was fastening the original torch in his hand to the wall. It helped add light to an otherwise darkened corner of his home, which Freya couldn't help but think was an extremely large home for a tree trunk. She didn't recall seeing any trees in the forest thick enough to house so much space. But nonetheless it was worth a peek at what else the home had to offer.

Freya gasped.

"Are those bones?"

"Aye," he answered proudly.

Freya saw he had the same expression on his face as when he was staring at the beads' reflected lights, though she couldn't understand why. She tried to uncurl her lip, but the thought of some dead animal's, or, worse yet, person's bones in his home was repulsing. "Uh, wouldn't it have been better to bury those in the ground?"

"Ah," a hint of hurt replaced his pride. "I reckon your kinsmen fare the seas."

Just as she was about to ask him to why that would make a difference, it suddenly all made sense— the reason the boulders in the National Viking Graveyard were placed in oval formations: to resemble ships. Her father had taught her that those who didn't own ships, but who still led a nautical life, were buried amongst such graves. Never, though, had she given any thought as to where the families with non-sailing connections buried their dead...or *didn't* bury them.

"No, no sailors here. But neither do we have any bones. We do have family ashes, though, from my Morfar, on the mantelpiece in our living room. Well, *most* of his ashes."

A look of worry shot across his face. "Ashes?"

"Yeah, my Mormor had him cremated after his death."

"Cremated?"

"That's when your body is burned instead of buried."

"Burned! Foul shame such a deed! My clansmen descend from the mightiest of hunters. To burn them would vanish the powers of their nogle."

"Well, I don't really believe bones, or nogle if that's what you call them, can actually have magical powers."

"Indeed the contrary. Nogle is the lifeline to Midgard. The spirit may be gone, but the nogle remains."

What he was saying made zero sense to her, having never heard her father mention anything about nogle before, but it did make her wonder if he even knew about it. She eyed the nogle to see any of the so-called special powers emitting from it. But just as she'd guessed, all she could see was a pile of bones lying perfectly still. There was, however, a stack next to the nogle that was rather familiar.

"Is that kubb?"

Erik's eyes followed where she pointed. "Your time destroys nogle yet plays kubb? It is a strange place where you are from."

"Yes, well, you live in a tree and don't have internet so I could say the same of here."

Erik cocked his head, oblivious to what internet was.

"I can't believe we both know kubb. My father taught my sisters and me how to play as soon as we were big enough to learn the game. But I've never seen a miniature set like this one. Ours is much larger since we play it outside."

"The forest is too dense to play outside here."

"Fair enough. Yet how fantastic! I never thought of tabletop kubb. Hey, wouldn't it be wild to see if the rules I learned were actually the right way to play? I mean, this is so weird, I'm talking to a real-life Viking. I could ask you anything. I could check everything my father's ever researched." Freya's eyes twinkled at the thought. "He'd love to know that his lifelong work was correct. And I'd love for him to be proud of me. Just think, when I go home tomorrow, because I will, I could confirm all he knows is right. Maybe even about the mythology." The twinkle in her eye faded as the memory of her worried father came flooding into her mind. "Erik, what's in the realms?"

Erik grimaced. "Vile creatures and the dark magic they control."

"Where I come from there is no such thing as magic."

"Then you come from a very special place indeed. I should long for a home with no magic."

"But if the realms get opened wouldn't the dark magic cross into my time? How would we protect ourselves against it?" Before Erik could say anything Freya already knew the answer. It was why her father was so worried about the break-in, the egg, his theory; he knew if magic came to their time, no one would be able to stop it.

"Aye. Alas, only magic is capable of defeating magic."

"Then why summon *me*? I haven't got any magic. Ugh! This is so frustrating! I wish the Norns were here now to tell me why they brought me here."

"Then let us to bed. We will rise early and be at Yggdrasil

before the day sets into night."

"How can I sleep when my head is full of questions?"

"Then let us away this eve. Lo, I understood you would not desire under the darkness of night another meeting with efoi."

"No, absolutely not." So she caved, knowing he was right. It wouldn't be easy waiting for morning to come, but she knew it was a safer option. With that she pulled off her shoes and climbed atop the crunchy hay. As it turned out the hay was much softer than she thought it would be and the plush wool was warm, inviting a good night's sleep. While she made herself cozy, Erik busied himself by extinguishing the torches.

The light in the tree home was beginning to fade and Freya caught sight of a small plug to another viewing hole just above her head. She gave it a push. Much tinier than the one Erik had shown her, it was nonetheless big enough for her liking, for hundreds of brightly shining stars greeted her with a twinkling sort of Morse code.

"I'll be home soon," she whispered to them. It felt good to think her family was with her in this distant land. But it also made her think of Erik and she wondered who he had.

"Erik?"

A muffling sound from the bench came as he positioned himself for the night.

"Hmm?"

"Were you born a Berserk?"

The room fell quiet until he softly cleared his throat.

"It was the thawing of my seventh year," he began faintly, his voice drifting in the memory of the story. "The spring snow had just begun to melt when the chieftain came to my kin. My father, top hunter in our clan, was on very favorable terms with the chieftain." He paused before continuing. "An honor was bestowed my home that day, but I could not have known its outcome. I was seven and consumed with excitement at the invitation of my first hunt. How proud they all were." A tone of regret filled his voice and Freya felt a saddened sense of loss for him.

"My thoughts were consumed by anticipation of the hunt. Many moons slept I not one wink for excitement of the coming adventure engrossed me. Fresh milk, still warm from the sheep's udder offered me by my mother in hopes to help me sleep extinguished not my sleepless nights. How could it? Everyone was proud, proud and hopeful that I would follow in my father's footsteps by becoming as successful a huntsman as he," his voice faltered at the comparison. "If only they had known."

Freya hung on every word.

"It was morning's light when we made our way into the forest. I remember the cool air casting shapes with my breath, but I wasn't cold; the adrenalin pumping through my blood kept me warm. My mind focused on spearing a meaty red deer, a prized feast for our thorpe. Prior to the hunt I was counseled in the art of hunting: stay low and downwind of the buck, follow hoof prints still soft to the touch, and trail broken branches or the rubbed off tree bark damaged by passing game. The huntsmen donned me with a spear, cut and sharpened for the special day. I carried it proudly at my side.

"Soon we discovered the fresh prints of a solitary buck and my belly rumbled, eager to taste the feast we would enjoy from this kill. Lo, the succulent meat we would dine on that day would not be venison.

"Our hunting party was swift, shooting through the forest like a feathered arrow steadied on its target. The earthen prints grew wider apart; our prey was in full gallop. Trees, creeks, and fields could not slow us from the buck. Then, in a clearing, we laid eyes on a prize more savory than the deer, for its meat was yet tender and its protector nowhere in sight...a lonely bear cub.

"My father nodded my way—this was to be *my* kill.

"Crouching low with feet planted to steady my throw, I bore the spear in my right hand and flung it soaring in the direction of the bear.

"My father's admiration rings yet in my ear. 'A perfect hit!' I heard him declare. My chest swelled with joy. Ah, how the huntsmen loudly cheered, lifting me to their shoulders in a parade of victory back to our thorpe. The feast was glorious, and the meat—mmm, so tender."

She could hear him smacking his lips trying to taste the

memory of the roast. As for herself, the lack of today's dinner along with the talk of a succulent supper made her stomach rumble with hunger; her appetite wanted a taste of the fine meal, but her curiosity wanted to know more of the story.

Erik must have gotten his fill of the memory, for his lip smacking quickly stopped.

Outside, Freya could hear leaves tapping at the sleeping chamber's walls much to the same beat the grandfather clock in their living room kept ticking away the minutes. She lay listening to the taps wondering why Erik hadn't resumed his story.

Did he think she had fallen asleep?

To signal she hadn't, Freya rolled to her side, purposely crunching the straw loudly as she turned.

A quiet sigh, weighted heavy with memory, escaped him.

"Hunting tradition decrees the coat of a slayed bear be awarded its victor. My mother, most proud that I, the victor, hurried in her needlework to fit the fur to my form. Curse be that day.

"Placed upon my shoulders was not the sizing she had measured, 'twas not room for youth to grow into man. Lo, horror struck my thorpe, myself, to witness the coat wrapped tightly upon my body as if it were my own skin. I had become—a Berserk.

"Shrieking cries pierced my ears. Villagers ran. The power of Berserk was strong in me, and I lashed out. Brutally tearing into the nearest flesh, I flung my mighty wrath upon my victims, deaf to their screams for mercy. Battle axes could not fell me, my coat an immortal shield to every hit and blow. Alas, no attack against a Berserk would bring them survival; their only hope was to hide.

"Winters earlier, my father had spoken of the many monsters and creatures I might in my future encounter. Little did I know it would be my own self. Berserks are rare. Upon explaining the powers of a Berserk, he said they calm and subside only when none left are standing to battle.

"With the clansmen of my thorpe now all in hiding and the person I had fought lifeless at my feet, the coat loosened and instinctively I knew to shed myself of it. Nothing, absolutely nothing, could have prepared me for what I saw," Erik choked on the words to come and he cleared his throat. "My own beloved mother lay victim at my hand."

Freya gasped.

"I ran to the forest; I ran from what I had done. I sought everywhere for a reversing curse. Alas, none exist which can lift the hurt I caused at seven winters old."

CHAPTER V

RAGNAR

a warm ray of morning's light tiptoed through the tiny viewing hole in the sleeping chamber, stirring Freya slowly awake. Yawning in half-sleep, her arms began to make their way above her head, but instead of extending fully they abruptly knocked against the chamber's upper wall. Freya's eyes shot opened. The dream of being back home sound asleep in her own bed jolted her from peace as the reality of the branch met her face to face.

She pulled the window plug back into place then scrunched her way down the sleeping chamber. Her socked feet landed hard on the wooden floor. Erik, she noticed, was standing on the table, his upper body poking up through the large viewing hole.

"Um, good morning?"

"Good morning," she heard from outside the window. "Here is bounty enough to share before our journey that we may fill our bellies with." He popped his head down to greet her. "And to quiet yours."

Freya's stomach let out a low rumbling roar demanding to be fed. How embarrassing. She knew she'd gone to bed hungry but hadn't realized her hunger pangs would affect Erik's sleep. It was like the time her aunt and uncle had come for a visit and she had to sleep on the floor of her parents' room. She hadn't slept a wink due to her father's snoring.

Her stomach rumbled again, rather loudly too, as if to one- up the level of noise her father's snoring had produced. It was a terrible noise which she didn't care for one lick.

Mmmm, a lick.

Thoughts of last night's display of meats, cheeses, and breads danced in her head like sugarplum fairies. Grimhild's thorpe couldn't be that far away, she thought, and surely there'd be some leftovers they could offer her.

She shook away the notion of leaving. Erik was getting breakfast ready and soon she'd feel full. After all he was busy scrambling to get food down from the branch. Scramble? Her mind drifted to scrambled eggs. He couldn't possibly have chickens up there. Unfortunately after yesterday's events, she was quite turned off of the idea of eating any form of egg, chicken or not. Unless of course it would be an egg that would send her home.

Trying to wait patiently for him to come down with whatever it was he'd be serving up, she occupied her mind by putting on her shoes and getting ready to leave as soon as they'd eaten. She found her sneakers lying near the nogle. The pile of bones possessed an air of creepiness, but Freya refused to believe they could possess anything more.

Piled neatly in an interlocking log cabin formation, the nogle didn't look to Freya like it had any magical capabilities. One of the larger bones was so near her shoe that upon reaching for the sneaker she dared herself to touch it. Ever so slowly, she extended her pinky until the fleshy tip above her nail lightly brushed against the bone.

Nothing happened.

She knew it wouldn't. It couldn't.

She grabbed her other shoe without the need to touch a second bone, and then sat on the bench waiting for breakfast.

Erik emerged from the window with a basketful of gooseberries. The berries were large, the way her Mormor grew them, and juicy as Freya soon discovered after helping herself quickly to a handful of them. If it was a race to see who could eat the most in the shortest amount of time, then Freya was winning.

"Please, fill your belly to its fullest," he commented on her inhalation of the breakfast.

"I'm so sorry." She knew better than to talk with her mouth full but today she simply couldn't help it. "I'm absolutely famished."

"Go on, Yggdrasil is a good day's walk from here. You will need to build your strength now."

"Oh, right." Guessing there wouldn't be any restaurants along the way, she eyed her backpack and wondered how many berries she could fill it with.

Erik followed the direction of her stare and raised a brow. "Fire-eyed fury, fret not. I know of a creek where we may sup upon fish before we reach the Norns."

"Was it that obvious?" she swallowed her mouthful and turned her eyes to him.

"Aye."

"Ok. I think I'm done now." But for good measure, she popped one final berry into her mouth.

Erik rolled his eyes in friendly banter. "Then let us away."

He turned and picked up two flat stones from the shelves. Striking them at the tip of a nearby torch he lit it before climbing up on the table and closing the viewing hole.

Without the morning light, the room was drastically darker, one torch barely enough to brighten the area beyond the length of his arm. But Freya knew it was all they would need in the tunnels, and just as she suspected, Erik grabbed the torch from the wall then pulled up the trap door flooring.

"To the Norns," he said, gesturing her to enter first.

Freya's heart thumped with excitement. "To the Norns!"

The descent down the rope ladder was much easier on

Freya's jelly muscles than the climb had been, and they landed in the tunnel much sooner than she thought it would take. With the dim light in front of him, Erik took the lead and led the way; a sharp turn to the left followed by a sharp right, then another left. The two climbed up the shorter ladder where ascending it Erik doused the torch in some dirt before hanging it in the holder she had seen him retrieve it from last night. Then, with a push on the secret door, they were back in Walden's Forest.

Freya looked around; the trees were still tall, nothing different about that, but now with the morning's sunny rays casting a friendlier light than the moon had, their branches no longer gave a sense of wanting to reach out and grab her. Gone too was—Freya did a double-take. Then another.

"It's not there. How's that even... You were with me. We both sat. We both drank. Where's the creek?"

Erik didn't do a double-take. "Walden's Forest is a 'living' forest," he replied with no concern at all.

"All forests are *living*. But streams don't just dry up overnight and get replaced by flowers in full bloom." She grabbed ahold of his shoulders and whirled him around to view the bed of flowers now growing where yesterday's creek had once flowed. "Or are you going to tell me little elves did this?"

"Deafen your ears! Elves in Walden's Forest? Impossible." The look on his face though, couldn't have disagreed more.

In any other circumstance Freya would have argued the existence of elves but at this moment her choice battle was with a missing creek. "Then how do you explain its absence?"

"I already have."

"No, you haven't. All you said was this forest is a living forest."

"Precisely."

"That doesn't explain anything."

But Erik had turned away to head off for the Norns and gave no further comments on the subject.

"Well then," she remarked to nobody but herself. "I guess I'm left to believe it just came to life, decided to change its course, and simply reroute itself to some other part of this living forest. Pfft. How absurd." She gave the area a second look and caught herself asking, "Isn't it?"

They travelled on in silence. Any conversation to be had was played out in Freya's mind, and it wasn't with Erik. Instead, she role-played the reactions of both the Norns and herself as how it would be when they finally came face-to-face.

"Oh, silly us," they'd say. "Remember how we appeared to you in a dream. Well, guess what? You're dreaming now. Wake up and you'll find yourself back in your bed. No egg, no summons, no problems."

"Wonderful."

"What?" Erik's voice pulled her away from any hope she had of waking in her bed. She scowled at the back of his head while continuing to follow his stop and go zigzagging pattern through the forest.

Another left. Another pause.

"Oh honestly, Erik, why do we keep stopping? And what's up with your crazy hand ritual? Are you measuring the size of each trunk or something?"

But before he had time to respond, the cawing of a crow called in the distance. Erik spun in its direction, his eyes wide and ears perked. "Birds?"

Freya didn't follow.

"They do not house in Walden's Forest." His hushed tone told her that these birds weren't birds at all.

"What persons are these who dare tread in Ragnar's Forest?" a voice deeper than Erik's came blasting at their right. "Men, surround them!"

About twenty men came closing in on them, each armed with various spears, battle axes, and heavy swords. The warriors, outfitted with round wooden shields painted in various patterns and colors, came at them fast. Their brutish bodies moved ruggedly like ogres, and for all she knew they could very well have been ogres for their faces were concealed by thick rectangular bronze nose plates extending down from metal helmets.

Why Erik called this place "Walden's Forest" and the

men "Ragnar's Forest" she didn't know, but one thing was for certain, it probably wasn't wise to tell them she was the Summoned One.

A tall brutish man carrying a long rectangular shield and wearing a mail corselet stepped forward from the group. His hair coloring struck Freya odd, for she had never seen a man with blond hair, red sideburns, and stranger still—a brown beard.

He looked Freya over but as he caught sight of Erik, a wry smile spread just above his beard. "Take them."

Two broad-shouldered warriors grabbed Erik and Freya and tied their hands with a coarse rope. With the rope leads in tow, the men stepped out swiftly, making it difficult for Freya to keep pace. As her gait behind the men widened, the rope grew taut, scratching at her wrists and tearing her skin, rubbing it raw. She stumbled, trying to pick up speed in hopes of loosening some slack in the rope, but her efforts required more energy than she had stamina for. There would be no sympathy, she knew, if she were to cry out in pain or ask the men to slow down. But she had to do something to relieve the agony of rope burn or soon her wrists would bleed.

Erik nudged her with his elbow, catching her attention, and then jutted his wrists forward for her to see. With one glance her eyes understood the message.

Mimicking what Erik had done with his tunic, she tucked the end of her own shirt between the rope and her wrists. The padding felt good.

"Extra mead to us all for a superior catch," called the leader over his shoulder.

An excitement of hoots and hollers filled Freya's ears like a loud stadium of sports fans.

"Mead was on last night's menu," yelled back one in jest. "Tonight let us have bear instead."

Freya looked at Erik as a thunderous roar of laughter shot out. Erik wasn't laughing. To his right came a burley, thick-necked Viking. He struck Erik across the back in a mock friendly gesture. "Skinning this one will be easy." Erik couldn't retaliate; the ropes prohibited him from striking back. Smiling, the man took ahold of Erik's bearskin coat, adding, "Do watch your distance. Ragnar wants you delivered alive." Then with a forceful pull he swiped the coat away from Erik's belt and threw it over his own shoulders. Erik wrestled with all his might against the ropes to try and snatch it back, but the Viking at the other end found the game fun and pulled the rope even quicker.

"Take warning," Erik spat at the man with his coat. "I will have my revenge on Ragnar."

"Nay, Berserk. Ragnar will have his revenge with you." With that, the man planted his feet and watched as Erik was led forcefully away.

Freya saw Erik tense. She looked back at the man just as the leader came and gave him a shove. "Move on, Mutwik.

Not here. Not today. Not by you. My uncle's revenge will be had by him alone." Ragnar's nephew swiped the coat from Mutwik, then quickened his step and walked at pace with Erik. He didn't, however, return the bearskin coat to him.

Only the sound of trudging through the forest was made after that. And although Freya attempted several times to catch Erik's attention to secretly communicate an escape plan, a way out, why they had his coat, or why Ragnar wanted revenge on Erik, he never once looked her way.

So on she walked in silence like the rest.

Unlike the zigzagging path she had taken with Erik, these Vikings' walking pattern was a straight line, minus the occasional dodged tree. However, if they could have bulldozed down those trees the way they trampled over everything else, they would have. They stomped on ferns, cut bushes in half by crossing brutally through them, and hacked branches in two when the slightest of overhang obstructed their progress—all without giving any second thought to the destruction they left behind. Freya gave it a lot of thought; it was all she could do as any conversation with Erik would be overheard. She thought and wondered about Walden's Forest being a living forest and the life it seemed to have of its own last night. But more importantly, she thought how terrible it was that this part of the forest didn't have any efoi.

By the time the party emerged from the forest, the sun was already high in the sky. Where they came out, Freya noticed, was at a path lining where the land sloped into a grassy valley. How she wished she could push the whole group of men down it. Unfortunately, it was almost the reversal, for their galloping speeds nearly sent her snowballing down the hill instead. Catching her footing as the hill finally leveled off, she found herself before an intricate design of huts and fields. Somehow she had missed seeing all of this from atop the hill. Opposite the huts sat a longhouse similar to the replica in the museum's Viking Antiquities Wing. Only at the museum there were no onlookers duplicating the stares she and Erik were receiving from the locals here. Another yank of the ropes and Freya and Erik were led straight to the longhouse.

Inside it was dark; the only natural source of light was the door they had entered and a small hole in the middle of the roof allowing smoke from the fires to escape. To brighten the space were several torches larger than those at Erik's, though similarly affixed to the walls through the loop of a leather strap. Between the torches were stacked beds bunked two in height and covered in furs and woolen blankets—all of which would make her father proud to know that the research he had done for his own replication had indeed produced a model most identical to the original. Now all she had to do was get home and tell him.

Staring eyes were as prevalent in the longhouse as outside of it, pairs of them followed where they walked. One set belonged to a woman in a long red tunic dress whose face was marked with a gashed scar. The woman marched herself up to Freya and Erik's captors, demanding in a raspy voice, "What despicable creatures are these?" A spray of spittle slapped Freya's face, causing her to inadvertently turn a lip up in disgust. This did nothing to improve their situation, for the woman quickly took offense. With one swift swoop, she jerked backwards on the ropes at Freya's wrists, forcing them free of their protective covering and sending them scraping up her forearms.

"Ahh!" The pain shot through her entire body followed by a ripple effect of throbbing.

A satisfactory smile creased the woman's profile. "Bring them to Ragnar."

The ropes cut into Freya's wrists again as they were tugged forward toward a man seated at the end of the longhouse. Nearing him, Freya saw that he looked to be from a page in one of her history books depicting the intimidating image of a ruthless Viking warrior. His broad shoulders, wide enough to seat two adults each, supported the solid muscular stump that made up his neck. Several deep scars on his face documented the numerous battles he'd fought, though the mere presence of him alive and breathing before her signaled he had returned home each time the victor. How many of his enemies could say the same? She doubted if any.

His hair, she glanced again, was colored in the same

spectrum as the leader of the warriors: Blond on top, red sides, and a brown beard.

Ragnar planted his palms on the table in front of him and rose, towering over Freya and Erik like a chiseled statue in an Italian museum. He met them with a grin on his lips and evil in his eyes. "A pleasure," he greeted them coldly.

Neither Freya nor Erik responded.

As Ragnar slowly rounded the table, his right ringed index finger slid along the outer edge of the carved wood. He stopped in front of them, closing the distance just at arm's reach. His grin grew into an untrusting smile. "Where now are my manners? Erik, we meet again. Do share news of your beloved brother's well-being. Word reaches me your father has not yet been robbed of life by him."

Erik lunged at Ragnar, but the two warriors were equally swift and skilled in predicting an enemy's movements. They yanked on the ropes binding Erik's wrists and sent him stumbling backwards. "You will fall before you witness that day!"

Ragnar laughed.

"I warn you, Ragnar," Erik roared recovering his stance.

"Warn me? Nay, I disagree." Ragnar played with the skinny wooden block dangling from his neck. "Pray tell, Erik, where have you to hide with a Raedsman as kin?"

Freya shot Erik an inquisitive look.

"Fortune is yours these past two winters," Ragnar went

on. "Your brother's transformation has yet to take hold. Lo, when it does, it is he who will own the position to give warning, not you." He turned his head in the direction of the scar-faced woman. "Helga! To the fire rooms with the girl. I will concern myself with her tomorrow. Tonight she will aid in the celebrations."

Helga grabbed Freya's ropes, pulling her harshly away from Erik and the men.

"Fire rooms?" She didn't even know what those were. "I won't leave Erik! No!" she struggled to remain, but the stocky woman proved stronger than she. "Let me go," she pleaded, trying to wriggle free of the ropes. Helga only pulled harder.

Outside she was led past various sizes of huts, tables, patches of gardens, and penned animals. Weaving between the thatched huts, Freya tried to get her bearings. If, no *when,* she managed to escape she'd need to know her way back to Erik to get him out of here. On her left was the hillside they had climbed down. She could just barely make out a few of the treetops from Walden's Forest. She refused to call it Ragnar's Forest. As she walked the length of the village getting a sense of its enormity, she couldn't believe all of this had been overlooked from up on the hill. It wasn't as if there were trees in this valley to hide the huts, which, as she thought about it, the smoke from fires would have risen high above, and she hadn't seen that either.

At the outer edge of the village was a hut no bigger than

the size of her living room, its entrance guarded by two bulky Vikings.

"In with you," Helga pushed her forward through the rounded doorway.

The hut was lit by various cooking fires. Under an open ceiling was a central pit burning strongly beneath a roasting pig, to the left was a smaller stone enclosed fire heating the belly of a cauldron pot, and beyond that one was a brick oven of sorts with its fire baking several loaves of bread. The delicious smells coming from the foods caused Freya's stomach to rumble.

"The fire rooms," Freya guessed.

"Or death," Helga responded with a grin. "Lo, some argue they are one in the same." She glanced away, still smirking. "Hilda, Chieftain Ragnar has another captive."

Off in the corner, an overstuffed woman who, by the looks of her, had been working in the fire rooms for years, turned and with a roll of her eyes snapped, "Another one?" She made her way slowly to her new worker, making sure to stop and taste each dish being prepared as she came. Her clothes were spotted with hardened food and her skirt showed signs of fire damage, suggesting it had swept one too many times against the flames of a soup cauldron. Her face was hard and upon scanning Freya she reached out and gripped Freya's right arm, squeezing up and down her bicep. Hilda quickly let go, clearly annoyed. "Like so many others here, capable only of stirring soup."

"Work them harder," Helga suggested before she turned and left.

"It served you well," Hilda quipped. Then she slapped a wooden spoon into Freya's hand and waited.

Freya stared back. Was she to stir the soup with her wrists tied together? "What about the ropes?"

"Keep them from my soup." Hilda snapped before turning to boss another young girl into kneading more bread dough.

With no choice left to her, she dipped the large spoon into the hot cauldron and stirred the soup without caring if it spilled or burned. When no one was looking, she sampled the soup. "Not too bad." She'd need her strength to escape, so she helped herself to more. Freya kept a careful eye out so as not to get caught in case Hilda took her off the task—a duty she found rewarding if for no other reason than it offered her the chance to fill her appetite.

The fire rooms never quieted from the crackling of flames, the chopping of ingredients, the stirring of pots, and the commands from Hilda. "More carrots! You, girl, I want a roaring fire, not a campfire. Cheese cannot slice itself!"

It was like listening to a bad cooking show, but as long as Freya was left alone with her pot of soup and thoughts of escape she could care less who Hilda ordered about.

"More logs under that cauldron."

It was Freya's cauldron this time, but Freya barely took

notice of the girl bent at her feet. She was lost in devising a way to start a commotion and escape. Perhaps she could kick over her pot of soup or catch the thorpe on fire.

"Help me with these logs," whispered a soft voice.

Freya looked down to see a dirty-faced girl with sunken cheeks staring up at her. "Um, sure, of course." When she squatted down to help, the girl gently grasped the rope at Freya's wrists and revealed a small knife hidden among the logs.

"Brilliant." A feeling of hope swelled in her chest. "My father always said not all Vikings were bad," she whispered as a thank you.

The girl's powder blue eyes smiled. "I am no Viking. My name is Noora." Her voice was light and airy. "And you come not from here," she said, sawing at the rope with the knife and a nod at Freya's clothes.

In an unconscious reaction, Freya found herself smiling back at the girl's kind expression.

Noora glanced away from Freya, cautiously looking to see if she was being watched, then whispered, "Were you summoned?"

The blunt question shocked her. "You know? Who else knows? Do you think Ragnar knows?"

Noora shook her head. "Only those of Walden's Forest." The rope broke loose and she added it along with two logs to the fire. "Quickly back now. Do not let Hilda see you tarry from your chore."

"Oh, right." Standing up to stir the soup as she had been doing, Freya leaned and whispered, "Do you know a way out of here?" But Noora's response was drowned out by Hilda's barking.

"Have your ears deafened upon arrival?" A ladle smacked Freya across the back. "Out with the soup I said."

A second woman standing with Hilda pushed Noora to the side. She grabbed a handle on the cauldron with her bare hands and tossed Freya a look to do the same.

"I can't do that. That handle's boiling hot. I'll need a towel or something. Unless you want me to drop the soup." There was a cloth on the cutting table and Hilda threw it at her. Freya took it willingly but could still feel the piping hot handle warming her fingers.

The cauldron was heavy indeed, nearly causing Freya to buckle under its weight, yet somehow she managed to help deliver it to its serving position alongside the other dishes in the smorgasbord. Her eyes darted this way and that, searching for any signs of Erik's whereabouts. She spotted none.

Several warriors looked busy doing nothing other than chitchatting. One came over with some bread, which he dipped in the soup. Upon swallowing his sample he turned to the woman and asked, "Have the fire rooms learned of Astrid?"

"Oh, Olaf, unless we are to cook the dead beast, when do

interesting tellings ever reach us?"

He let out a hearty laugh, his belly jiggling with each staggered breath. Freya didn't get the joke, making it easy to zone the two of them out and continue her search for Erik.

"I say to you," the man began to gossip. "Mutwik heard Oslow announce a resurrection."

The woman raised a brow. "Of Astrid?"

"Chieftain Ragnar keeps company with Volvas—his powers ever growing."

She nodded in agreement. "'Tis true. The ristir at his neck has done him well."

Freya's focus came whirling back to the woman. Ristir. She could spell it in her sleep. R-I-S-T-I-R. It was the last thing she'd overheard her father say at the museum. Oh why hadn't she stuck around to hear him tell the police what it was? If the ristir, like the woman said, was around Ragnar's neck then she could guess it was the wooden block she'd seen him play with but more than that she didn't know. She certainly hoped though that it didn't mean Ragnar had anything to do with the break-in at the museum. Either way she knew she had to get the ristir from him. Taking it might not put a stop to whatever his plans were but at least she could bring it back to the museum and her father would know what to do with it.

"Come away and steal a look at Astrid while he yet cannot attack."

"I think I ought to if what you say is true."

With that, the two walked off together leaving Freya completely unattended.

Of the few Vikings in view, none seemed interested that Freya was alone. They were all too busy stringing flowers, setting up tables, or rolling out barrels of mead to take notice of her. Freya knew her chance at finding Erik might be short-lived should Hilda catch her doing nothing, so she picked up a platter of cheese and pretended to deliver it to one of the tables. Only she pretended to deliver it to each and every table. Moving from one to the next, she craned her neck to view between huts, around huts, and in huts. One such view offered nothing but an empty room aside from a row of stacked bunks lining the far wall. With the tray of cheese in hand, she headed off to the next table. Round wooden shields hung neatly in a row. Underneath them lay battle axes and swords. Freya swallowed back a lump in her throat. Escaping alive would be harder than she thought. Carefully, she moved the cheese platter to the next table. The hut viewable from there was too dark to see inside, and she dared not call out Erik's name for fear someone else would come answering. One more hut to check, one more chance to find Erik. Hopeful this would be the jackpot location, she headed for the final table.

"What on Midgard is this?" snapped Hilda's voice. "You, maid, in the ridiculous tunic."

Freya whirled around with the cheese platter in her hands.

"Just delivering this."

"To the fire rooms with you!"

Defeated, Freya plopped the platter down and headed in the direction of Hilda's bossy pointed finger.

The fire rooms lay outside the ring of tables and huts. If snooping around hadn't helped her find Erik, it had at least helped her get her bearings. Thus she now knew enough to head behind the empty hut with bunks. As she crossed through the circle of tables, she felt Hilda's untrusting eyes follow her. Now wasn't the time to make a break for it. But now *was* the time to use the opportunity of Hilda's absence from the fire rooms to get more info out of Noora. Freya kept her pace steady, trying not to look too eager to return. She passed the darkened hut on her right and stepped out into the breezeway between it and the one housing the weapons.

"Stand aside," called a voice between the huts. And a good thing too or Freya would have collided with four men and the large box they were carrying.

Her eyes widened; the box was large enough to carry a human inside. "Erik?"

"Stand aside," grunted one of the men, shoving her away with his gorilla-sized hand. The force of it pushed her right into an onlooker, or so she thought. Freya twirled around to make her apologies and came face to face with Helga and her scar. The mark was long and thin rounding her temple. Whatever had caused it had just missed her eye by a hair.

Helga caught her staring, and struck her against her cheek. The sting of the blow throbbed but something inside Freya told her not to show any weakness. She looked Helga dead in the eye and steadied her hand, withstanding the desire to rub and soothe her cheek.

Helga smirked. "Up front with you, or have you not heard the horns blowing?"

No, she hadn't. But apparently everyone else had for they were coming out in droves and filling seats at the tables.

Erik, she thought, her hope renewed. Freya did an about-face from the fire rooms and quickly scanned the crowd for the box. It had been placed at the front near a small table set for one. Ragnar's. She curled her lip. Opposite the table and box lay a very still dog, which was either completely undisturbed by the commotion of the gathering or...dare she think it? The dead dog, Astrid—a.k.a. the beast to "be brought back."

"Not possible," she said half to herself. How could a dog be brought back from the dead? Why? What purpose would it serve?

A forceful shove to her shoulder, and she like many others, stepped to the side to part the way for Ragnar's grand entrance. The sight of him excited the villagers, who began to clap and cheer loudly. Ragnar swam through their praise, taking notice only of it and not of them. Eye contact wasn't met, handshakes weren't returned, his shoulders jerked to toss congratulatory pats away, and sneers told others to keep their distance. As he reached the table, the Viking warriors from the forest took their place behind him. Only his nephew Askr, whose Neapolitan-colored hair was a spitting image of his uncle's, was allowed to stand close to him.

Ragnar raised his right hand. The crowd silenced immediately.

"I have made a promise to those who follow me. You shall rise HIGHER than the gates of Valhalla." An orchestra of noises swept over the thorpe, and there were grunts of agreement, pounding of goblets, and claps of hands as all rejoiced wildly.

Raising his voice above them all, Ragnar commanded as if ready for battle, "Let it be known—our ascent sets forth today!"

The thorpe exploded with shouts of excitement. No one cared that Freya didn't share their sentiment. They called to each other over her head, threw arms around one another, caring little when she got caught between them, and even included her in the merriment with a smile when she made eye contact with them. She needed to tread lightly if she were to make it out with Erik unharmed. Slowly, she began her way to the front hoping she could sneak Erik out of the box while no one was looking. The Vikings let her pass by, too busy conversing with their friends and fellow warriors.

"I knew Ragnar would be the one."

Freya pushed past the comment and the man who spoke it.

"Aye. Unlucky be the day our foes should meet us now!"

Their laughter filled her ears as she headed forward. Weaving around the labyrinth of sweaty bodies, large bellies, and loud voices, Freya finally came just a few people deep from the front when Ragnar raised his right hand again.

All eyes met his. All voices ceased.

"In this box," he began with a booming voice in no need of a microphone, "we build our army. The Nine Realms will be ours to rule. Every living creature and being will bow to us or fear their own mortal destruction." Everyone drank up his words as he continued. "Dark magic will fail at the command by those who dare threaten its use against our very existence. We will power ourselves as casters of spells and master the inhabitants of Yggdrasil's realms—both of the day we live and of the generations to come, from now throughout eternity!"

The villagers went wild and Freya could do nothing. She couldn't put a stop to Ragnar, not here, not now. She couldn't free Erik with everyone interested in the box. And she couldn't run without rescuing Erik first. How would she face herself if she left him behind?

Ragnar raised his hand to the crowd once more, then motioned with a nod of his head to a warrior behind him. The man stepped over to the box and unlatched the metal lock at the top of it.

"Shield your eyes," Freya heard someone nearby whisper to a neighbor before the front panel fell forward. She didn't question the advice and quickly looked down at the ground.

"Mutwik," Ragnar called out.

"Aye, Chieftain Ragnar!" Freya recognized the bellowing voice as that of the man who had taken Erik's bearskin coat from him.

"Let your appetite for curiosity be quenched. Look upon what I have conjured."

A dull thudding sound came and the ground began to shake. Freya didn't dare look up. The crowd took to life with grunts and cries as this one bumped into that one and that one stepped on this one. Then, a thunderous crack whipped above the commotion, though the clouds were white and the skies were blue.

Mutwik fell.

With her eyes still low, Freya could see him. He lay still, his body frozen. No one came to his aid.

To her horror, dense swirls of smoky white poured out of his temples, forehead, and crown, intertwining above him while morphing and mirroring the very shape of his paralyzed body. She could see him staring back up at the ghostly figure. The only movement from him was the fluttering of his eyes as he blinked furiously in protest. Neither sounds nor lashing out came from his otherwise lifeless body.

The Vikings of the thorpe kept their distance, all but one.

At first Freya mistook the person who was concealed behind a dark brown cloak to be just that—a person. But he wasn't. *It* wasn't. If mud could take form and walk about, then this would be that form.

From out of one of its long sleeves came a hand, as cracked and muddied as its feet. Holding a small leather pouch, the cloaked creature loosened the drawstring of the pouch, then, spreading the mouth of the pouch open, it lowered the bag to just above Mutwik's head. Instantly the ghostly figure floating above darted into the pouch.

With a tug of the drawstring, the creature sealed the figure away.

Ragnar's voice came booming, "It is done. I have taken his spirit." He eyed Mutwik who lay powerless and still, save for his continuous blinking. "I am your chieftain lest you forget it." Then, opening his palm wide, Ragnar turned to the Viking at the wooden box and demanded, "The pouch."

The Viking wasted no time in retrieving it for Ragnar, and Freya wasted no time in making her way to the very front of the crowd where she was quick to notice that so, too, had the conjured creature. As if the clock of time were rewound, the conjured creature had returned to the box it had only moments earlier come from.

As a precaution, she shielded her eyes from it and its box for fear she might become the next victim.

Ragnar held the pouch up for all to see as if it were a rare and precious jewel on display. "Many a brave warrior has fallen too soon, battle-death seizing them. So I say to you foul shame that they are gone."

Shouts of "Aye" sang out in unison.

"Oleg was the fiercest," confirmed a woman. "To the death with Harald!"

Others picked up her sentiment and repeated, "To the death with Harald."

The only Harald Freya knew was Grimhild's father. If he was the Harald in question and therefore deemed as Ragnar's enemy, then that was reason enough for her to like him.

A slight wave of Ragnar's hand brought the group quiet again. "Aye, Nessa, Oleg was the fiercest. And *will* be again."

The villagers exchanged glances of confusion.

"Death lacks life, nothing more," Ragnar explained. "And what is life, but a spirit." He held the leather pouch higher. "Mutwik's spirit, the spirit of one in exchange for life in another."

Freya's stomach sickened at the swelling excitement.

"Those alive only in memory shall live once more! Our army shall rise! We will rule those who do not join our path."

The excitement rose from those eager to reunite with their fallen heroes.

"Mutwik dared venture from this path." Ragnar's eyes narrowed on Helga, sending a message of warning. Helga, whose hands held each of Mutwik's, released her grip and backed away. Ragnar extended a finger and pointed at the box. "Dark magic in the ristir at my neck has afforded us this grogger, this spirit snatcher. It will afford us another, and another. Every grogger conjured is one grave emptied of our own. Let us refill those graves with the bodies of our enemy!"

"Aye!" The responses buzzed all around.

But Mutwik wasn't dead, Freya wanted to shout, her face as worried as her father's now that she understood what a ristir was.

Ragnar raised his hand.

All fell silent as they watched Ragnar stroke the head of his beloved dead dog.

"Draw your final breath, Mutwik, for you shall cross me no more." Ragnar took hold of the ristir at his neck and opened the pouch. He pulled the ristir before him and began reading from its side. "Skila honum fra gurum!"

Suddenly the dense swirls of milky white poured out of the pouch spilling over and landing on Astrid. A gasp for air strangled in breath sounded from the crowd.

Mutwik.

Freya turned and saw his life was no more.

"Mutwik!" Helga's voice cried out.

A man next to him knelt and checked for breath. "Dead," he proclaimed.

Everyone, including Freya, about-faced. Astrid, now sitting, was energetic and alert. Full of new life, he nudged his nose into the palm of Ragnar's hand just as the grogger dematerialized.

"Hoo-rah for Chieftain Ragnar!"

"Down with Harald."

"The Nine Realms will be ours!"

"Hoo-rah," they all sang out. "Hoo-rah, hoo-rah!"

A sinister smile spread across Ragnar's lips, causing Freya to shudder. "Ah, my fellow clansmen, our festival has only yet begun. My nephew, knowing how to please his uncle, has brought us the most perfect sacrifice for today's celebrations."

Askr motioned to some men inside a neighboring hut.

"I shall take great pleasure," Ragnar continued, "with this sacrifice in particular." There was a wild look upon his face as he addressed the crowd.

The group of men appeared from the hut with Erik in tow.

Freya's heart raced.

"Boo," a child cried out.

The man next to her snarled, "Vile Berserk."

"That one killed his own mother," yelled a woman.

"Then attacked the chieftain's own nephew," hollered another.

"Death to him!"

Freya panicked as the mob grew angrier. She bolted in between them to get as close to Erik as she could.

"Behold," Ragnar bellowed, holding up Erik's bearskin

coat. "A Berserk's lifeline."

Freya saw Erik struggle to free himself from the ropes. Ragnar saw him as well and laughed. "Desire you your coat?" he asked, moving several paces from Erik, then wiped the smile from his face and snarled, "I will destroy you."

Erik began to cough and tried to catch his breath. He lunged forward, but the warriors holding the ropes tight were stronger.

Ragnar continued to distance himself from his captive, causing Erik to choke and gag. "Lo, how many paces away from your coat are necessary to suffocate you? This, after all, is the only way to slay a Berserk."

Erik gasped for air.

"What say you? Eight? Nay, perhaps you spoke nine." Ragnar increased their distance one step more.

Freya couldn't believe what she was witnessing. She couldn't let this happen. Her panic grew, and without thinking, she screamed at the top of her lungs, "NOOOOO!"

The sudden outburst jolted Ragnar, who turned on Freya with rage in his eyes.

"Would you rather it be you?" he laughed wickedly, raising his finger and pointing at her.

Freya felt something pierce inside her as if his finger had gone straight through her stomach.

"Would you rather it be you?" The piercing stare now turned to pain. She grabbed at her sides and turned to see Erik grabbing at his throat.

"I won't let you strangle him," she yelled at Ragnar. Wanting to run and grab the coat from his hands, she couldn't. She doubled over and fell to the ground from the cramping pain inside her. She screamed in agony. The crowd near her stepped back. So did Ragnar.

Freya lay on the ground, wriggling in pain as the coughing and gagging sounds from Erik began to grow weak.

She struggled to stand. In excruciating pain, she stared Ragnar down with boiling anger and screamed out, "ERIK!" just before the world around her went dark.

CHAPTER VI

1-2-2-0

"**B**ring her back!"

A white light flashed in the darkened void, and in its wake appeared hundreds of blue-flame faces.

Freya spun upwards, her hair whipping down in her face. "WAIT," she shouted at the flames, though her own voice was soundless to her ears.

The flames flickered wildly.

"The Raedslen powers are too strong!"

"It's too dangerous this way!"

"For the sake of the Nine Realms, we must hurry!"

Flash!

A white light blazed before her eyes. A scene illuminated. Gathered before a stone altar were three cloaked women standing by Yggdrasil.

The Norns.

Freya sped upwards at a frightful rate.

"HELP—I'm not ready to leave!" Her voice still soundless.

Flash!

The scene was gone and the sky was blue, her feet on solid ground.

Everywhere she looked were the familiar tall boulders in their oval formations.

"I have to get to Father!"

"Pardon?"

Freya whirled around. A few graves over was an employee from the museum filling in the hole she once thought to be the perfect hiding place for the Raedslen egg. How long ago that all now felt to her.

"Darn kids digging in a historic landmark," he huffed over his shoulder. "No respect, I tell you. I warned the curator to install security cameras out here. Well, too late now."

"Um...that is too bad." Not about to tell him the culprit was the very person he was speaking to, she quietly tiptoed away, then when out of sight, sprinted for home.

While dodging in between boulders, hurdling the graveyard's stone wall, and flying over Salt Creek's wooden bridge, her mind was fixed on one thing only—the belief that her father would know how to put everything right, her transformation curse, the Nine Realms, Yggdrasil, Ragnar, and especially Erik. She couldn't bear the thought of him dying at Ragnar's hand.

Nearing home, she dashed across the backyard and bolted through the kitchen door yelling, "I'm home," at the top of her lungs. "I'm home, I'm home!"

The kitchen was empty so she raced for the living room.

There, she found her sister sitting in an armchair reading a ridiculously thick science book.

"Susanne, didn't you hear me? I'm home!" She beamed widely, her arms outstretched to embrace a welcome.

Susanne shut the book with a loud thud, but didn't get up.

Glaring at her younger sister she snarled, "Oh happy day, you've decided to return. Do you even know what kind of trouble you've caused for me?"

Freya was dumbfounded. For her?

"Father told us where you went, about your dreams, about the stolen object. He told us he gave you that thing to hide, the thing I said for you to give to me. But you never listen! You swallowed it, Freya!" Tears were welling in Susanne's eyes. "It haunts me having watched you disappear before my eyes! And I—I did nothing. I could *do* nothing! I couldn't protect you. I failed you as a sister."

Freya shook her head fervently. "No, no, you didn't!"

Susanne reached up to pull her sister near, grabbing ahold of Freya's wrists.

"OW!"

Susanne's fingers had pressed directly into the rope burn sores. Susanne turned her sister's palms up, shrinking back at the wounds and flayed skin. "What happened to you?"

"It's a long story," she answered, removing her hands from view. "But it's why I need to talk to Father."

"He's not here."

"Is he at the museum?"

"No. He left in search of something called a 'Nimrah.' He said it would help to bring you back."

"But I'm back now."

"Look, I don't have all the answers but he said he *had* to find it. He also said if you were to come back while he was gone to tell you that he placed something in his office for you."

"In his office? Why not just leave it here?"

Susanne shrugged her shoulders. "I don't know. His only instructions were to look in your 'special spot.'"

"What special spot?"

"What do you keep asking me questions for? I thought you'd know what he meant."

Freya shook her head full of worry. "Not a clue. Then we'll just have to search the whole place looking for it."

"We?" a twinkle of delight sparkled in Susanne's eye.

"Of course. I can't do this without my big sister."

"That's right," she threw an arm around Freya's shoulders giving them a gentle hug. The affection was returned. "Come on; let's go find what he hid for you."

"Like an adventure?"

"Ah, Freya, you and your search for adventures. Haven't you filled your appetite with this one?"

"My appetite…" that word had lost its appeal since eating the egg. "Su-su, did Father tell you anything about the object he gave me?"

"Just that he didn't want us to worry more than we already were."

So he knew what he had given her.

After leaving a note for their mother, the girls jumped on their bikes and sped to the museum.

They found the museum back up and running again, no police tape or blockades prohibiting visitors. From the looks of it, today was a typical busy day for the museum, the parking lot full of vacationers' RVs and tourists' cars. Even the bike rack was packed.

Eerie as it was for Freya to see things return to normal so quickly, it somehow gave her hope to know that life *could* be normal again.

"Did they find what got stolen?" she asked, dismounting her bike.

"No, and Father's extremely worried they never will."

Susanne pulled open one of the tall front doors and held it for Freya to enter. Inside, the Great Hall was swarming with visitors and tour guides. The sisters had to reroute their path to the employee door about a hundred times to avoid smacking into various groups of photo-takers.

Inching their way past the Tapestries Wing, something caught Freya's eye. Hanging on the wall against a yellow background was an intricately woven scene depicting a forest and brown bear. "Look at that. I think it's a Berserk."

Never having shown much knowledge in Viking history, Freya didn't take it rudely when her sister threw her a questioning look.

She opened her mouth to explain, but…

"I didn't mean to eavesdrop into your conversation, Freya. I heard you identifying the Berserk in this one. I didn't know you were into tapestries."

"Oh," she panicked, her judgment no match for the head of the Tapestries Wing.

Maren's brows raised in friendly encouragement for her to continue. "Don't be bashful. You were right; that bear does represent a Berserk."

"Nice one, Freya," Susanne quietly complimented.

Whispered or not, her sister's sincerity deeply moved her; for with all the many "pulled a Freya" remarks aimed her way, she had never thought she could ever impress Susanne. And now she had.

With her newfound confidence, she began. "Although I really don't know much about them, I have thought maybe they are tamer than people think."

"My sentiments exactly," agreed Maren. "We have many tapestries depicting the monstrosities of their might, so clearly the Vikings saw them as beasts, and thus history dictates we should too. However, there is a tapestry here that I unearthed years ago. After seeing it I've always questioned if the view on Berserks was accurate."

"What does it show?"

"Oh the tone is very peaceful, very calm, in fact. It depicts a Berserk and the Norns in a completely noneventful confrontation."

"The Norns? You know the Norns?"

Maren sweetly laughed. "I should hope so, since I've dedicated my lifework to the study of Viking Era tapestries. I wouldn't be an expert in my field if I didn't know who the Norns were. You know, if you're interested…I have a tapestry that I'd love for you to see."

Freya glanced at Susanne whose only response was a shrug of her shoulders.

"Sure, I guess. As long as you think it won't take too long."

"We don't mean to be rude," Susanne jumped in quickly, jabbing Freya's side. "It's just we're running an errand for our father."

"Completely understandable; I'll be quick. This way then, shall we?" She led them up the row of tapestries from which she'd come and to an employee door neither Freya nor her sister was familiar with. Punching in the security code, Maren opened the door into a room full of tapestries in need of repair.

Scores of them hung on movable rods for easier access in cleaning and repairing. About a half-dozen men and women could be seen around the large room. Many on scaffolding, lying down or standing, some sitting in chairs on the floor, and even a few on short stilts walking around passing materials and tools to the artists. Everyone was there to restore the museum's many thousand-year-old tapestries yet to go on display. One man, busy reworking the hem of a dark-colored tapestry, pulled a large needle threaded with thick black wool through the bottom of a tightly woven outdoor scene; at a smaller tapestry, a short woman holding a bottle of clear cleaning fluid in her hand was wiping a cloth rag over a faded corner area. Elsewhere, another woman was using a crude broom of branches tied to a metal handle with twine to beat out dust; one tapestry lying flat on the ground was being steam cleaned, while another depicting a Viking warship complete with sails and steering oar and filled with Viking men was being vacuumed; and still there were several more tapestries waiting for workers to reweave broken strands of spun wool.

Maren wove the girls through the intricate labyrinth of scaffolding, making their way to the back corner of the conservation room. There, hung by a myriad of fastened tabs to hold its heavy weight, was a tapestry of the grandest scale; its entirety viewable only by cocking one's head.

"This is it," Maren said in adoration. "A magnificent wonder."

"Oh, wow. Well it's um..." Freya tried searching for a complimentary word, but as far as she was concerned, its appeal to museumgoers was none and the decrepit thing was better off hung here on a back wall than out in the Tapestries Wing. She saw no fancy patterns in it nor anything of interest that paying tourists would want to look at; there was no fringe, its colors were dull, and its border had no intricate design. It didn't even have any inscriptions woven into the scenery to at least entice viewers into wondering what the mysterious script said. There was, however, a wide tear in the middle of it where the strands of wool were frayed. Perhaps someone could find that interesting, but she didn't.

"I think what my sister means to say," Susanne jumped in, thrusting a reproachable jab in Freya's side, "is that it's remarkable such an old artifact still exists."

Shooting Susanne a nasty glare, Freya rubbed her elbowed ribs. "Yeah, that's what I meant."

Maren whirled around clapping her hands together. "Oh, you don't know how happy I am to hear you say that. These tapestries are priceless to me. They are my life's work. Then the other day I had a feeling, an inkling of a feeling, that you might just be as passionate about them as well."

"You did?" The words spat out quickly from shock.

"Oh yes. When I saw you at Yggdrasil the other day—the

130

way you were looking at the tree, the concern you had for its well-being; it confirmed my feeling."

"About...tapestries?" Freya didn't follow the connection.

"Precisely. Yggdrasil is the tree of life; its protectors are the Norns, the very weavers whose tapestries hold the key to guarding Yggdrasil."

"The tapestries hold the key?" her widened eyes darted across the tattered wall hanging. The answer to foiling Ragnar's plan was staring her in the face, right here— somewhere—in this tapestry. She could kiss Maren! "What does this one say about Yggdrasil?"

"Oh." The excitement dwindled from Maren's expression. "I was hoping... *you* might have some insight."

"Me?" Disappointment punched her like Susanne's jabs to the side. "Are you saying you can't read them?"

"Freya," whispered Susanne. "Don't be so rude."

"Oh I can. Well, in a way. You see, it isn't the question of ability, rather...hmm. Freya, there are some things all the research in the world can't teach us."

This was zero help. Freya needed answers. And she needed them now. If her father was gone, if Maren had nothing, if she was stuck in the present, how was she to stop Ragnar? More than ever she needed whatever it was her father had hidden to be that missing puzzle piece—her solution to the problem, the key, the answer.

Trying to gather some composure so Susanne wouldn't

poke her again for being rude, she began to make her leave with, "Well, gee thanks, for the interesting tour, but my sister and I really do have to get back to our father's errand."

"Please wait. There's something I'd like for you to see."

Susanne nudged her sister to stay, frowning at the rolled eyes she received.

Caving in, Freya cordially responded, with the tiniest of polite smiles, saying, "Let's have a look."

A flush of excitement returned to Maren's expression as she quickly lifted the flap of frayed threads to plug the gash in the tapestry. "Now then, we'll start small. I want you to list all the objects you can identify—doesn't matter where you start." She pulled a laser pointer from her pocket, offering it to Freya who took it reluctantly.

Beaming the red light randomly at the first image she spotted, she said, "That thing, right there. I see, I don't know, it looks like a brown blob of some sort."

Maren clasped her hands together. "Excellent."

It wasn't exactly the reaction Freya had expected. "But I don't know what it is."

"Ah, yet you know it *should* be something. This tapestry is not at all in good condition, so we'll need to do some guesswork as to what your brown blob could be. We know this weaving dates to the Viking Era because we've tested the fibers in the wool. And we also know Vikings loved their tapestries to depict action. So, as there is only one brown blob in the picture, I think we can safely say the brown blob here was acting on its own, which rules it out as being a horse or sheep, as they tend to roam in groups. But these faded figures nearby—we know them to be human forms. However, they don't appear to be hunting the blob. Though they do have their weapons in hand, the weapons aren't aimed."

One? Brown blob? Freya almost gasped. Could it be a grogger?

"Maren, do you have any other tapestries with similar brown blobs?"

The bushy blond hair haloing Maren's face swayed to the rhythm of her head gesture. "No. This is the only one of its kind that I've ever seen. Though, bravo you, for thinking to compare like images as a way of extrapolating its identity, excellent research skills. You must often make your family proud."

Freya's chest swelled at the compliment, even with Susanne's stifled snigger.

"Should I go on?" she asked, the laser's red beam fixed on a thin tan rectangle.

"Please do."

"This looks familiar, but I don't know what it is." The object was long and marked by black runes. She'd seen a similar version hung around Ragnar's neck, but wasn't about to explain that to Maren.

"Ah, yes. It's called a 'ristir.' You saw it here in the

museum; Dr. Andersen excavated it himself. Yet regrettably, that was the object which was stolen."

Freya already knew everything Maren was sharing. Rising to her tiptoes for a better view, she eyed the curious oblong believing it to be the one Ragnar had. "What exactly does it do?"

Still examining the tapestry, Freya sensed Maren shift her gaze to her. There was something in the delayed response that made her eye Maren.

"You're right to assume that it does something." An astonished smile crept into the corners of Maren's mouth. Freya had seen such a smile once before when she gave a response in class to a question her teacher thought none of the students would answer correctly. "Though you wouldn't want to ever experience any of its capabilities. Dark magic brews inside of it, and in the wrong hands a ristir can conjure the most devastating deeds. Believe you me, the museum has every available detective out there looking for the ristir now."

She let the torn flap dangle down again, and moved to the side of the scene. "I'd like to ask you, if you can, to point out something other than an object. Is there anything else you can see in this hanging?"

Suspecting this was a test of some sort, Freya shifted awkwardly, hoping not to be a disappointment with her next find, and gazed once more upon the tapestry. The new angle caught the light differently and Freya jerked her head back, her eyes wide with interest.

"What is it, what do you see?" Maren asked, prodding for details.

"I see…" she hesitated. This was the second time she'd seen a tapestry with this feature, but she worried the oddity was just that—an oddity.

"Go on."

"Well, I see a single silver thread—there." With the laser beam, she traced the winding trail of the unique strand.

Taking her by the shoulders, Maren looked deeply into Freya's eyes. "I was hoping you did."

The words trickled coldly down Freya's spine.

"Not all tapestries were made by the Norns. This one was. That silver thread, as you call it, is their signature marking; separating their tapestries from all others. We've tested the fibers and know the strand is there, but until now you are the first to confirm seeing it."

Out of the corner of her eye Freya saw Susanne rush to the tapestry, straining to find the silver thread.

"I don't see it," she heard her mumble.

"It is a gift, Freya."

"A gift?" A gift the Norns knew she possessed? But what was she to do with it? What did it mean to be able to see the silver thread? She needed to get back to the Norns. She had to ask them what she was to do.

"Thanks, Maren, for showing me this. It definitely was

worth it. But if you don't mind, we really have to run that errand for our father now."

"It's absolutely all right with me."

"Thanks."

As quickly as she could, Freya led Susanne through the labyrinth of tapestries, out into the Great Hall and straight for the employee door. Without a moment to lose she punched in the security code on the number pad: 3-6-6-7, a number she could always easily remember because it spelled D-O-O-R.

With Susanne following close behind they bolted down the corridor, dodging the many artifacts protruding from the boxes stacked all around them. Both were eager to find what it was their father had left for Freya.

They opened his office door and came to a screeching halt.

"Who would do this?" Freya asked, gaping at sheer vandalism.

Everywhere were broken artifacts, upturned drawers, disheveled papers, and empty shelves, their contents destroyed or scattered across the floor.

Susanne pushed her forward. "Hurry, get in. And close the door behind you."

Both in shock, they stood and stared at the wreck. Their father's framed diplomas and hung artwork all ripped from the wall leaving gray frames of dust imprinted on the wallpaper where they had sat for years. Crates of uncategorized antiquities, jimmied opened and searched through, were callously thrown into the corner of the room. Even her favorite excavation of his, a seventh century enameled chest, was scratched and split in two, its lid torn off the hinges.

Susanne waded her way through the room, unable to step anywhere free of papers strewn about or crushed pieces of shattered artifacts. "Whatever Father left you, let's get looking for it and hope it's still here."

Freya's stomach sank. "You think someone could have taken it?"

"Does this look like Father's version of redecorating to you? Clearly someone was after it. And if it's still here, well, what if they decide to come back and search again? Now let's find it and get out of here."

"But, Susanne, if those burglars couldn't find it, how will we?"

"Think, Freya, think. Where would you have a special place in here?"

"Calm down, you don't have to bark at me." Shirking out of the line of fire, Freya stepped awkwardly over to their father's desk. She glanced around at the mess. "I don't know why Father thinks I have a special place here. Maybe he meant you did." On his desk was a picture of their family, before her grandfather had passed away. It had always been a favorite picture of hers, so before leaving it for someone else to claim, she picked up the frame, pulled away the picture and placed it inside her backpack's side pocket. In doing so, the broken glass from the frame spilt into a little pile on his desk.

"Of course I don't. I never used to play in here like you did."

"You think that's what I was doing? I never played in here. I came here to…to…to get away."

"From what?"

"From being invisible. I'd come to work with Father and journal. Hey, wait a second."

"What, what? Did you see it?"

"No, but when I think of it, under his desk is a secret compartment where there used to be this panel of wood you could remove. It made the greatest storage spot for my journal. But I stopped using it when I found a place in my room— never mind."

"Then that's got to be it."

The girls rounded the front of the desk, pushed aside their father's chair and squatted low. Freya reached at the back right panel and pulled. The board came popping off in her hands. Inside the hollow cavity of the desk was a red metal box.

"I've got it, Su-su. I've got it." Excitement rushed through her as she removed the case. Slapping it on the desk, she lifted up on the lid but it wouldn't budge. "It's locked."

"Try the combination wheels."

"With what numbers?"

"I don't know. Try your birthday—try the date 20th of

December."

Freya turned the lock to 2-0-1-2 as she was told.

"Nothing. It won't budge."

"Reverse the date."

1-2-2-0.

Click!

The lid popped open.

"The Raedslen?" Susanne read out loud.

Freya's heart stopped. It was the book she'd seen on his desk when she came to tell him about her dream. Only at that time she had no idea what the word meant.

"Why would Father leave you a book?"

"I don't know," she lied. Their father knew perfectly well the ramifications of what she had swallowed or he wouldn't have spared the family the information. And if he wouldn't say, then neither would she. But one thing was for certain: He wanted her to know what was in this book.

"Come on, Su-su, we've got what we came for. Let's go home now."

CHAPTER VII

IN SEARCH OF ANSWERS

"**F**reya, you're home!" In one loud clop the back door burst open, overextending its hinges and freeing her mother's outpouring affection. "I wasn't sure. Your note said you'd gone to the museum. I only got home myself just now." She held her daughter's shoulders at arm's length to have a good look at her. "Oh, never mind, come here." Pulling her into her arms, she smothered her with a hug. Freya melted at the embrace.

"Mother," Susanne whispered rather sternly. But her mother was busy planting a bouquet of kisses atop Freya's head. Susanne shrank back. "Just remember," she tried warning, but her caution fell on deaf ears.

"Su-su, you found her!" Bouncing out of the kitchen door came Charlotte, who was as quick to reach them as her questions were. "How'd you do it? Why'd you stay away so long? Will Father come home now? Did you meet any Vikings? Father said it was okay to talk about it with each other but not with friends. What was it like? Was the food good? Did you bring me back a souvenir?"

"Now, Charlotte, let your sister have a chance to breathe."

Little Charlotte squeezed her unwelcomed self into the hold Freya was clinging to with their mother. Standing her ground, Freya protected the sacred hug her disappearance had won her and gripped her even tighter.

"Come." Their mother pulled away, placing an arm around Charlotte and while leading her back to the house said, "I'm sure Freya will answer all your questions once she's had a chance to clean herself up a bit."

Gone for days, met Vikings, and the first thing her mother said was, "take a shower?" Freya looked at Susanne for help or an explanation but most importantly, for some love.

"Phew, that was a close call," Susanne rushed. "Think of Mother's reaction had she seen your wrists. I suggest after you shower you change into a long-sleeved shirt to hide the markings. You wouldn't want Mother worrying."

"Are you kidding me? That's exactly what I want her to do." She thrust her wrists at Susanne. "I want her to see what happened, to know how serious all of this is. I'm not just going to shower and wash away everything that happened. It doesn't work like that. Besides, what if I need medical attention? What if my sores are infected? Shouldn't Mother know? Isn't that her job? To care? To worry?"

"Freya, you don't know what it was like here while you were away. And they don't look infected to me. You're home now, and Father will be back soon. That's all that matters. In the meantime, go shower and afterwards we'll look at the book he left you."

So that was it? She was fine, everything was fine, and life would go back to her being ignored? In her mind the answer was yes. After all, the warmth of her mother's embrace was quick to cool in the speedy departure with Charlotte.

"Won't long sleeves in summer look suspicious?"

"Nah, it's unseasonably cool this year."

It made no difference. A winter coat couldn't win Freya her mother's attention even if it were ten sizes too big and sweltering outside.

After her shower she met Susanne in her room, where she immediately shut the door. Freya pulled open her backpack and dumped its contents onto the bed. Tumbling out came her journal, a second magenta permanent marker, a pack of gum, loose coins, a mechanical pencil, and the book.

"Here goes," she declared with nervous optimism.

But instead of jumping to open it, both girls stood perfectly still, wrapped in silence as they stared at it. A cloud of seriousness loomed over them and the book. Its red leather, the color muted through the wearing of centuries, was cracked and wrinkled. A loose strap, stretched through the aging of its leather, barely held the book closed. To open it would require little effort. Yet now that Freya was safe at home and face to face with the possible unpleasantness of discovering what its pages would have to tell her, her fingers recoiled at the mere thought of touching the book.

"Go on then. It's your book. You should open it."

Freya glared at her sister, who obviously also wanted nothing to do with the task. Unfortunately, of the two of them only Freya really knew exactly what lay at stake if she didn't learn what her father had intended for her to read. Knowing its importance, she squared her shoulders, unclenched her hands, and took hold of *The Raedslen*. The flap fell open and without hesitation Freya turned the cover. The page was tarnished, its wavy edges lined with a thick yellow coloring, its binding weak and torn.

She turned the page.

"You've got to be kidding me."

"What, what do you see?"

"Runes. Father left me a book of runes." She shot her sister a look of concern.

Susanne eyed the ancient text.

Freya leafed through the first few pages. Not a single one of them could she make any sense of and nowhere was there a translation to be found. She saw no signs of her father's handwriting, no notes, no highlights, no nothing. She flipped page after page until "Blank?" Turning chunks of pages at a time, she fell upon blank page after blank page. "It's all empty. Now what? It's not even a full book!"

"It's something. Otherwise Father wouldn't have left it to you."

"Oh come on, Su-su, it's hopeless. We don't know the first thing about reading runes."

"*We* might not, but we know people at the museum who might."

"Like who? You know Father takes Mr. Taberlig on every dig with him."

"Right, so keep thinking."

"You mean Maren? I've never seen her read runes."

"Simply because you've never seen her read them doesn't mean she can't."

"Maybe it does."

"Oh Freya, you're always so quick to give up on everything. It's as if you second-guess all that you think or do when really you ought to approach things more scientifically. If one variable gets eliminated or doesn't work out, try another. And another. And another until one does work out."

"Okay, we'll ask her to read it."

"No, it's not okay. Don't you see? Father left you this book for a reason. A book he knew you couldn't read. Why not translate it for you? No time? I'm not so sure. Why hide it? Why not just give it to me to give to you? I think it's safe to say, after seeing Father's ransacked office, that he knows more than he's letting on. Something's in that book that he doesn't want anyone else to know about. Something others could read if he had translated it. Freya, I should tell you, he looked frightened when he said there was something urgent he needed to do back at the museum. But I only thought that's because he was worried about your disappearance."

"Wasn't he?"

"Of course he was, and still is. My point being is that when he came back home and told me he had hidden something for you in his office, I thought nothing of it. Until now. Now I think he was worried someone else was after that book. You've got to find out what's inside that book before anyone else can."

"Then what about Maren? If he didn't leave it in her care then maybe we shouldn't let her know it's in ours."

"Exactly. Oh, I know! We could tell her we're doing a research project and we'd like to learn how to read runes. Then we wouldn't need to show her the book."

"Su-su, who would ever believe I was doing a research project in the summer?"

"True. But she would believe you wanted to learn to read runes so you could teach them to your friends and have your own secret language when passing notes in school."

"That's brilliant! She would believe that. Anyway, why didn't I ever think of it before? My notes are always getting confiscated."

"Then stop passing them."

"Never going to happen."

Freya caught Susanne eyeing the book, the playful look between them suddenly gone. "I hope it never does."

"Su-su?"

Her sister didn't look up. "Father said you'd come back."

"And I did."

"He also said…you wouldn't stay for long."

"He did? Did he say how long is 'long?'" A floodgate of thoughts opened, filling her mind with a multitude of scenarios she wasn't sure she wanted to face. Would she stay long enough to transform before her family's eyes? Or would she return to where she'd left and be forced to watch Ragnar kill Erik?

"I don't know how long. He didn't say. Maybe the book can answer that and maybe it can help interpret the dreams you were having."

Freya shot her sister a look. It was the second time she'd mentioned knowing about the dreams. "And how do you know about my dreams anyway? I never shared them with you."

"Father told us."

"How does he know about them? I never had a chance at the museum to share them with him." Suddenly the answer came perfectly clear to her mind.

"Now Freya, don't get mad."

It was too late for that. "Is there never to be any privacy for me?"

"It's just how Charlotte is. She doesn't know any better; she's just a baby."

"She's seven! If she's old enough to snoop around and read my diary then she isn't a baby. She knows perfectly well what she does."

"Well..."

"Are you for real? Are you honestly defending her?"

"Yes, I am. You weren't here to see how grateful Father was for the information."

It was the biggest blow to her ego. She wanted to be the one to please her father by telling him everything he'd learned about the Vikings was indeed true. And now perfect little Charlotte had stolen her thunder. If only she had made her father listen to her at the museum, made him hear about her dreams firsthand, then being grateful would have been a result of her actions and not Charlotte's.

"I still don't know why you never speak up for yourself. You're always so silent. Perhaps Charlotte wouldn't have to read your diaries if you shared with us what you share on those pages."

"Because..." no one ever listens; that's what she wanted to say had she been given the chance. But as always, someone with a stronger voice took the floor.

"Look, Father said your dreams were like an omen or

perhaps even part of a calling."

So Erik *was* right.

"You're part of something huge. I know he meant dangerous, but he wouldn't go into detail. That is why we have to get this book translated." Susanne picked it up and shoved it into Freya's backpack. "The museum opens at eight in the morning. Let's get there first thing and hope Maren can help."

She needed her sister's support and was glad to have it. "Deal. I like the story about learning runes in order to pass notes. I think she'll buy it too, but I also want to ask her about the Nine Realms."

"Why the Nine Realms?"

"Because I want to know what's in them, or more importantly, how to keep what's in them from getting out."

Her sister eyed her curiously. "What do you know that you aren't telling me?"

"Just that I need you to help me pack."

"Already on it." She pulled a flashlight from her top drawer and tossed it to Freya. "Put that in your backpack," she commanded with older sister flair, then dashed to their closet and threw over a clean pair of socks and a sweater. "These too." Then from a desk drawer she pulled out a zipper bag and a tin of mints. "You may not need mints, but take the tin just in case. Oh, and don't change into your pajamas tonight."

Freya laughed. The absurdity of sleeping in normal

clothes was too much.

Her sister whirled around. "What if you vanish at night, while sleeping? You wouldn't want to get caught back there in cartoon jammies, would you?"

"No, I guess not." Freya rolled her eyes but obliged.

That night she slept well, even if Susanne *did* instruct her to sleep with her backpack on. In the morning the two filled themselves with a breakfast of their Mormor's heavy gooseberry pastries, one of which she put in the tin, then wasted no time in getting to the museum. However, Dreaded Hill forced them both to walk their bikes up.

"Let's go round back, Su-su."

"Fine with me. The tourists only get in the way when trying to cross the Great Hall anyway."

It wasn't avoiding the camera-happy tourists that Freya was concerned with; it was Yggdrasil. She needed to see what state of health the tree was in.

"Hey, Freya, wait up! This isn't a race."

Ahead of her sister, she rounded the museum without a care to Susanne's request. Skidding to a swerving halt, her stomach dropped.

Yggdrasil was alive and strong.

"What does this mean?"

"What does what mean?" Susanna asked, pulling up along side of her. "My stars, I've never seen Yggdrasil look so healthy."

"Hurry Su-su, we have to find Maren."

Freya quickly punched in D-O-O-R on the keypad and unlocked the back entrance. As the dim light of the hallway encompassed them they made their way through the tunnel of boxes. The first door on their left, their father's office, was closed. Freya didn't bother to check and see if it had been cleaned up; something told her it hadn't. They walked on. To their right the long corridor leading to the Great Hall was equally congested with boxes of artifacts as the short passageway they were in now. A few steps further and another room on their left told them they had arrived at their destination. Its door, cracked ajar only the tiniest amount, let out a single sunbeam, which shimmered across the engraved nameplate of Maren Lind and Neil Taberlig's shared office.

Freya tapped against the door three times, each tap gently forcing the wooden door to creep open wider.

Inside the room Maren could be seen leaning over her desk with a magnifying glass in hand, examining what appeared to be a very tattered tapestry.

Freya knocked a little louder, this time catching Maren's attention.

"Oh, hello. Come in, come in, please come in." Waving her magnifying glass she gestured for them to enter. "To what do I owe this pleasure? Freya, have you come back to discover more fascinating tidbits about tapestries? I've a wonderful example right here if I do say so myself." With her free hand she patted the tapestry atop her desk as if to clarify which tapestry she meant.

Tapestries weren't exactly on Freya's mind unless they could give some sort of clue as to how to defeat Ragnar. "No, sorry." She stepped forward awkwardly, unsure of how to approach the subject of Yggdrasil. Searching the room for some inspiration to the topic, she fell short, spying only carpet color pallets, an antique loom, strands of yarn taped to the walls, and sketches of what she could only assume were of tapestries. And that was just the side of the office Maren occupied. Mr. Taberlig's offered no inspiration either, albeit his side was more orderly. His boasted neatly stacked books, a framed diploma, and a cup of hot coffee placed perfectly centered upon his desk.

"Um, we just came by to…" Lost for how to continue, her attention focused on the cup of coffee. Its steam rose in staggered jerking motions as if on a roller coaster slowing up a steep incline. She hated roller coasters, especially that part.

Turning her eyes away she noticed a black and silver container. Up on a filing cabinet on Maren's side of the office was a thermos. "Your coffee," Freya said.

"My coffee? Oh, yes, of course, where are my manners? Would you like a cup of coffee? Do children even drink coffee?"

"No, we don't. I just mention it because it doesn't look all that sturdy up there." Freya pointed at the leaning thermos atop a pile of haphazardly stacked papers then nodded in the direction of the roller coaster and added, "Whereas Mr. Taberlig's cup isn't at risk of spilling on anything."

Maren let out the sweetest of laughs but Susanne caught on immediately to Freya's observation. "Is Mr. Taberlig not with Father?"

"No, not this trip." Maren grabbed her thermos and placed it on the windowsill where nothing else had yet been piled. "The worries of the stolen artifact have been indeed pressing on all our minds; it's no wonder he keeps himself busy here. So, getting back to you girls—what brings you back today? Another errand for Dr. Andersen?"

"Actually," Freya began, "we were wondering about runes. How to read and write them, that is. You see Susanne has this brilliant idea that we could teach them to our friends and pass notes in school. Genius, huh?"

Maren tried hiding a smile of agreement. "I'm not so sure your teachers would be paying Susanne such a high compliment when they confiscate your notes. Yet I doubt any could read them."

"That's the beauty of it." Freya could feel Maren taking the bait. "So you'll help us?"

"Oh, if only I could. But I'm afraid I'm not skilled in reading runes myself. Dr. Andersen is a whiz at it and even Mr. Taberlig can do a decent job. I'm sorry to disappoint, but I'm just not your go-to for learning the runes. However, if it's tapestries you're after…"

Freya wasn't about to be lured by Maren's wide grin into playing another I Spy game with the woven threads. "Perhaps a rain check."

"Do you know anything about the Nine Realms, Maren?"

Freya threw her sister a look to kill. Something about seeing hot coffee on Mr. Taberlig's desk told her they should keep their mouths shut. But leave it to Susanne to always speak up.

Maren reached for the locket at her chest. "What would you like to know?"

"What's in them? Are they linked together?"

There she goes again, shooting off her mouth. Freya glared at her now to stop.

Fidgeting with her locket, Maren went to her desk and pulled open a filing drawer, except there were no files inside. Instead it was filled with long narrow canisters, each tied with a different colored ribbon. She pulled out one with a rainbow striped ribbon on it and unscrewed the lid. From within, she removed a rolled piece of parchment. "The first lesson in learning about the Nine Realms is this: Yggdrasil is the gateway to the Viking's universe."

"Speaking of Yggdrasil, have you seen how alive it looks?" Perhaps it was best for Susanne to ask the questions, for she was getting to the heart of everything Freya wanted to know. "It's as if it found the Fountain of Youth and drank it dry. I have a project in mind for the science fair; it has to do with plants. Maybe I should get the name of the gardener. If he or she can perform this sort of miracle on a thousand-year-old tree, I'm a shoe-in for top prize. Do you have his name?"

Maren wasn't wearing the same enthusiastic expression as Susanne when she answered, "If only I did." She then unrolled the parchment atop the tapestry on the desk, placing a paperweight in each corner to keep them from curling. In the center was a large tree. And from its trunk were eight fat branches, each with a colored sphere at their ends.

"These are the Nine Realms," Maren explained, pointing to the circles. "The Vikings' other worlds."

Freya took a good look at the circles. These were the realms Erik had told her about—the ones Ragnar wanted to control.

"Could the Vikings travel to them? Like we can to the moon?" she heard the words come flying out of her mouth and knew Maren interpreted the questions as more than just mere curiosity.

With the locket in her hand, Maren stared directly at Freya. "Yes. They could."

Silence filled the room. Freya didn't know how to respond or how to get Maren to stop staring at her. Luckily Susanne jumped in and began tracing her finger across the drawing. "Eight circles. So there were eight realms?"

Maren shook her head as if snapping out of a trance and

focused her concentration on the drawing. "No. There were nine. The trunk is the ninth. They called it Midgard. The modern translation would be 'Middle Earth.' 'Middle' because it was the center of all the realms, and 'Earth' because that's where the Vikings and Norns lived."

"The Norns being tapestry weavers," Susanne recapped.

"And protectors of Yggdrasil. But you are correct. They knew how to keep the Nine Realms from being opened and wove those secrets into their tapestries."

"Opened?" Susanne shot Freya a look. A look that said she knew her little sister wasn't telling her everything.

"Indeed." Maren grasped her locket. "Though it would take a powerful mind to open them, and they would need very dark magic to do so."

"Would a ristir contain enough dark magic to open the realms?" It was as if Susanne was working through all the mental notes and was now piecing them together one by one.

Freya turned her attention to Maren as any respectful listener would, yet her insides were exploding to know the answer.

"I believe yes. If the holder of the ristir knew what they were reading, then I believe it could very well aid in the opening of the realms."

"Do you know what lies in those realms that would make someone want to open them?" This time Freya was quicker with the questioning than Susanne.

"Danger. A Viking could cross into the other realms without much difficulty. We know this from many of the tapestries woven depicting their experiences. If you girls are truly interested, I wouldn't mind one bit to explain the Nine Realms to you."

"Oh, we'd love it!" Susanne nudged Freya to show a little less excitement. "That is, it's summer and we have nothing better to do."

"It would be my pleasure. Tapestries, the Norns, the realms, Yggdrasil, they are my life's work. I enjoy passing on what I know. I happen to have a meeting though in five minutes. If you could come back in an hour, the rest of the morning is yours. I'll fill your ears with details of information and by the end of it, you'll each be experts."

"How perfect." Freya looked with wide eyes at her sister. Their plan couldn't be going any smoother. "Isn't that so wonderful, Su-su?"

"Yes," but her eyes weren't as wide as Freya's. "Wonderful."

CHAPTER VIII

THE NINE REALMS

The girls went out back and sat beneath the shade of Yggdrasil while waiting for Maren's meeting to be over.

"You're awfully quiet, Su-su."

Susanne pulled at the grass near her knee. "I'm still processing everything."

"Yeah, I know what you mean. To have met Vikings, and not the kind at fairs, but real live, actual ones absolutely baffles me."

"No, not that. Everything Maren said, or didn't say."

Freya looked at her like her hair was on fire. "You're having a hard time processing what Maren said and not that I met Vikings?"

"Oh please, I've known for years that, scientifically, time

travel was possible. But now we're talking opening realms and dark magic. Science has nothing on that. And you, little sister—did you already know the realms could be opened? Is that why you wanted to ask Maren about them? Fess up, Freya. What is it you aren't telling me?"

"No way. Nice try. You already know more than I do thanks to Charlotte discussing everything with Father. You answer my question first. What did Father say about the summoning? About my dreams?"

"That's two questions. I'll answer one, then you answer one of mine."

"Fine."

"Father's been on a kick about Viking mythology for awhile now."

Freya lit up, recalling the conversation he had had with her at the museum. "Yeah, he told me he had reason to believe it was all real. He said…"

"The Vikings believed it to be real and now we have reason to believe the same."

"Yeah, that's exactly what he said! But what does that have to do with me?"

"Can I finish?"

Freya shut her mouth. She knew her sister well enough to keep quiet or pay the penalty of having the conversation end right there and then.

"Like I was trying to say, Father has been on a kick about

mythology for some time. I think it started when they unearthed the ristir. The ristir has actually been in the museum for over a year, he told us. Probably in one of those squished up boxes outside his office door if you ask me. At any rate, I'm not sure why or when he decided it should be showcased in the museum, but out it went on display about two weeks ago. The museum whipped up stories about its magical powers—you know how Mrs. Iver likes to build press—but Father always downplayed that side of it. I don't know what changed his mind, but all of a sudden his research turned to everything 'mythology.' And now to the part about you. Somewhere along the line he learned of a Viking omen, but what it was meant to forewarn he didn't say. All he told us was a summoning would take place; a summoning of the person who could put a stop to whatever was in that omen."

"But how did he know from my dreams that it was me?"

"Nope. You had your one question answered. Now it's my turn. Why did you want to ask Maren about the Nine Realms? You've clearly learned something while you were away, for you knew there were nine."

That was true. In fact, she had learned a great many things, not all of which she felt comfortable sharing with Susanne. For starters, she had no desire saying anything about becoming a Raedslen. Since it didn't appear their father had said anything, then neither would she.

"Well, go on; I didn't wait all day before answering your

question."

"Hold on. I'm thinking, I'm thinking." She couldn't just jump right in and say there was this bear she followed to steal the egg it stole, which then skinned itself and turned into a boy. So she began with, "As you know I met some Vikings. They were very interesting, to say the least. One of them told me about the realms. He said there's this bad man, a very bad man, Ragnar is his name—the bad man, not the Viking—and Ragnar wants to open the realms to rule them." Her sister was listening as if Freya was confirming what had already been suspected. "Su-su, I met Ragnar. He's the most terrible, horrible, vile man in all the world. Ragnar said he'll stop at nothing in order to rule the Nine Realms. And in ruling them he'll be able to rule the future as well."

"Then we'll just have to find out what's in those Nine Realms and find a way for him to not rule them. Come on, the hour is almost up. Let's get back to Maren and learn what we can."

They darted for the door when Susanna paused. She looked back over at Yggdrasil and asked, "How can a tree just bounce back to life like that?"

"Do you think it's a good thing?"

"Freya, that tree is the heart and soul of Viking mythology. With everything that's happened, I don't see how it could possibly be a good thing at all." She typed D-O-O-R on the punch keypad and the girls entered the corridor.

Maren was already in her office by the time the girls arrived and welcomed them in before they even knocked on the door.

"Wonderful, you've come back. Here, I took the liberty of taking two from the gift shop." She handed the girls a postcard each. "They aren't exact copies of the map I've laid out before us, but that's because the museum didn't use my sketch and insisted upon using some cartoonist's drawing instead. You'll get the gist and can follow along. Besides, those cards you can take home. So unless you have any questions, I say we dive right on in."

Freya and Susanne looked at each other and both shook their heads no.

"Good. Then ladies, may I be the first to introduce you to the Nine Realms." Freya and Susanne eyed the colored sketching. "Let us step into the minds of the Viking world, shall we? Come to the window. It's important to understand Yggdrasil before we begin." The girls followed Maren to the window and looked out at the tree they both thought they already knew. "Do you see the branches?"

Of course they did. They nodded.

"They are the gateways into the Nine Realms. Now I know you're asking yourself how come there are eight branches, yet Nine Realms, and you're right to ask that. What you may not know is the ninth realm is not accessed through a branch, rather through its trunk. And it is there where you will find the most important realm of all: Midgard. Literally, its name means 'Middle Earth' for it is the middle realm, the one connecting all the others together. You girls are already acquainted with Midgard, did you know that?"

Freya shook her head. She'd heard Erik use the word but wasn't about to let on anything about how she'd met *him*.

"I tend to read science books and leave Viking history to Father," Susanne responded.

Maren smiled. "No, Midgard isn't a place of fantasy you'd read about in books. It's here. It's where we live. Midgard is the Viking Realm and would have looked like you'd imagine it—with trees, pastures, villages, livestock and farms, rivers, lakes, and oceans, and of course Vikings. But their beliefs and customs were very different than ours are today. For starters, you don't have people going around crossing into other realms like you used to." Maren paused, and Freya saw her take hold of her locket. "Well, you shouldn't at any rate." Freya and Susanne exchanged glances. "But I digress. If we return now to my drawing I'll explain why it was that Vikings wanted to cross realms. Risky as it might have been, they did have a reason."

The girls followed Maren to her desk where her colored sketch depicted Yggdrasil's eight branches, each grasping a gigantic sphere.

"I say risky because crossing realms wasn't simple. One didn't just walk across a branch and voila, was in another realm. No, in fact quite the contrary. One had to first do something in the realm they were in before even being considered access to leave. Then came the task of entering another—a whole other set of rules applied for that. First there was permission granted by the Norns to even climb the tree."

"The Norns?" Freya interrupted. "I thought they just wove tapestries."

"Ah, you forget—the Norns also protect the tree. So of course they would allow Vikings to cross through the realms if the greater good of Yggdrasil is at stake."

"Ok, so only good Vikings could cross through."

"Hmmm, the Norns' decision process as to whom and why one could cross is a bit more complicated to research and understand. Easier is to explain how one managed crossing. Take for example, Midgard. In order to leave, one would need to sacrifice something.

"Yummy. Pig roast time." Freya's stomach rumbled gently at the thought.

Maren smiled again. "No, not that kind."

"Ew, then their firstborn?"

"No, not that either. Nothing as gruesome as you would think considering we're discussing Vikings. This sacrifice didn't require any killings. The sort of sacrifice meant here was more in the way of giving something up. A quality perhaps, or a bad habit."

"Well, that doesn't sound too difficult."

Susanne rolled her eyes. "You honestly think you could give up watching television or even journal writing?"

"I wouldn't have to. She said this sacrifice didn't include killing, and if I gave either of those up I'd die."

"Then it appears your chances of leaving Midgard would be grim," Maren teased. "For television didn't exist and only rune masters—most of whom were males—could read and write runes. However, let us say that you succeeded in sacrificing something dear to you. And let us say the Norns allowed you to cross. Now along with knowing how to survive the beasts and land of whichever realm you'd enter next, you'd also have to know how to have that realm be opened to you. Otherwise there was no hope of even entering it. There isn't much in my research that's told me what that may encompass; I only know it exists."

"What do you mean 'be opened to you?'" Susanne asked.

"From what I understand, the best way I can describe it is to liken it to a code of entry, like the keypad on a security door. If you have the code, then you can unlock the door."

"But Vikings could get the code?" asked Freya.

"Of course they could. There are so many stories, both written and oral, as well as tapestries all depicting the adventures and happenings that took place in the other realms. These have all been passed down through the centuries. Unfortunately not so much has been said about the codes."

"Then I guess my next question is what exactly *is* in those other realms?"

"Glad you asked, Freya, because that information I do know."

Maren dropped her pointer finger on the sphere that was completely white. "Alfheim or 'Elfin Home.' As the name suggests, Alfheim is home to elves. But be forewarned, these are light elves. Cross them and their dark spells would be cast most unfavorably upon you. One story that comes to mind is of an old man named Broddi. He spent many years in Alfheim as a rather peaceful farmer. He came to do trade with the light elves, then found Alfheim so much to his liking that he stayed. One day he learned of his daughter's poor health and wished to go be by her side. Well, unlike Midgard, leaving Alfheim didn't require a sacrifice; it required confessing one's most inner desire. But Broddi's most inner desire was not to be at his daughter's side; it was to become one of the very light elves who ruled the realm he had come to love and hold dear. Inner desires didn't have to be granted, simply confessed, though confession tended to result in consequences, so those who had desires best kept secret should tread lightly. Naturally the light elves learned of his desire, took offense and turned him to stone."

Freya's lip curled. "That seems harsh."

"I never said the light elves were kind."

Susanne eyed the sketch. "I'm guessing a lot of the realms have stories with harsh endings."

"They do, but there are also many with positive outcomes too. Remember each crossing plays an intricate role in the protection of Yggdrasil. Try this one," she pointed to a sphere on the opposite side of Alfheim. It was on a lower branch and filled with purples, blues, and reds. "Asgard. It means 'City of Heroes' because it houses the secret location of Valhalla. Perhaps you've learned about it in school?"

"Father said it's where the spirits of fallen warriors go when they die in battle."

"That's right."

"Good job, Su-su," Freya mocked. With an answer to everything Freya wondered why Susanne hadn't been summoned instead of her.

"Naturally Asgard was a great fascination to many a warrior. Their battle skills would one day honor them with eternal rest in Valhalla. For some, that day would be sooner rather than later. It was this thirst to remain alive, the thrill to battle and not fall, too soon at any rate, that had many warriors seek out Asgard as a sort of training ground to hone their skills. Those who crossed into Asgard were there for one reason: truth. And what truth would a warrior wish to seek? The truth in knowing how good their skills actually were. However, one couldn't gain the truth until one left Asgard. And, in order to leave Asgard, one had to battle all the spirits of Valhalla. Trust me, battle-thirsty Vikings kept Valhalla well stocked. Failure meant dishonor and a one way ticket to

Helheim—I'll get to that realm in a minute. Success, however, meant the ultimate glory and honor a warrior could ever aspire to achieve: the title of superior warrior. I know of only one Viking whose name goes down in history for ranking so highly: Beardless Braided Beard."

"What a funny name." Freya couldn't have agreed more with her sister.

"I think you'll come to find many Vikings had outrageous names. Though, for me, there's something about this Viking. I would love to know more about him for his story intrigues me. He's buried in the National Viking Graveyard here in Aalborg."

"He is?" Susanne and Freya asked in unison.

"Yes, though unfortunately it isn't allowed to exhume him. You'll often catch me eating lunch near his grave if I'm not sitting under Yggdrasil. You've been past his grave if you've ever taken one of the tours. The guides stop right at it. It's marked with runes, several of which are shaped similarly to the capital letter B."

"Hey I know that grave," Freya blurted out a little too excitedly. It was the only one she knew thanks to those Bs.

"Then you'll be happy to know no damage was done to it. I learned yesterday that someone had been digging near it." Freya felt Susanne give her the evil eye. "Luckily they dug outside the grave itself; think if they had tampered with Beardless's remains. All that history could have been lost forever. It's precisely why I push each year to have him exhumed. Learn what we can now before something happens. Again, I apologize, I digress."

"Oh, completely understandable, Maren. Father tells us all the time that the National Viking Graveyard is sacred property. Doesn't he Freya?"

Freya threw her sister a look saying let it go. "Yes, he does."

"Where to next?" asked Maren.

"The blue one," Freya offered.

"Ah, Jotunheim. The Mountain of Giants was home to the Frost Giants. Although hostile creatures, they are gifted riddle masters. For our more intelligent thrill seekers, a riddle was like charting a treasure map. Bring one to the Frost Giants or get one from them; a Viking's only way of leaving Jotunheim was to solve it himself."

"And this red and grey one?" Freya asked, pointing to a small sphere next to Alfheim.

"That's Nilfheim, or 'Dark Mist' as it is often referred to. Here lived the Valkyries." Both girls looked blankly at her. "The Valkyries were female warrior spirits. Their job was to collect the spirits of those who died in battle. They'd swoop down on their flying horses checking the dead and delivering only the spirits of the courageous to Valhalla. However, it's been said Valkyries also played a role in creating the dead, if you catch my drift."

They did.

"Nilfheim was also inhabited by a breed of dwarves called Nibelungs who were the guardians of a secret treasure. Some believe the treasure to have been the Valkyries themselves, while others believed it to have been jewels and gold."

"What do you believe?" Susanne asked.

"I guess a bit of both really. They say everything was created in Nilfheim. And if you've ever questioned why you were created…"

"All the time," sighed Freya.

Maren laughed. "Sometimes being a middle child will do that to a person. I should know." She gave Freya an encouraging wink, then continued with her story. "You can find out why here. Discover your purpose and you're free to leave." She then placed her finger on a yellow sphere above Asgard. "I've colored Svartalfheim yellow to represent precious metals. Although this is the 'Underground Realm.' I thought the dark elves could use a little lightening up. They're tricky little blacksmiths, placing nasty curses upon all their wares. One never knew if one was paying for the fine craftsmanship of a sword or for the threatening curse placed secretly on it."

"That doesn't sound fair," Susanne said.

Maren just laughed. "Again, we're dealing with elves. Besides, should the buyer pay a dark elf a large enough sum of money the curse could be lifted. Pay them an even larger sum of money and they'll forge a curse to work in your favor."

"Curses could work in your favor?" Freya was curious.

"Sure. Let's say someone needed to find something, a cursed stick could point the way. Or, perhaps someone wanted to harm their enemy and needed a cursed sword that would kill only the intended. But curses aren't something to take lightly. If you want to leave Svartalfheim, you'd have to place a curse on one of the dark elves themselves. It is said that a curse on a curse-maker could reveal secrets, but be careful because curses like these often backfired."

"With all those double dealings, I think you should have colored Svartalfheim black instead of the one over there," Freya said, placing her finger on a dark circle under Nilfheim.

"The Dark Realm you've pointed to is Helheim. I mentioned it earlier. It is the opposite of Valhalla. Here reside the spirits who *didn't* die in battle. Those may include death by old age, hunting accidents, drowning, or even curses. Although this may sound odd to us today that ordinary deaths passed eternity in a separate place as those who died in war, Vikings believed dying in battle was the only way to die honorably. It was a horrid thought to die and go to Helheim where your spirit sat in darkness on an overcrowded rowboat with nothing more to do than float up and down the icy cold waters of the fjords."

The girls' lips curled at the nasty description.

"Who would ever want to cross into this realm?" Freya couldn't fathom that Viking.

"You'd be surprised. As ruthless as Vikings could be, they were still human. And being human often means having fears. Unfortunately in life, it is often fears that block a person from moving forward. One might feel blocked for whatever reason and possibly not realize the cause is a deeply rooted fear. Crossing to Helheim will reveal that fear to you. It's the ability to get over it that will get one out of Helheim."

"All this talk of Helheim makes me feel I'm there now." Freya shuddered away the thought. "Let's go to the colorful pretty one here." She pointed at the large sphere to the left of Alfheim.

"Indeed, much, much lovelier." Maren smiled with an air of relief as if she too had just ventured out of Helheim. "Although I guess you could argue anything to be lovelier than Helheim. This one is called Vanaheim, or 'Land of the Vanir.' Vanaheim is the most beautiful and fertile realm thanks to the nature sprites, or Vanir. Its soil can grow anything or restore any other soil back to being fruitful."

"Is that why someone would cross there?" Susanne asked.

"No, those who came to Vanaheim came to discover what they were capable of producing themselves. Yet as lovely as all of that sounds, the Vanir were no dummies. In exchange for their help, they would ask for something in return. Unfortunately we have no records of any dealings that didn't end in death for the requester."

"That's horrible," Freya protested.

"It's horrible we hardly have any records, but I'm sure many came back alive, otherwise everyone must be failures and incapable of producing anything in their lives."

"Oh, right."

"This orange one is the last realm, then?" Susanne brought their attention to a small sphere at the bottom right of the tree.

"Yes, Muspellheim. It's orange because it is the Realm of Fire. This is the get-out-of-jail-free card as far as what realms had to offer. Vikings went here for almost anything. If the Fire Giants favored you, they could melt away, so to say, whatever you bid of them. If they didn't favor you, well, I'm sure by now you can guess."

"You didn't get to cross back." Freya and Susanne answered in unison.

"See, I told you I'd make you experts on the realms."

"Absolutely." The sincerity in Freya's voice caught Maren's attention.

"You girls had asked if a ristir could be used to open the Nine Realms and I said indirectly if one knew what they were reading."

"Can it do anything else?"

Freya tried blinking away Maren's locked gaze on her; it was Susanne's question after all. Why wasn't Maren addressing her?

"I believe a ristir can give one the strength to defeat the elements of the realms."

Bingo! That's what Freya had come to learn. She could kiss Maren for the information. Ragnar needed the ristir; without it he was powerless. All she had to do was get it from him. Or better yet, "Can a ristir be destroyed?"

"Freya," Maren said softly, taking ahold of her locket. "You saw the tapestry's silver thread."

That wasn't the answer she was looking for; it didn't even make sense.

Maren leaned in close to Freya's ear and whispered, "Ask the blue flames."

CHAPTER IX

WALDEN'S FOREST

In the corridor and out of earshot, Susanne flung Freya around demanding to know, "What is it you aren't telling me?"

Freya's shoulders sank. "Oh, Su-su, where to begin?"

"How about from the moment you disappeared."

"You said yourself—Father said I'm part of something huge. Do you think Maren knows I vanished and where I went?"

"Not a chance. Father was explicit about us not telling anyone. I even doubt Mr. Taberlig knows why Father left in such a hurry. I still can't believe he didn't go with him."

"I know."

"So? Go on—what is it you're keeping from me? What did Maren whisper to you?"

An unsettling nervousness tingled in her stomach. Butterflies, perhaps, butterflies that she was involved in something much deeper than she could comprehend. Another tingle came, stronger than the one before. The tingles turned to pain.

She yanked Susanne's arm, forcing her around the corner and out of sight should Maren come walking out the office door. "It's happening again!" In pain, she sank to her knees, biting her lip to keep from screaming.

Susanne pulled away, her eyes wide with fear.

Grabbing at her sides, Freya twisted and wriggled positioning herself to find even but a second of relieving comfort. Then when the pain suddenly subsided she looked up at her sister and all went black.

She fell much quicker this time, landing without any flashes of white or encounters with talking blue flames. Unfortunately, her skills at bracing her fall were equally as poor as before.

In an attempt to stand up slowly while rubbing the pain out of her butt, the only available cushioning to break her landing, she checked her location.

Instantly recognizing the hilltop she was on, she dove behind some neighboring trees to keep from being seen. Below her was an empty valley—a valley she knew to be the location of Ragnar's thorpe. And although he and the village itself were somehow secretly invisible as if by magic, she knew *she* was not.

Craning her neck above a wall of branches, she sighed at the empty valley below. No plan came to her as to how to sneak into the thorpe and rescue Erik. So she was left to hope he had escaped and that she'd find him waiting back at his tree home. Besides, it was much nicer to think something would work out smoothly since her return home had left her with nothing but unanswered questions.

She turned to set off for Erik's tree home when the undaunting challenge of navigating through the thickly wooded forest hit her. Which way did he live? And how, for that matter, did he even know where to go when landscapes such as creeks could simply wander off and move locations? Maybe heading down into Ragnar's thorpe *was* the easier decision.

She shifted her footing amongst some exposed tree roots to take in the vastness of Walden's Forest, and noticed the appearance of a smaller tree come into view.

Freya's eyes lit up. She leaned to the left; the little tree vanished, blocked by the tree trunk she was standing in front of.

"He's brilliant!"

Without a moment to lose, she lifted her hands to either side of the trunk, double checking her theory, and when she lowered them the little tree to the left was standing tall, marking the direction her path should take.

So to the left she headed, until she reached her marker tree.

It was too skinny to block any distant trees, and not seeing the one Erik used to enter his home nearby, she knew she still had farther to go.

Next to the skinny tree was a tall, fat, gnarly old chestnut tree. Aligning herself to face the same direction as she had been walking in, she approached the tree careful not to trip and fall over its exposed roots.

"The roots. That must be what he was looking for when he entered the forest from Harald's thorpe."

Giving it a try, she placed her hands to either side of its trunk, lowered them and saw a young sapling appear where her right hand had been.

Off she went to the right.

Zigzagging deeper and deeper into the forest with her hands as her guide, she felt sure to find his home. At the next large tree, she repeated the navigation trick. This time, she created a guessing game.

"I think…to the right." As she dropped her hands, she checked first to the right and saw, "Grimhild!"

A mane of red hair spun as the girl turned sharply at her name. The two girls locked eyes and Grimhild's face lit up with a smile. "Freya! I bid you welcome! Come and join our hunt. Look quick, my brandished spear." She shoved a long metal spear forward with its tip pointed to the sky for Freya to view.

"A hunt?" Freya took caution as she approached Grimhild. Having nothing to defend herself with, she could only hope they were out hunting deer and not Ragnar's men.

"I have been made a warrior." She looked away and called over her shoulder, "Father, it is Freya. Come and greet our lost friend." Then she quickly addressed Freya, asking, "Have you not found your Aalborg?"

"No, well, actually I did, thanks."

"That is good to hear. And you have returned for more adventure! Do say, is this spear not the envy of Valhalla? Father had the Fire Giants of Muspellheim forge it for me."

Freya couldn't believe her ears. "Your father's crossed realms?"

"Aye. Lo, my tongue gave him quite a beating of words for passing me by on this trip. Alas, this gift did help soothe my temper. Spy the shaft. Do you see it?"

Freya saw some intricate design etched into the metal handle but couldn't say for sure what it was Grimhild was trying to point out.

"Our golden plunder. The warrior spirits wanted none, lo, I craved the beautiful markings of this bracelet. What delight to have it cast in the shaft." Grimhild was beaming with joy. "I do not know who loves whom more—Father, me or me, Father." As Harald approached, Grimhild threw her arms around his waist.

"Tidings, Freya," he said while hugging Grimhild back. Several more members of their thorpe arrived with him, each carrying spears of various lengths. "Are you returned from your home, or have yet to find it?"

"Oh, no, Father, she's returned. Alas, too soon to behold the splendors of our hunt."

Freya shifted awkwardly "Oh, sorry. I hope I didn't scare off the deer you were tracking."

"Deer?" Grimhild laughed hysterically. "The blood of huntsmen fill not *my* veins. My calling is that of warrior. Look upon my clansmen. Our spears soar the skies, the tips double-edged, the craftsmanship elfin made. We are dragon slayers."

Freya's heart raced and her head jerked up. "Dragons?" But the sky, at least what was visible through the canopy of leaves, was filled only with clouds.

"Our hunt today was mere practice," Harald said calmly. Perhaps he'd seen the fear in her eyes. Hopefully that's all he saw. She needed him on her side. She needed him to help her defeat Ragnar. And most importantly, she needed him to *not* know she had eaten a Raedslen egg. "Your day will come, Grimmy," he said affectionately to Grimhild. "On that day you shall spear the fiercest of dragons. All the races will hear of your name and tremble."

Grimhild's eyes widened dreamily as she envisioned the scene. "A Raedslen."

"Aye, niece." Freya turned and recognized the man who

spoke as the man who mouthed the words "the omen" to Harald back at their thorpe. "Spear a Raedslen at nine winters old and you'll have *me* trembling at your name."

The hunting party laughed together at the joke.

"Pride will swell you till you burst, dear Uncle Karl. I will be the youngest dragon slayer in our clan."

"Pride swells me already, Grimhild." He leaned down and ruffled the top of her head. "I doubt little you will not see your tenth year before slaying your first dragon."

Grimhild beamed. "Ooh, I cannot wait! Mother shall have a necklace from its talons."

Freya found herself unconsciously placing her hands in her jeans pockets. There were no signs yet of a transformation, but perhaps dragon slayers had keener eyes and would notice what she was to become with just a quick check of her nails.

"Slain be the beast!" Grimhild called out in battle cry.

"Slain be the beast!" roared the others.

"Come," Harald gave Grimhild a gentle nudge. "Let our lesson conclude for the day. Light leaves us soon and we needn't be venturing the forest at night. There will be plenty more days for practice."

"And when King Walden nests the egg, I will be ready!"

Freya's ears perked at the talk of an egg. Erik had an egg, their egg. But that King Walden had an egg. Was it Erik's egg? She wanted to know. There was only one way to find out. "Grimhild, it was really good seeing you again but I have to get going. I'm meeting up with a friend and, well, like your father said, it's getting dark." Her stomach turned at the thought of any efoi lurking about.

"Then swift travels to you! Lo, stay away not long. Visit soon for you shall hear the tale of my first slay!"

An uncomfortable smile and a slight nod of her head were all Freya could muster up for a fake agreement.

Then as she and Grimhild's clansmen parted ways, Harald approached her and said, "If your friend is absent, my thorpe will welcome you for the eve."

It was an odd offer to receive, yet all the same she found herself saying, "Thank you." She didn't want Erik to be *absent*. But the reality was there, and whether or not Harald knew of it, she was indeed thankful for the offer.

They left each other with that, and Freya continued navigating through the forest with just a few remaining rays of sun to light the way. It wasn't long before she came upon a tree—*the* tree—the one with a shower of dangling branches, and smiled proudly.

"I did it!"

Next all she had to do was find the door release. She parted the branches copying Erik's breaststroke technique. There must have been thousands of thin wispy branches, all covered in little round leaves. Yet only one was the one she wanted: a leafless switch.

"Where are you?" she felt like calling out after quite of bit of lost time spent in searching for it.

Continuing to wade through the cascading boughs, she painstakingly checked each one that brushed against her hand. This one had leaves. That one had leaves. They all had leaves. This one had many, that one had few. This one had—none! The bare branch surfaced in her hand. With an energetic tug she pulled down on it with all her might until she felt it refuse to give further, then released it quickly letting it spring back up into place. The cutout door in the tree's trunk pivoted slowly outwards. As soon as her body could fit through, Freya dashed inside. Erik's torch wasn't at the entrance.

"He's home!"

She hurried to grab the flashlight from her backpack, grateful to Susanne for packing it, and bolted down the ladder in almost one bound. The earthen passageway, warmer than she remembered, perhaps because she was so elated to see Erik alive and well, was quick to navigate—no wrong turns, no dead ends. Things were working out perfectly for her. Even the net ladder was no match for her ironman skills today as she hauled herself up with ease.

BAM! BAM!

Using the metal barrel of the flashlight as a door knocker she announced her arrival.

"Erik! It's me. It's Freya."

BAM! BAM!

Again she pounded at the under sheath of the drop floor.

"Let me in!"

Footsteps shuffled above and the cover slid open. Erik stared down at her.

"You have returned?" he asked, sounding rather confused, though offered her an arm up all the same.

She grabbed ahold and pulled herself in.

"Aren't you glad to see me? I'm certainly glad to see *you*! I thought for sure Ragnar had..." She couldn't finish her sentence. He was alive and that's all that mattered. "Forget it." She flopped down on the bench to catch her breath and changed the subject. "How did you do it? How'd you escape?"

Erik's brow rose.

"Oh, come on, you can tell me. How did you get away?"

He cocked his head. "You truly know not."

"How could I?" What an odd thing to say. As if she were able to see into the past while at home.

"Most odious are they with ability to vanish."

"Who?" She shifted uncomfortably as he looked at her like a guilty suspect under a sharp detective's incrimination. Panicking what to say, how to explain, where to begin, because she herself didn't even know, she couldn't help but notice the faintest of grins curling in the corners of his mouth.

"A Volva indeed; you do cease to amaze me." He was almost laughing.

Was it okay to laugh along if she didn't have a clue what he was talking about?

"Hee hee hee, ha ha ha." she tried, but it was the fakest of laughs. "Indeed."

"Aye. Lo, I fear you not. As for Ragnar..." he could hardly contain his laughter. "A She-Volva!" he mockingly screeched. "Fire-eyed fury! Madden her not! Release the Berserk!"

Freya stopped the fake bounce in her shoulders. She stopped the fake laughter. She stopped believing her ears. "Ragnar's afraid of me?"

"Liegeman's joy fears *he* you, for my life has been spared because of it."

"Why? What does he have to fear?"

Erik pulled his chair closer to the bench, the gaiety spread wider on his face. "The wrath of a Volva would fell his vision, would fell the man he desires to be. A foe to one is the very peril of his death."

It wasn't the first time Erik's words confused her, but now her head felt as if it was drowning instead of swimming.

"I don't understand you at all. And I've never heard of a Volva before."

"Wand-bearers. It is only *their* casted spells that could have conjured the grogger in his thorpe."

"Volvas are witches? Ragnar thinks I'm a witch? This is perfect! If Ragnar's afraid of me then I guess we won't be hearing from him anymore."

Erik's serious expression dashed her high hopes.

"It is a game, Freya, a calculated risk worth taking. In favoring you by my release, Ragnar believes to be in your good graces. Think not that your dealings with him have concluded. Nay, in contrary, take care, for he shall seek repayment of his deeds."

A chill ran down her spine as she shuddered to think Ragnar would be coming to look for her. "What *kind* of repayment?"

Erik shrugged his shoulders. "More groggers?"

"But if he finds out I can't conjure up groggers he'll kill me for sure. We have to get to the Norns. We have to know why they summoned me before Ragnar can find me."

"Agreed. At first light we shall head out."

"Perfect plan. I vote now we get some sleep. The sun was setting as I arrived, which means it must be something like ten o'clock. I'm beat."

"Aye. Let us gain rest and start refreshed in the morning."

The two readied themselves for bed, following the same routine as the night before. Only this time when Freya reached above her to open the viewing hole she told the stars she was coming back a hero. Tomorrow the Norns would explain how to stop Ragnar, and Freya would soon be home for good.

After breakfast, consisting of more gooseberries and some bread—Freya didn't bother asking how he had baked it—she and Erik grabbed their things to go.

Erik went to remove the floor covering, then dropped it

suddenly back in place. "Plagued as fools are we should Ragnar have a second grogger we know not of." He walked over to the pile of nogle and picked up two bones. He handed one to Freya.

Mortified by the skeletal offering, she jerked backwards knocking into the bench. "What on earth do you expect me to do with that?"

"Fire-eyed fury, Freya. I counseled you, lest you forget. Nogle possess powers great enough to destroy dark magic. Brave yourself with this gear. Then, should a grogger appear in your path…fell it."

"You want me to kill it? Are you mad? I saw what it did to Mutwik. I don't want my spirit snatched; no thank you, I like it just where it is."

Her pleas and concerns had no effect on Erik. "Look not in its eyes," he coached her while placing the nogle in her backpack. "Or you too shall suffer Mutwik's fate. Approach quickly, then when not a foot's space lies between you both," he looked her dead in the eye, "strike the nogle hard against the creature's chest and destroy the conjured magic within."

She swallowed hard. "I can't do that."

"You must, or rather you lose your spirit to Ragnar's cause?"

"No, of course not. But isn't there another way? Couldn't you just go Berserk on the grogger or something? Then I wouldn't need to get close to the thing or bother having to whack it with a bone from some dead guy."

Erik sank back, his eyes falling on the nogle in his hand. "These bones come not from 'some dead man' to me unknown. They are the remainder of my mother's life."

Freya opened her mouth to apologize but "sorry" didn't seem enough.

Looking back up at her he said, "My powers protect me not from a battle with magic. Thus a grogger will yield never to a Berserk. I bade you, we must arm ourselves with nogle. Should our path cross with one of a grogger it is we who shall be the victors. My mother will not fail us. Of this I am positive."

Without hesitation she took ahold of the nogle and gestured to the floor covering. "Then let's find the Norns before Ragnar or his groggers find us."

In the forest Freya followed behind Erik, her eyes scanning the area with each twist and turn they made. She ducked under low-lying branches, hopped over fallen logs, and stepped through a patch of wild mushrooms.

The scenery was beautiful, fooling her into thinking their walk was a peaceful one. But with the possibility of Ragnar's men looking for her she knew to keep her eyes on Erik as much as on the forest. In doing so, she couldn't help but notice something. "Erik, if I can figure out how to find your home, don't you think Ragnar and his men could too?" She stepped softly through a blanket of small white flowers.

"Nay. The forest sees to keep it hidden."

"Oh it does? It *decides* that? Sometimes you don't make any sense."

"I? It is your ears which do not comprehend—not *my* words which make little sense." He pushed a wispy branch from their path.

"See, there you go again."

He stopped and turned to her. "Freya, Walden's Forest is a land of secrets; revealing the path to my home means revealing a secret. If Ragnar is set upon conquering the forest by dethroning King Walden, do you actually believe the forest would reveal any secret to him?"

"No, I suppose not. But then why do you always have to use the trees to find your own home? Don't you just recognize the way around this forest?"

He smiled wryly. "Aye, if my home were to stay put." Turning on his heel, he twirled his back to Freya to continue their journey to Yggdrasil.

"Oh no you don't!" She hurried ahead of him, and jogged backwards to face him. "You can't drop a bombshell like that without an explanation. Are you saying that your house *moves*?"

He pointed to a fallen log for Freya to not trip over. "Aye."

"How can a humongous tree, with all of your stuff in it, just get up and move?" She hopped over the log and stopped, her mind still trying to wrap itself around the idea.

"Such pondering would be better directed at King Walden himself," he threw over his shoulder. "For, alas, I know not the workings of these secrets. Lo, did you not witness the vanishing of the creek yourself?"

It was true, she had. But she never thought it was his home that had moved and not the creek. Or both. The log at her feet lay perfectly still, and as Freya eyed it, wondering if it too could move, an idea hit her. "Ok, smarty." She called out, then hurdled a patch of creepy efoi-looking vines while running to catch up with him. "If your home can move, and its location is a secret only for you to find, then how come I was allowed to find it too?"

He ducked under a low swaying branch. "I have no belief that Walden's secrets are revealed to all. I should think the forest finds value in you, as you are summoned by the Norns, or the path to my home would not warrant being shown. Lo, these are my thinkings; true answers I have not."

Erik stepped sharply to the right, but Freya, still focused on his response, didn't take notice and stepped forward. Before her foot landed in front of her, she felt Erik grip her wrist tightly and yank her backwards.

"It is best to not walk into that," he said, pointing to a giant spider bug web in front of her.

She looked up and in the middle of the stretched web she saw a tiny insect that looked to be a cross between a spider and a beetle.

"Is it poisonous?" she asked.

Erik shook his head. "Nay, the harm lies not within the spider bug but rather in its silken nest."

As she stared at the web, the intricately spun fibers glistening in the morning sun, she cautiously asked, "Is the web the poison?"

Responding only with a devilish grin, he bent down and picked up a small stick. Then without warning, he tossed it into the web. The clinging silk managed to slow the momentum of the stick, but the forceful blow still broke the web. Yet instead of the stick knocking against the neighboring tree or falling to the ground, it simply vanished into thin air.

Freya did a double-take. "How did it…Where did it go?"

With a shrug of his shoulders, he answered matter-of-factly, "Somewhere else in the forest. I myself have on several bored occasions vanished through a spider bug's web only to appear elsewhere each time."

"Seriously? When I'm bored I usually play video games. Does it hurt when you come out the other side?" She was thinking of her own bruised landings.

"Nay." He flashed a flexed arm at her to show off his pain-defying strength, but Freya only laughed at the display.

"Yeah right. You probably hit your head against a tree trunk or two, which is why you think those little welts on your arms are muscles."

"Little welts?" he mocked. "Young maiden, I am a Viking."

"No you're not; you're a Berserk. And to tell you the truth, where I come from Berserk means 'crazy.' So, yup, you're definitely a Berserk."

"Oh?" he asked taking the jest. "Well, in Midgard 'Freya' means…" but he didn't finish. A faint screech of a falcon suddenly clacked in the distance.

Freya, still caught up in their joking, was about to protest when suddenly he slapped a hand over her mouth and motioned with his finger to be quiet.

"Walden's Forest houses no creatures of flight," he whispered.

She remembered. Taking his cue, Freya followed without question as the two dove behind an overgrowth of tall bushes.

The movement of the leaves concealing their hideout had just come to a rest when a man's voice shouted, "Fire-eyed fury, where is she?"

"Vanished again," answered another.

"Nay. She is yet in this wood." The man took a long breath in through his nostrils then slowly exhaled, "I can smell her."

The rustling of large leaves sounded nearby and Freya panicked knowing the men were searching through bushes and plants looking for her. The flora cracked, shifting under the weight of several axes hacking away at them. With each slashing noise Freya's heart beat faster and faster as if it was gearing up to take flight and flee the scene without her.

"We shall not leave here empty-handed," the warrior with the keen sense of smell said.

"Aye."

A strong, loud sneeze overlapped the other's short response signaling many more warriors were lurking about.

Erik shoved her closer to the ground and whispered harshly, "Stay low."

No sooner was her face in the dirt when shouts of excruciating pain came roaring from the men.

"We are attacked!" one yelled as he hacked once more at a bush.

The sneezing came again, followed by more yells of pain.

Whooshing noises of arrows being launched soared all around them pelting the ground and vegetation like raindrops. Their hideout was under attack. The leaves concealing her whereabouts caved under the blows. Freya didn't look up; she didn't dare move her head above the level of the ground, even though the sounds of men retreating would otherwise mean she was safe. The whooshing noise and pelting sounds around them continued. She panicked, wondering if she and Erik would be the next victims.

With the Viking warriors fleeing the scene, the yelps of pain subsided.

When finally all fell silent, Erik tapped her on the

shoulder. "Come, we are safe. Let's away."

Freya hesitated, peering between the bushes just to double- check.

Everywhere were tiny toothpick-sized spears; the sides of trees were covered in them, the ground full of them. Leaves were pierced, flower heads and mushroom caps too.

"What are these things?"

"Nettles from the nettle berry bushes," he answered as if impressed by their appearance.

No sooner did she stand up than the nettles began to dissolve into whatever object they had struck.

"One nettle will sting with the power of a hundred bees, or so says my father. I am not one who willingly seeks to disprove his wisdom."

"Neither am I. I'm allergic to bees and would swell up like a parade balloon if I got stung."

"Harm befalls only those who heed not the warning call."

"Their warning call?"

Erik faked a sneeze.

"You mean that sneezing sound was the bush?"

"Aye."

He walked over to a colorful yellow and green bush weighted down by hundreds of purple berries.

"Eat not of the berries for inside lie the nettles. Nor should you brush against one of the berries as you risk aggravating the plant. The whipping action of the nettles is the sneezing sound we heard."

"That's absolutely crazy."

"Nay, it is a secret of Walden's Forest. Look around you; every bush, tree, and mushroom plays a role in protecting the forest and King Walden."

She looked around and saw a beautiful blanket of white flowers, lush green bushes in all shapes and sizes, sturdy trunks from hundreds of trees, and a canopy of thick summer leaves. But unlike forests she knew, the white flowers here covered strangling vines of efoi, bushes shot deadly stinging nettles, and the trees with their leaves hid more than just the forest floor. It was finally dawning on her that this place called Walden's Forest was more than meets the eye. She turned and looked at Erik. "What about you? Do you play a role in his protection too?"

"I could not live here if I did not."

"You said Walden's Forest has no birds. Why is that?"

"All creatures of flight—birds, insects, *dragons*—cannot be trusted. They are double-crossing betrayers hovering in the skies seeking out their prey to spy upon."

"You mean to 'eat upon,' not 'spy upon.'"

Erik shrugged his shoulders. "If so you believe."

Of course that's what she believed. She had no reason to think her friend's parakeet, who rarely ever left his cage, was a skilled spy. Absolutely absurd. Even ridiculous.

But, then again, she reminded herself, so too were the

ideas of forests housing secrets, creeks and homes that could move, and realms connecting through a tree. Until now.

"Come away." Erik turned and headed left of the nettle berry bushes. "The Norns live not far from here."

CHAPTER X

LEIF

They ventured on for quite some time and Freya noticed the sun now high above the treetops; its position along with the rumblings in her stomach signaled it was lunchtime. To her exhausted delight, Erik led them to a strongly flowing creek of crystal clear water filled with fish.

"I thought we could rest here and fill our bellies with herring before continuing onwards."

"Oh how perfect." She flopped on the ground, cupped her hands and lapped up the cool refreshing water.

Erik too drank from the rushing water.

A thought came to her as she was hunched over quenching her thirst. She peered down into the creek and asked, "How did you find this so easily if everything can relocate? You weren't navigating with the trees to get us here."

Erik wiped his mouth against the back of his sleeve. "Snobek Creek belongs not to Walden's Forest. Its waters flow through the forest; they do so only here. Its source is Aal, a town a journey of two moons away."

She sat up listening to his answer and waited for him to finish the explanation. When he didn't continue she realized that *was* his explanation. "Um, that didn't help me at all."

"Fire-eyed fury, Freya, how are you the Summoned One when you fail to comprehend what is obvious?"

His comment didn't offend her when there was no point in arguing what she herself had already wondered. Why choose someone to help who knew nothing from the era?

"Snobek Creek is protected not by the powers of King Walden and his forest. It ventures in and makes its leave in the same position as the day before and every day before that."

"You mean that it never relocates."

"That was my meaning from when I first gave answer."

"I get it, I get it. It's just…" she let out a sigh of defeat.

Erik looked at her. "You believe victory to be Ragnar's as knowledge of our ways comes not naturally to you?"

"Exactly."

"Then you must be schooled."

"Oh, and you're going to teach me?"

"Have I not already?"

"Well, you do answer all my questions. I guess I thought you meant something more formal, like special training." She jumped up and struck an imitation karate pose. "We could be spies or Ninjas or both. Ragnar won't know what hit him. Hoo-waa!"

Erik didn't flinch at her high kick aimed at his chest but simply rolled his eyes. "Perhaps you ought to gather small twigs and bits of wood."

"Ooooh, is that to be my first lesson?"

"Nay. Unless—it is for you to know; here we cook fish over a fire and wood *builds* fire."

"Ha, ha, ha, har, har, har. I'm not that stupid."

"Let us see your kindling before I am to disagree."

She punched him in the shoulder and smiled as she turned, having seen his need to rub the pain away. There was a soft splash of water and as she looked behind her she caught a glimpse of Erik with his hands plunged into the creek. A couple seconds later, he stood up gripping a fat, squirmy fish.

Well done, she noted, and turned her head just in time to catch herself from walking straight through a spider bug web. Her heart pounded in her chest at the close call of being transported to who knows where else in the forest. She stepped back slowly and kept her gaze forward as she went looking for firewood.

There were plenty of small branches and broken twigs to choose from so she didn't need to wander far. The difficult task was to carry them all back without dropping the pile as Grimhild had done. Thinking she could outperform the little Viking, Freya grabbed ahold of the bottom of her T-shirt and stretched it wide in front of her. Then she knelt down and began placing sticks into her makeshift basket.

After collecting enough dry branches and twigs she made her way back to the creek where she found three caught fish waiting for the wood. She dropped the kindling next to the fish just as Erik came over with a thin flat rock. He restacked the pile of wood into a pyramid before placing the stone on top. Then from a leather pouch hung at his hip he withdrew two small stones and struck them together. Sparks flew. One jumped onto a small twig where it held onto a patch of dry bark with fierce determination, its orange glow burning brighter and brighter and reaching for the sticks all around. Another twig began to glow and another. Soon, a small blaze grew, crackling loudly as it ignited each little twig. Erik stepped away and walked over to the creek. He knelt low and plunged a hand into the cold water for just a second then pulled it out without shaking his hand dry. He came back to the fire and let the droplets of cold water drip onto the rock where they sizzled like bacon.

"Let us begin," he said, gesturing to her to hand him the fish.

Once they had eaten their fill they readied themselves to leave.

"The creek will carry away the bones. As for the ash, spread it about the earth and I will sink the charred stone."

"Good idea. I always think it's much nicer to leave nature looking untouched."

"Nay, Freya. It is nicer to leave no trail for Ragnar's men to follow us."

"Oh. Right." If she was going to put a stop to Ragnar, she told herself, then she really needed to start thinking like a Viking.

On their way, Freya watched as the sun slowly slid from its lunchtime position high above them to a sunken position ahead. The sky was still bright enough for them to travel, but Freya knew the afternoon hours had settled in and were stretching out behind them. They had stayed deep in the forest throughout the day, but now she noticed Erik leading them closer to the forest's edge. She could see the tree line thinning and could make out open lands of fields and soft rolling hills as the sun was setting in that direction. Before too long they emerged from the forest at a valley most unlike where Ragnar hid his thorpe.

This valley was lush, the backdrop of the land filled with smaller hills colored purple in the distance, and the foreground painted green with patches of thick grass that pocketed down the hill where they stood.

It was here that Freya finally heard the very word she'd been longing to hear ever since she first arrived in this Viking time: "Yggdrasil," said Erik, his eyes full of wonderment.

She needed no introduction. Growing out of the ground amongst those all-too-familiar exposed roots was a thick gnarly trunk supporting eight massive branches. This was Yggdrasil in its prime, looking as it should with each branch stretching in youthful might along the horizon. This was how she envisioned the tree: a sort of Hercules here in the era when it *should* look vibrant and strong. Why it had lost its fragility in the present day and was growing stronger instead of weaker was a question she wanted to ask the Norns.

She had reservations about meeting them though, wondering if they'd scold her for eating the egg or if they would just reverse the curse and get down to business telling her what to do.

Erik passed glances with her, giving a "now or never" nod of his head toward the tree. The two dashed down the hill toward it, adrenalin pumping their legs ever faster.

Being more steeply sloped than she had realized, her careful stepping turned into an out of control gallop. The bumpy terrain full of small rocks, pebbles, clumps of dirt, tufts of grass, and thickets of flowers commanded her eyes to stay focused on what she was treading over rather than where she was heading. Then, just as she had predicted, her foot caught on something hard, tripping her up and sending her face-first down the slope whacking flower heads as she went.

While her sliding slowed to a halt, laughter filled her ears.

She spat out the dirt in her mouth and lifted her head, only to see that the roaring was coming from Erik. The chortling was all too familiar, sharing a similar rhythmic tone to Susanne's mocking phrase, "Looks like you pulled another Freya." She picked herself up off the ground like a wounded soldier, her feelings hurt by the display of amusement at her expense. Anyone could have fallen down such a steep hill, she tried consoling herself, but of course that "anyone" had to be her. Next time she'd make sure to grab his ankle and take him shooting down as well. But for now she did her best to ignore his gasping attempts at catching his breath and instead focused her attention on the tree. However, when she scanned the land it sat isolated upon, instead of finding the Norns waiting for her, she found something else unbelievable. Lying in the grass was a smooth grey rock with three white stripes.

"Impossible."

"Hmm?"

She ignored Erik, who was attempting to regain composure, and stepped over to the rock. Her eyes narrowed like a detective's as she inspected it. "You don't have a magenta line through your stripes," she said as if it had ears.

Perhaps it did for without warning, the rock began to shake, its tiny tremors taking hold, springing it into the air. Freya jumped back in surprise. The rock somersaulted through the air and landed on the ground in the form of a very short man.

Erik rolled his eyes. "Sprites," he mumbled. "Always so dramatic."

The sprite eyed Freya, then glanced over at Erik. "Berserks, always concealing their bearskin coats as if to hide a dark secret they believe no one will uncover."

Erik curled his lip but gave no retort.

The sprite stood no taller than Freya's knee, his head full of disheveled brown hair and his grey shirt and pants just as untidy. He carried a slingshot in his hand and wore an armor of stone complete with pebble knee and elbow coverings.

"Sprites unite!" commanded the little man with a booming voice.

Almost instantly hundreds of rocks scattered about the hillside rolled into a formation surrounding Freya and Erik. All were marked by three white stripes. Then just as the sprite before them had done, they shook fervently and sprang into the air uncurling themselves from their rock shapes and landing on the ground in little man forms.

They loaded their slingshots with tiny rocks pulled from their armor and aimed them at Freya and Erik.

"State your purpose," the first sprite commanded.

Freya stepped forward to respond, but Erik pulled her back. "Sprites are guardians of Walden's Forest. Their weapons are poisoned. Be they small pebbles, lo, contact with one will render you witless for life."

The rock sprites steadied their aim warning Freya to make

no sudden movements.

A sly smile spread across the leader's tiny face. "You have a secret to share?"

She had a huge secret, but letting them know she'd eaten a Raedslen egg was the last thing she planned on sharing with them or anyone for as long as she could.

The leader studied her face. The longer she waited to respond the more she knew he was aware she had something to hide.

"I put a magenta line through three white stripes on one of your sprites."

A commotion of whispers ignited, swarming her ears like the buzzing of bees.

The leader signaled one sprite to draw near.

In response, the requested sprite lowered his slingshot and walked the inner arch of the circle toward the leader. His head was held high, but his little blue eyes darted quickly from the leader to Freya, as if he was asking her to keep a secret herself. Freya was confused. What secret? Keep it from whom?

"Is this true, Leif?" the leader asked of the sprite. "Is this the girl responsible for the marking on your back?"

Leif nodded slowly.

The commotion of whispers grew louder.

"Then this is the Summoned One! This is the one the Norns sent you to retrieve," one of them shouted.

Freya eyed Leif. "You're how I got here?"

A sprite wedged himself into the line of her focus. "You've come to protect the Nine Realms."

Another took ahold of her pinky finger and shook it. "To protect Walden's Forest."

"To protect the king!"

"The sprites!"

They all began congratulating her with hoots and hollers and finger shaking.

When she finally managed to turn her attention back on Leif she could have sworn he puckered his lips and mouthed "shh;" Or was he blowing a strand of tattered hair from his eye? Oh, why wouldn't everyone just get out of her way so she could ask him how he did it? How had he brought her back? How had he managed to pull her through time without being near her? She noticed him in her backyard, at the museum, but never once did she see him in the graveyard.

The commotion was out of control and Freya couldn't hear herself think.

The sprites continued to line up, to pay their respects to the Summoned One. They dipped their head low in turn, though still in constant conversation with the next. The majority kept their eyes down even if they had to reach up to shake her finger. Leif didn't. She returned his congratulatory shake and quick glance with a puzzled expression.

Finally the leader approached her and when he raised his

head he said, "Good luck to you; we are at your service." Then he snapped his fingers and the sprites spread out before somersaulting into the air and landing back down as rocks.

Freya turned to speak, but Erik put a finger to his mouth shushing her. "Sprites acquire most of their secrets through eavesdropping," he explained and pointed at the lifeless rocks scattered about the hill. He motioned for them to walk away. Freya followed slowly and in silence down the rest of the hill.

The Tree of Life was even more impressive up close. At the museum, visitors were required to stay behind a roped border far away from the stilts and old branches. Here though she could climb on its roots and swing from its boughs if she liked. So she did.

"It's so massive! We can't touch the one back home because normally it is very frail. I mean for us it's got to be over a thousand years old. But for you—I wonder how old it is here. Any guesses?"

Erik's eyes narrowed. "*Normally*?"

Freya heard the hint of suspicion in his voice. "You find it odd too then, right?" She dropped from a branch and looked at him. "I was hoping the Norns could tell me why. But to be honest, I think it won't be something good."

"Aye. Time ages the living. A reversal to youth suggests dark magic. Lo, I know not what purpose it serves."

"Me neither, but I bet it has something to do with Ragnar."

"I wager you are correct."

"So where are they anyway, the Norns?" Freya circled Yggdrasil's trunk in search of them. At its other side was an altar made from several heavy stone slabs piled one on top of the other. The uppermost layer was adorned with four extinguished candles, each one as dark as midnight and set at opposites corners of the stone.

"I've seen this slate before, in a dream," she said to Erik when he saw her staring at it. She surveyed the altar. It was warm under her touch, though she wondered if that was due to being heated by blue flames and not the setting sun. "I'm not sure about the candles. Those weren't in my dream."

A breeze swept softly over them. Freya stepped away and took in the enormity and strength of the tree. Standing under its branches Yggdrasil seemed to stretch out forever. Its leaves canopied where she stood, shading the last of the sunlight from reaching the ground. And its fat roots curved like a sea serpent slumping in and out of the earth.

"I thought the Norns would be here. What do we do now?"

"We wait."

"But if we don't know where they are then how do we know when they'll come back?"

"Yggdrasil is vulnerable without their protection. If they fear Ragnar to open the realms, then it would not be wise to stay away for long."

"Any guesses where they might have gone?"

"None." He shook his head in emphasis.

"Well there's a first. You're normally a wealth of information—full of insight and details."

"All right then. They have gone to deliver a tapestry. Does that suit your liking?"

"Actually it does. I saw some of their tapestries at the museum. It's kind of weird now to think that maybe one of those is being delivered this very minute."

He chuckled lightly. "And for me it is strange to learn their tapestries are still in existence in your time."

"Yeah, right. Well, some are very tattered and aged of course. But I bet Maren—oh, she's an employee at the museum; she knows *everything* about Viking tapestries—I bet she'd love to see what they looked like in their original condition. Sometimes I think she or my father should have been chosen to help here instead of me. You wouldn't have had to answer as many questions, that's for sure, and besides, this era is their life, they thrive on it. I…well I…"

"You will do fine."

She didn't share his confidence. The fact that she had eaten a Raedslen egg changed the equation completely. It pushed everything into overdrive. What would happen if the Norns couldn't reverse the curse? Would she become a dragon before stopping Ragnar? Then what? Her family was already in danger to the opened realms. She couldn't bear the thought. Something had to be done quickly. Oh, where were those Norns!

Freya peered about the landscape and saw nothing but the grassy hill. There were no nearby villages or voices of others, no Norns or Vikings or anybody; she and Erik were all alone—or so she thought.

A rustling came from the grass and before she realized what had caused it she saw Leif, in little man form, standing before them.

"What are you doing here?" she asked, jumping up abruptly, as did Erik.

He approached them slowly, his gaze never coming up high enough to meet Freya's. He stopped at a root, stood still and said nothing.

Freya exchanged glances with Erik who seemed to be less curious and more annoyed by Leif's sudden arrival.

Patiently they waited for Leif to say something—well, Freya waited. Erik sat back down and rested against Yggdrasil's trunk. Seeing him close his eyes, Freya thought he was ruder to Leif than she had ever been to Charlotte. And she had just cause to be.

"You weren't planning on standing there all night were you?" she finally asked him.

He gave no reply.

"Ok then. Perhaps you'd care to share how you brought me here. Do you have magic?"

Erik stifled a snigger.

She shot him a stare that would have made bossy Susanne proud. "Since you brought me here I think I have a right to know how you did it."

Finally he looked up, his eyes big and round.

"Sprites don't keep secrets from each other," he said so softly that Freya had to lean in to hear him.

"So...?"

His eyes fell and she saw him begin to nervously twiddle his thumbs.

"We are guardians of information," he continued in the same soft voice. "It is a job we do most proudly. Should our secret ever be found out by any non-sprite," he looked up and met her eye. "We would be cast out forever—to remain in rock form for all eternity."

Erik groaned. "Be away with you, Leif. We are but non-sprites, the very you speak of. You have no secrets to share here. Be gone."

"Erik," Freya gritted through her teeth. "He clearly came here for a reason, so let him get it out. What is it you want to say, Leif?"

The sprite wavered, his mouth opened to speak but no words came out.

"Go on, clearly you have something to say," she tried to encourage.

Leif looked from her to Erik, then back again. "There is something more, but alas I cannot say." With that he somersaulted into the air, landing far from earshot and back in the form of a rock.

Confused, Freya turned to Erik. "Well, that was mysterious."

"There is little mystery in the ways of a sprite. They have secrets and they taunt us with saying they have secrets. Users, not helpers, are they. Your secrets are *their* gain."

"What could they possibly have to gain by knowing someone's secrets? I think it sounded like Leif wanted to help. He wanted to *tell* us something, not blackmail us."

"Take heed, Freya, what you share with a sprite."

"Why? What's the big deal? If they're guardians of secrets then it seems to me my secret would be safe with them."

"Precisely—with *them*."

"And where's the problem in that? They're too scared of permanently turning to stone to ever spill what they know. You saw Leif just now; the others are sure to be the same."

"Fire-eyed fury, Freya! My warning is not for the sprites to keep abilities of transformation. It is for you. Share a secret with a sprite and it becomes theirs. They own it. Not you. Where they have memory of such a secret, you will have none."

"You mean...I'll forget what I told them?" She couldn't fathom losing her memory by simply confiding in someone.

"Aye. If you are to defeat Ragnar, tell no sprite of your

plans. Watch your words with Leif, Freya, or he shall be your undoing."

She was speechless. It didn't make any sense. If Leif was sent to get her, to bring her back to defeat Ragnar, then how could he be her undoing?

She leaned against one of Yggdrasil's roots, her mind swarming in confusion. All she could do now was wait for the Norns to return and hope they would make sense of everything.

CHAPTER XI

VERDANDI, URD, & SKULD

The setting sun's orange rays melted into red as it touched the horizon. Freya yawned. The task of waiting for the Norns to return had gone from boring to downright tiring and her mind, eyes, and legs were feeling the toll.

Rubbing her eyes and losing an attempt to overcome another yawn, she asked, "How much longer do you think?"

"I know not." Erik too yawned.

"It's just, I'd hate to leave and miss them when they come back. But on the other hand," she looked out at the darkened hillside fearing what might be lurking there, "how safe can it be to stay here all night?"

"Yggdrasil will protect us."

"How? By stomping down our enemies with its branches?"

Erik looked at her. "Know you something I do not?"

"I was kidding."

"Oh. Nay then, branches not. My father once instructed me that life remains, lo, does not end, in the roots of Yggdrasil."

"And my teacher 'instructed me' that that's how *all* trees work: Roots provide nutrients and water to keep them alive. It doesn't make Yggdrasil different or special, Erik." She snapped at him a little too harshly.

"Fire-eyed fury, Freya, are you to ever comprehend? Life *remains*—it cannot expire. I speak not of trees. I speak of you and I. We are the life. Wrap yourself amongst a root. In doing so no harm shall befall you this eve. Your life will remain."

"Oh" or "sorry," or perhaps even a "thank you" for the insight he was constantly sharing with her should have been her reaction. Instead she said nothing. Sleepiness was making her grouchy. Not finding the Norns was making her grouchy. Trying to interpret the meaning of things she had no way of knowing about was making her grouchy. She kicked her heel at the soft summer ground. It gave way under the force of her shoe and she found herself concentrating harder on digging a hole in that ground than digging herself out of the one she was in with Erik.

The silence between the two of them grew. Finally Erik

stood up and while making his way to the nearest arched root said, "I counsel we retire."

The sting from her biting remark was obvious in his voice. Again this would have been a perfect opportunity to apologize, but she couldn't bring herself to make a peace offering even if she did agree sleep would be for the best.

He said nothing more, at least not with words. He curled up quietly beneath the arch of the root, purposely positioning his back to her. Resting his head in the crook of one arm he took the other and laid it limply across his eyes. Even if Freya were to walk right up to him, stare him in the face, and wildly jump up and down, he wouldn't see it; he wouldn't notice. He had blocked her out completely.

Fine then! She felt like childishly yelling at him. But it wasn't fine. She couldn't afford to lose his friendship, to turn him against her, to make him Berserk. He'd tear her to shreds. Then who would stop Ragnar since *she* was the Summoned One? Who would protect her family and save them from the opened realms?

She circled Yggdrasil looking for just the right sized root under which she could wedge herself. With the sun almost completely set and the canopy of leaves shading what little light was left to be had, Freya found she had to feel her way around the darkened landscape of protruding roots and tall grass, not to mention the eight low-stretching, heavy branches, in hopes of finding protection. It was protection, after all, that she was hoping to find. Her mind though, in the act of helplessly searching the dark with nothing more than the sense of touch, began to fill itself with horrific thoughts of finding other things—none of which would protect her. A grogger lurking through the night? No, not under this small root her hands were currently on.

If no grogger was there to snatch her spirit, then how about a sprite? Could it be that Leif was back to take her secrets and all her memory of them?

She backed away from the puny root and continued her search, stepping aimlessly about the area.

Halfway round the perimeter of the trunk her fingers fell upon a thick sturdy root strong enough to use as a seat and hold her weight—she checked—and tough enough not to snap in two—again she checked. It was important to be shielded well while sleeping, not just for her mind's sake, but also should an attack come from one of Ragnar's warriors or her neighboring root's Berserk.

It would do.

Yet, however safe Erik painted Yggdrasil's powers, she simply couldn't get her mind to cozy up to the idea of completely dropping her guard while lying under the root. This wasn't home, and this wasn't safe. Therefore, in case of a quick getaway, her sneakers stayed on, as did her backpack.

She lay down, then scooted under the root, doing her best to find a position that would keep her in constant contact with the wood. For more security, she wrapped her feet around the end of the arch where the root went back into the ground and locked her ankles together. Nothing about how she was lying could she describe as comfortable, not physically, not mentally.

And yet, somehow, when she closed her eyes she was overcome by peace. Sleep consumed her.

In the grassy hillside a playful breeze swept up and tiptoed buoyantly from one flower head to the next, while clouds above began to swirl ever so slowly. Thickening clouds expanded as the breeze continued to play up and down the hill. Darkness pulled a curtain gradually across the sky until, one by one, it choked away the light of every star. The breeze dashed through Yggdrasil's umbrella of leaves, shaking them noisily like the rattle of a rainstorm.

Night was black and still.

Freya slumbered on.

"It is time," came a voice.

A dim haze of blue formed on the horizon of Freya's sleeping mind, approaching her with an increasing intensity of light. As it strengthened, the blue haze shifted into forms, molded into faces, and flickered wildly as a hundred little blue flames: the ancestral Norns.

"She is here," said the one with angular features.

No other flame responded.

The angular flame waited before speaking again. It looked

about the gathered flames as if aware of what they were thinking, then commanded, "Awaken the others."

Sparks flew and the flames disappeared.

Freya shot her eyes open and discovered it was morning. She also discovered that, ironically, in her search last night to distance herself from Erik, she had actually come almost full circle around Yggdrasil and took a root neighboring his.

There he lay asleep facing her, his eyes closed and his body still folded under the protection of the tree.

"Erik?" she whispered.

He didn't stir.

"Erik?" Her voice a little louder this time. Perhaps a little too loud for all at once the ground began to tremble. Then in the blink of an eye the tremors intensified, shaking Yggdrasil's branches and leaves as well as Freya and Erik.

Erik bolted awake.

"What's happening?" Freya asked frantically, clinging to her root for stability.

"I know not."

They searched for an answer. Suddenly the arch of a root came to life. Creaking and cracking like a set of old stairs, the root slithered up out of the earth. Its wooden frame stretched outward, lengthening itself beyond the reaches of the altar and perimeter of the eight branches. Loud cracks thundered as it moved.

"What do we do?"

Hiccough. Her nerves got the better of her.

Erik offered no response. He was too busy plugging out the rolling noise with his fingers to have heard a word she said.

The root jolted, swooped upwards toward the sky, then pivoted 180 degrees and came shooting down, plunging its entirety below the surface of the ground. The force of it crashing into the earth caused the land under Freya and Erik to shift about wildly both sideways and forwards. Freya held onto the root in her arms for dear life. As the animated root continued its descent, the hole in its wake began to widen.

"We can't stay here!" she yelled at Erik.

Hiccough.

"Run and you risk being swallowed."

The hole was a landslide, taking everything in its path: grass, flowers, pebbles, and even a small frog as its victims.

Freya gripped her own root with both arm and leg muscles and stayed put.

Then as quickly as it had all begun, the tremors weakened. Yggdrasil's branches stopped bobbing, its leaves stopped shaking.

Freya didn't trust the new serenity. "What if our roots are next? Erik, we should run."

"Nay, all is well, look." He pointed at the hole.

The hood of a cloaked person ascended the hole with ease. Then came a second, and a third. The first to ascend carried with her a lit torch. She had a soft facial outline, Freya guessing a woman of thirty-five. From behind her hood emerged loose plaits of raven hair styled to rest in front of her shoulders, and although the woman was hidden by the cloak, Freya could tell that her physique was slender. She looked over at Freya with round black eyes and spoke.

"You have come," she said without any signs of emotion on her face as she walked to the altar.

Speechless by the arrival of the three women, Freya simply stared.

The second to assemble at the altar had the same round black eyes and expressionless face as the first. This woman, her face worn and wrinkled, had one long ringlet of pure white hair, which was fashioned like a decorative asp coiled around her arm.

The last woman to reach the altar was the most beautiful with heavy auburn curls draping to her waist.

The white-haired woman quipped, "You were summoned, though you did not heed our call!"

"*You're* the Norns?" Then what were the blue flames she'd seen in her dreams and darkened void. "I…I'm here now. If I didn't heed your call then how did I get here?"

"You are here by means of Raedslen," snapped the raven-haired Norn. "Its powers now breathe in you."

Freya's head swarmed with confusion. The egg. She had swallowed it just before vanishing. *It* brought her here? What about Leif? Of his guarded secret?

Hiccough.

She didn't dare look at Erik; just feeling his angry, disgusted glare was all she could handle.

Hiccough.

The three Norns turned and looked at her as if she had said something scandalous.

"The transformation..." the raven-haired Norn warned, then hurried to light the four black candles at the corners of the altar with her torch.

Freya panicked. "Can you reverse it?"

The Norns ignored her. "Quickly sisters, a forlansk. Urd, begin."

Urd pinched the tip of her white ringlet, pulled from it a single strand of hair, and laid it on the altar.

"Skuld."

Skuld combed her open fingers down her auburn curls and produced a single hair, which she too placed upon the altar.

"And as for I, Verdandi..." Verdandi unwove a braid, plucked out a black hair, and piled it upon the other Norns' strands.

Skuld moved forward, reaching her hair-wrapped arm across the altar. She closed her eyes and inhaled a long deep breath. As she exhaled, a soft scent of lavender filled the air. When she opened her eyes again she stepped back, carefully crossing one foot over the other in a long sweeping motion. Circling the perimeter of the altar she moved her feet, each time in the same side-sweeping pattern.

Freya held her breath, hoping whatever it was they were doing would undo the Raedslen curse.

Urd went next, swinging her arm across the altar before stepping in rhythm with Skuld.

Following suit, Verdandi waved her outstretched arm over the altar and stepped back, crossing her feet to the pattern of the others. As the Norns circled the altar, Verdandi withdrew a small pouch from under her black cloak and thrust her hand into it. Pulling her hand from the pouch, small lines of sand oozed from between the cracks of her fisted fingers. She draped a swirl of thin sand trails across the altar. Then with a clap of hands, the three Norns spoke in harmony, "Sands of Times, make us heard as Fate is in our hands."

Verdandi stepped forward and approached the altar. She picked up all three strands of hair and tied them together. Holding the knotted strand above the sand it began to sway like a pendulum.

Freya could see the hair take width with each oscillation, widening to the thickness of spun wool.

Hiccough.

A strong wind blew through the leaves of Yggdrasil.

Urd turned her back to the altar, placed one foot to the side of the other and circled around the ritual site four times.

Then she turned round and approached the black candle that had been placed at its northern side. "Ancestors' wind," her voice as hurried as wind itself. "Come hither and be my northern guide."

The sky darkened and a bolt of lightning shot through the clouds striking the knotted strands of hair. Sparks flew.

Wide-eyed, Freya watched as the sparks ignited into hundreds of tiny blue flames. In the center of them all was the angular-faced flame.

"She is here," it stated.

"Aye," answered Verdandi. "Ancestral Sisters of Fate, we seek your powers to create a forlansk."

Prolonging its response, the flame flickered, strongly growing in height and gazed out above the other flames at Freya. "She is Raedsman."

Freya hiccoughed.

Urd responded quickly, "Aye, though summoned was she nonetheless."

"Indeed." The angular face returned its attention to Verdandi. "Take warning, only a forlansk, one in number, can ever be created for her. She must be made to understand!"

"This I know."

The flame seemed to hesitate. Its silence killed Freya inside and she wanted to yell out "Just do it! Just help me!"

As if the flame had heard her, it suddenly announced, "So be it then." With that the flame burst into little amber sparks.

So too did the other blue flames. The amber fires grew in width, spreading into a seamless blanket of fire. They stretched to all four corners of the stone slab and just when Freya thought they'd leap down from the altar and set the landscape ablaze, they extinguished themselves.

The three Norns reached their hands to the center of the altar. Freya caught Erik craning his neck to see what they were after, though she had seen it before the Norns had even moved. On the stone slab where the knotted strands had lain was now a silver thread.

"Forlansk," Verdandi said, picking up the string.

"With this, guidance will be made," Skuld spoke to Freya. A gentle scent of lavender permeated the air as the words came out.

"How will it guide me?"

"What you seek, it will show," answered Skuld with breath of lavender.

"What I seek is a way to reverse this curse, and a way to stop Ragnar."

"Your gift of sight," Skuld continued, "will prevent the realms from ever being opened." She placed the string in Freya's hand.

Verdandi's dark eyes narrowed on Skuld. "The Raedslen's powers…"

"Her summoning was not made false!" Urd snapped.

"There can only be one forlansk!"

"Her gift will guide her," Skuld piped in.

"Please…" Freya tried intervening.

It didn't work.

Verdandi wouldn't let it go. "As a Raedsman…"

"The consequences of the egg will be *her* fate to write," Skuld informed them.

Freya froze. Her heart sank. Did that mean, "You can't reverse the curse?"

Hiccough.

Verdandi turned away in anger. "She heeds not our words." Picking up the dormant torch, she lit it instantly with a flick of her fingers.

"I do heed them!" burst Freya. "Just tell me what to do."

"The tapestries will answer what we cannot." A scent of lavender delivered the words to Freya's ears as the three Norns headed for the hole.

"And the curse? What about that?"

Freya saw Skuld glance at Erik before the three Sisters of Fate disappeared into the earth. Dirt rolled, filling the space, leaving no visible entrance to the home of the Norns.

Freya felt the forlansk in her hand and tightened her grip on it.

"That's it?" she whirled around to Erik looking for support. "A string and some tapestries? And they expect me to stop Ragnar?"

"Fire-eyed fury, Freya! A Raedsman? I shared my home

with you." He turned and stormed off.

"Hey, where are you going?" She chased after him up the hill.

"You fooled me once. Lo, I shall not fall again for your innocent inquiries. 'Erik, what is a Berserk? Erik, who are the Norns? Erik, what's a Raedslen?' You have used me most ill." He threw her a nasty glare over his shoulder and continued storming up the hill.

"Please, I'm telling you the truth. I really didn't have a clue about any of those things." Hiccough. "Look, you've got to help me." Hiccough. "Can't you hear that? I'm so nervous about everything I'm hiccoughing uncontrollably."

Erik stopped mid-step and whirled around. "Aye, those hiccoughs cannot be controlled. Hiccoughs signify the nearing of your first transformation—fire breathing," he ranted. "What a blubbering ox am I! The efoi sensed you right. You are evil through and through. As Raedslen, you cannot control it. You are a beast, a monster most hideous. Worse are you than a Berserk, for where a Berserk can choose to do evil, you cannot." He turned and crested the hill, leaving Freya behind.

Hiccough.

Alone on the hill she wiped her cheek. Where his words had smacked her face, a tear dropped.

She opened her fisted hand and looked at the silver thread. In a coiled ball on her palm, the string shone, reflecting the bright sunlight above. With her other hand she created a shadow over the string but saw it still emitted a silver light. "Eating an egg does not make me evil. The Norns said I have a gift. I'll show everyone I can do this. Tapestries, they said. If they want me to check out tapestries to put a stop to Ragnar, then I will."

Using Erik's trick for navigating, she headed off through the forest in search of his tree home. Only, along the way, she thought she heard a thumping sound every so often. When it became audible again, she stopped and listened. Someone was moving through the woods, she reasoned, someone heavy-footed.

She hid behind the widest tree she could find, no bushes in the area were tall enough to duck into. The thumping grew louder.

Hiccough.

Freya slapped a hand over her mouth hoping to mute any future outbursts.

She peered over the leaves of a fern looking for the source of the thumping. Then to her horror she saw it: the cloaked brown blur of a figure; muddied, cracked hands and feet...a grogger.

In a panic to act swiftly she pulled off her backpack and fumbled with its clasp, trying to get at the nogle. Checking the position of the grogger with each advancing thump she heard, she couldn't help but notice it walked as if with no real direction for where it was going, but perhaps that was how groggers walked.

Securing the bone in her grip, she jumped out from her hiding place and ran full force toward the grogger.

Glancing up to gage her proximity to it, her gaze fell upon two glowing green eyes.

"NOOOOOOO!"

There was nothing she could do; it was too late. The grogger flew at her, and before she could blink she felt a sudden blow to the top of her head. It throbbed excessively. Freya fell to the forest floor, unable to move a single muscle save those connected to her eyes. A thin stream of cloudy white drifted above her eyes.

Freya fought to regain movement, telling her legs to kick, her hands to pound, and her voice to be heard, but to no avail. She could hear though, but it sickened her to listen to the sound of the grogger closing the pouch. Nothing she could think of was worse than knowing the satisfaction it would give Ragnar to bring back the dead with *her* spirit.

"Over there." It was a man's voice but Freya didn't recognize it.

The sound of burlap trousers shuffling against themselves grew closer.

"Well, well, well. We find the Volva at last." A fat bearded face leaned over her face and into view. "Chieftain Ragnar will be pleased—pleased to return your spirit in exchange for conjured groggers." She could hear the laughter of two other men, but without being able to turn her head she couldn't see who or where they were.

Again, she commanded her body to react. Over and over, she told herself to punch the man in the nose—the Viking whose face was so close to hers that his laughing mouth would have drooled on her had his beard not caught the saliva first.

Her frustration was their entertainment. Their three unique laughs blended as one while watching her do nothing.

Suddenly, for reasons she couldn't see, one voice dropped out and only the laughter of two remained. She strained her eyes trying to learn why.

"You," roared a man whom she couldn't see. The Viking in her face turned quickly at the commotion.

The scene was out of view, but distant sounds filled her ears. There was a battle; the sounds were that of fists striking bodies. There were screams of agony. Someone was losing. She tried to turn her head but it wouldn't budge. She pivoted her eyes to the furthest corners of their sockets and caught a glimpse of brown fur.

More screams of pain and a loud thump. Someone had fallen. Another roaring grunt followed by the gurgling of choking on liquid. This man couldn't breathe. He coughed, then all was silent and he too fell to the ground.

For a moment she heard nothing and feared her own fate. A soft noise came; someone was advancing.

The grogger was still a few feet from her, but it hadn't

moved. So what had?

Out of the corner of her eye she saw Erik come into view. With a bone in his hand he turned to the grogger and whacked it full force across its chest. Then, as if the air itself had a mouth to swallow with, the grogger was sucked away leaving the leather pouch to fall to the ground. Next to it lay the nogle, shattered finely into a pile of dust. Erik leaned over and opened the pouch. From within, a cloud of white swirled up into the air and encompassed Freya's immobile form. She felt the cool gentle touch of her spirit descend upon her, reentering her body.

"Erik," she heard her own voice cry out. "How did you know to find me?"

"Your screams could have led a deaf man to you."

"I'm so glad you came! I don't know what I would have done." She sat up and threw her arms around him, grateful for his return. Erik shifted awkwardly. Freya sensed he was uneasy with her display of affection, but she didn't care. She hugged him tighter; it was the least she could do for saving her life. But with one glance over his shoulder, what she saw told her Erik had other reasons to feel uneasy. There in the grass lay the three Viking men, their bodies slashed and bloodied, dead by the brutal force of a Berserk's wrath.

CHAPTER XII

FIRE

S he released her hug and pulled back.

Erik looked away from her gaze. "Only you can stop Ragnar. And stopped he must be, for worse are his evil doings than the curse and wrath of any Raedsman." He looked up and met his eyes with hers. "This I solemnly promise: I shall protect you in your quest against him. Lo, fire-eyed fury, Freya, you must conquer him quickly; I take no pleasure in my Berserk form."

"Understood." She was glad to have him on her side again. "Then if I'm to put a stop to all of this, I'll need to have another look at your tapestry. It's the only one I know here, so let's start there."

Taking her cue, Erik headed for the nearest tree to lead them home.

Hiccough.

Her cheeks flushed. A surge of heat swept through her body and she could feel her chest warming from it.

Hiccough.

Her closed mouth had muted the sound, though when she went to exhale, a puff of hot smoke coiled out from between her lips. It was happening; the transformation was taking place.

"Erik?" she wiped the nervous sweat of her palms down her jeans. "Um, Erik?"

Hiccough.

He turned as a burst of sparks escaped her mouth. One spark landed on a nearby leaf, singeing the curly tip of the foliage.

She knew full well that a few more hiccoughs like these and the whole forest would burn down. "What do I do? What do I do?"

"Quickly, to Snobek Creek!"

The two raced between trees, dodging low-lying limbs, hurdling fallen branches, slipping on muddied patches of ground and trampling every flower and twig in their path. With her hand over her mouth as she flew through the forest, Freya could feel the flaming heat of each hiccough she blocked. Better to scorch her hand than the dry timber, even if it meant the painful sensation of each searing burn.

At the creek's edge Erik pushed her to the ground.

"Breathe." He pointed to the cool running water.

He clearly meant for her to breathe the fire into the river but her intentions weren't to breathe fire—she wanted to breathe normal. Cupping her hands, Freya lapped up mouthfuls of water hoping to douse the fire within and stop the transformation altogether.

Hiccough.

Like a sideshow act, a solid steady flame blazed out of her mouth. Stronger by far than the others, her ability to breathe fire was growing. The flame scorched the surface of the creek, causing steam to erupt.

Freya dropped her head in her hands. "It's not supposed to be like this. I'm supposed to be of help, not stuck here waiting for the next hiccough. If Ragnar opens those realms, it will be all my fault."

"Correct."

Her head shot up as she glared at him. "Gee, thanks."

Erik sat down next to her and drank from the creek.

Still annoyed by his heartless comment, she stared at him, half determined to aim her next hiccough straight at his head.

He wiped his mouth.

"Oh, do put your rage away. I have not brought you here to quarrel."

"Really? You could have fooled me. I thought you were on my side."

His brow rose. "I am. Lo, you spoke a truth of which you

wish me to deny agreement with? I understand not your anger. You have been summoned and thus are correct to say should *you* not stop Ragnar, then none will."

"Oh. But look at me. How can I stop him now?"

Hiccough.

She swung her head away just in time for the flame to miss Erik completely. It landed with a forceful splash in the water. Pockets of boiling bubbles popped along the surface.

Erik pointed to the water. "There lies the reason for coming here."

"Yeah, so I can put out the flame and not set the whole forest on fire."

"Nay, you understand me wrong. Aye, indeed it is safer here than amongst the dry trees. Lo, the creek acts not only to protect but also to practice."

"Practice?" The idea hadn't struck her until now. "Absolutely brilliant! If I learn to control it then I can get back to working on a plan to stop Ragnar. Genius, Erik. Let's get started."

She jumped up from her spot, faced the creek, and opened her mouth. Not a hiccough in sight. Then, swallowing some air she closed and opened her mouth again. Nothing.

"It's not working. I don't have any more hiccoughs."

"Can you not fake them?"

"How do you fake a hiccough? Oh well. Here goes." She wriggled up her stomach muscles, then with one quick upward thrust while sucking in a puff of air she exhaled fire. Hiccough. "I did it!"

He returned her enthusiasm with a wide smile.

Freya stood tall and wriggled her stomach muscles again. Fire sprayed from her mouth arching over the creek and ignited a patch of grass. Erik quickly jumped into the water, waded across, and doused out the tiny blaze. A twirl of smoke was all that remained of the extinguished flames.

"You have mastered the production of fire; now master your aim."

Freya bit her bottom lip, self-conscious of the potentially serious mistake she had just created. Then, drawing a deep breath she blew a fire straight at a brown submerged rock— and missed. The flame hit the water a few feet from the rock, catching a passing fish off guard.

The fish floated downstream, belly up, and into the hands of Erik. "An interesting way to cook a meal. I should think a few more of these would fill us for the day." He pulled himself up out of the creek and placed the fish on a flat stone.

"I'm glad you find it funny," she said under her breath. Aiming again for the rock, this time she checked if the water was clear of fish. With her gaze staring down the target, she felt the hot energy of fire escape her lips and saw it head straight for the rock. Spearing the water like an arrow, the blaze struck the rock, stirring up the muddy floor.

"Ha! Did you see that? I did it! Did you see?"

"Aye, well done." He gave a gentle clap of approval to which Freya mockingly curtsied.

Full of new confidence, she leaned over the edge of the water looking for a smaller target. "There. That pebble down there—I'm going to aim for it."

Erik looked to where she was pointing and raised a doubtful brow, challenging her to the task.

Before beginning, she closed her eyes and tried to envision the pebble. Upon opening them again she noticed her gaze was already fixed on the location of her target. Somehow she had sensed its exact position. She faked a hiccough and felt the blazing heat shoot up from deep inside and roar out of her open mouth. The force of the fire struck the tiny pebble with such a blow it moved several feet from its peaceful nook.

Freya was shocked at her own strength. "This is great." Peering up and down Walden's Creek she looked for another rock to test her skills on. "Which one next?"

Erik picked up a long stick and held it at arm's length over the water. "This one."

"You want me to light it?"

She hadn't expected that and looked nervously at the stick.

"If you cannot control your fire breathing…"

"I know, I know. Just give me a second." The stick was twice the length of his arm. It was basically a branch. Holding it out, it reached to the center of the creek. Freya wasn't sure

236

where to focus her aim; if she missed the tip, she could overshoot the fire and set the grass on the other side ablaze. Yet if she undershot her aim then she'd set Erik ablaze.

Freya drew her breath and blew a mighty flame. It arced below the level of the stick, plunged under the water, and lit the length of the creek in a shade of amber.

Erik shook his head. "Too big a flame."

"You think?"

Sizing up the length of the stick, Freya cocked her head thinking of a way to light the skinny branch and not the whole creek. She walked herself through what she'd learned so far about breathing fire when something clicked. "Birthday candles."

Erik furrowed his brows.

"Never mind," she told him. If blowing out birthday candles took all of one's breath, much like breathing a large fire, then perhaps using less breath would produce a smaller flame. It was worth a shot. Filling her lungs only halfway Freya gently released the air aiming straight for the center of the stick. A perfect hit.

"Liegeman's joys." Erik waved the glowing branch triumphantly as if it was the flag of a victor's army.

"Toss it in the creek and hold this one. But hold it straight up." She handed him another long stick, which he took at her command.

This time she chose to draw a deep breath, but when she

hiccoughed she didn't exhale it all at once. Instead, she rounded her lips and softly blew a narrow flame up and down the length of the stick.

Erik dropped the branch, his fingers dancing at the heat of the fire.

"I did it," she boasted, half wishing Susanne was here to witness the achievement.

"Aye, lo, it would please me to mistake not my hand for timber."

She bit back a guilty smile. "Sorry about that."

"Let us break for now. You may practice next on a bit of kindling. You fetch the kindling and I shall catch a second fish."

"Deal."

The two met back together a few moments later, Freya with a triangular stacked pile of wood and Erik with a flat stone and their lunch.

Freya, eager to test out her newly trained skills on something as tricky as a campfire, hunched low ready to fake another hiccough. "Here we go."

"Wait." Erik bent and surveyed the kindling. Checking each angle, for what Freya didn't know, he stopped at the opposite side. Pointing to a gap no larger than the width of two or three fingers, he said, "You have proven an ability to hit a target, but can you avoid nontargets? Try your luck at starting the fire from below, through this hole. Should you miss, you must catch your own fish."

Freya viewed the gap. It was basically impossible to send a flame through such a small space without lighting the twigs around the entrance. "Are you serious?"

"I am."

"If this is because I burned your fingers I already said sorry."

He just smiled.

"Oh perfect, a Viking with a grudge." She rolled her eyes at him then focused her concentration on the small opening. Envisioning the target, like she had done with the tiny pebble, she puckered her lips as if to whistle, then blew the skinniest of flames. It soared right through the gap, striking one of the bottom buried sticks. Then, much to her delight, a coil of thin white smoke came oozing from the hole. Freya puffed her chest up like a proud peacock.

"Hmm, let's see. I think I'll have the larger of the two fish, thank you very much."

"Oh?" he asked skeptically. "Have you lit the cooking fire? Or are we to merely smoke the fish all day? I do believe my words were you should *start* a fire."

"All right, all right, don't get all crazy. I did it once, so I can do it again."

She leaned down once more, drew her breath and released it slowly. Suddenly Erik jabbed her with his knee, knocking her to the ground. Shocked by the jolt, her mouth opened wider, releasing a much larger flame. The fire spewed all over the kindling, the muddy bank, and the creek.

Freya quickly tried to control the situation. She forced a strong push on the last of her breath sending it straight into the kindling.

"Are you crazy?" She rounded on him and punched him hard in the shoulder. "I could have burnt the whole forest down."

He barely flinched at the assault. "Sneak attack."

"What? There's no sneak attacking when someone's lighting a campfire. That's stupid Erik, absolutely stupid. What happened to you crying about your poor little baby fingers when now you'll risk being burnt entirely?"

"Nay, I disagree; stupid it is not. How would you respond to Ragnar or his men if attacked by them? Will you say to them, 'You may fight me so long as no sneak attacking is about?' Nay, you must train for everything, Freya."

Hanging around his know-it-all attitude was as bad as hanging around Susanne. She knew he was right. "Fine. But you cheated, so I'm taking the larger fish."

He chuckled lightly. "It is yours for the taking."

Erik grabbed the flat stone and laid it atop the fire letting it heat through. Then he dipped his hand in Snobek Creek's cool water, sprinkled the stone with the droplets and watched them sizzle. "The fire is strong—excellent creation."

With the fish cooking, Erik picked up three dry twigs and

fanned them out in his right hand. "Try to light only one."

"No pushing me this time?"

"Nay, not this time." But the gleam in his eye told Freya he still had something up his sleeve.

She focused her attention on the target, picking the middle twig as the one to light, and tried to keep Erik in her vision just in case he executed whatever he was planning.

She faked a hiccough and released a tiny fire that struck the very tip of the middle twig. It ignited on impact.

Erik nodded pleasingly.

"I thought you were going to make it more difficult."

"Ah, you speak with confidence. There are still two remaining."

"Easy."

"So you say."

She drew her breath and just as she exhaled, Erik flung the two twigs high into the air. Her flame missed them both and flew straight for the empty space close to his hand. Quick to recalculate the moving targets, Freya drew her breath again, this time focusing on the cascading twigs. With two swift puffing thrusts, one to the left and one to the right, she sent her flames soaring toward the objects. The twig on the left lit midair. The twig on the right came crashing down untouched by the fire.

CHAPTER XIII

WHAT IT MEANS
TO BE RAEDSLEN

The charred twig crumbled into a pile of ashes. There was so much to learn, and she hadn't even attempted her gift of sight on a tapestry yet.

Erik bent over to pick up the twig.

"Leave it. The practice was good, I learned a lot, but who are we kidding? My priority shouldn't be playing with fire. It should be putting a stop to Ragnar. Let's get back to your home and see what this forlansk can do."

Erik stood up and nodded. "Aye." He lingered for a moment staring at the twig before saying something more. "Lo, I would counsel you master this transformation."

The same thought had occurred to her as well. "Yeah, I get it. Don't worry, I have no intentions of burning down your home. I was actually just thinking maybe we could fill your bucket with some water when we get back. That way when I hiccough I can breathe the flame into the water. Nothing would catch fire then in your home, see?"

She smiled enthusiastically having found a solution to the problem. Erik, however, kept his head low and his eyes on the twig. "That we can do."

"Ok, then let's get a move on. Or else tell me what's on your mind because obviously your thoughts are elsewhere."

"Aye, they are."

"Is it the transformation? I mean, you brought it up after all. If you want, I'll stay by the creek then. You can bring the tapestry here if you don't trust I can keep the fire under control."

"Nay, it is not that."

"Then tell me."

He sighed. "As I always do."

"What's that supposed to mean? Fired-eyed fury, Erik! Isn't that what you always say to me when you get frustrated? Well, now I'm frustrated."

Her anger, or perhaps the use of local lingo, caught his attention. Whatever it was she didn't care now that he wasn't ignoring eye contact.

"How easy your questions fly my way, Freya. Lo, it has occurred not to you how difficult some answers are to relay. I know little of a Raedsman's transformations. Alas...I know much of their repercussions."

"I know." Her voice softened. "You told me. If there's no reversal to the curse…" she couldn't even finish. Owning up to her fate made it real. Superstitiously she feared saying it out loud, as if it would speed up the process. "I get it."

"Nay, I believe you do not. How do you envision life will be as a Raedslen?"

She hadn't thought of it.

"Do you envision hoarding gold and treasure? Swooping through the skies? Or of a life far removed from those you love?"

His eyes pierced hers, but he was staring right through her. Was he even talking to her?

"I will inform you of what fails your realm of knowledge. Raedsmen forget not where they are from, the families who birthed them, raised them, loved them. They forget not these things for one reason. Freya, your curse is not that you will become a Raedsman. Your curse is what you will do once becoming one. Dragons hunt; forget that not. Lo, Raedsmen are no ordinary dragons. As half-dragons they will hunt what they know, where they know…*who* they know. After the transformations take hold, mercy and compassion will cease to exist in you. You will hunt, and your loved ones will perish by your deeds. You will seek them out and you will…"

"Enough! Why would you say this to me?" Her vision blurred as tears welled.

"For I have a brother."

So what? She almost flew at him for changing the subject. Suddenly, the words Ragnar said to Erik flooded her memory—about having a Raedsman as kin.

"Two winters ago he came to me. Erlend, he is called. I should leave the forest, he counseled. Alas, I knew not why. I stayed for I had reason to: my family. Lo, as you can imagine, the loss of my mother weighed heavily on my father. I wish to believe the loss of myself also weighed on him, although this I do not guarantee. Consumed by gloom it was not long before his craft in hunting waned. My father, having been a respected hunter, was favored by our Chieftain who took pity upon him. He allowed my father to tend the lands instead of exiling him from the thorpe. I know of these events for Erlend shared them with me. Though my junior and younger than I when the events of that horrid day unfolded, he understood my emotions, my sorrow, my regret were true. My father did not. It is for Erlend's compassion that I have the nogle, kubb, glass curtains, and tapestry. There are no words descriptive enough to paint an accurate vision of the level and depth to his kindness. Thus, of all the treasures sacred to me it is he who I hold most dear."

It was the same for Freya with Susanne. As nerdy and bookwormy as she was, Freya couldn't think of life without her. Who, after all, always had her back, even when she "pulled a Freya?" Susanne. She was the person Freya wanted to be: smart, cool, loving. To think she could succumb to death because of this curse was unbearable. If only she had relinquished the egg to Susanne there'd be no fire breathing, no transformations, no curse. She tried concentrating on Erik's story but her own grey cloud shrouded her.

"I bring us now to two winters ago when Erlend came with words my ears denied to believe. Ragnar, a clansman in my thorpe…"

Freya's concentration suddenly sharpened "What? So that's how he knows you?"

"Aye. Lo, foul shame for it. Foe was he always to my kin, his wants most odious while his contributions severely lacking. Battle-blood hardened him and he used my father ill, destroying the crop he tended. Erlend intervened, but was met with gear of war. Ragnar and his men, along their many raids, had returned with a weapon used to fell an enemy along with all their kin: a Raedslen egg. Through force, Erlend was made to eat the egg."

It all made sense now why Erik hated Ragnar so much.

"But can Erlend harm you? You're a Berserk."

"His transformations are not yet complete, nor do I wish they ever be."

Her eyes widened. "You don't mean—you wouldn't— Erik, you said you love him."

"Fire-eyed fury! I seek not to harm him; I seek to reverse his curse."

"You can do that? Oh, Erik why didn't you say so? You made me get all weepy eyes thinking I was going to kill my whole family. That was the worst prank ever! So how do you do it? Is there a potion to concoct?"

"Nay, a potion not."

"Well, let's get cracking on whatever it is you have to do. Let's get this curse reversed."

"Slow, I beg you. You misunderstand. I know the how, alas, I possess not the craft."

"What do you mean? Are you saying you can't do it?"

He nodded. "Aye."

"Well, now what? We're no better off than before you told me all of this. Great going! Some story you shared, getting my hopes up like that."

"Agreed, there are complications, but I am learning."

She begged to differ. "In two years? I don't have two years for you to figure things out. I want to end all of this now. Stop Ragnar. Reverse the curse. Go home. Plain and simple. The end."

"I have learned that to reverse the curse the mother dragon must be slain. That is why I went to Borg; that is why I took the egg."

She was taken aback. How long ago it all seemed now. She'd practically forgotten all about that egg.

"So what will you do with it?"

"I will destroy it. The connection between it and its

mother will call the mother to it. When she comes, I will slay her."

"Do you know how? I mean, have you ever killed a dragon before?"

Erik sighed. "Nay, I have not. Lo, try I will. And if success is not met, if this was not the mother who laid the egg Erlend is now cursed with, then I will find another egg. And another and another. Should I wipe the entirety of the Raedslen race from all the Nine Realms in trying, then so be it. I will succeed; this oath I gave my brother."

It was admirable, his determination. But it wasn't the quick fix Freya was so heart-set upon having. "I believe you will."

An appreciative smile curled across his face.

"Where is the egg now?" she asked.

"In my tree home."

"Then I suggest we get going."

"Perhaps you would care first for one last round of fire, to devoid yourself of the need until we next upon cool waters."

"I'm actually good, thanks. I guess I used it up faking all those hiccoughs. Ha, maybe I'm even cured."

Both she and Erik knew better, but didn't say so.

They set off in silence with Erik leading them through the forest. For Freya, enough had already been said and discussed.

Erik turned sharply to the right.

Now was time to take action, to think, to plan.

A quick left and a bit more speed in their step.

How, she wondered, was she supposed to stop Ragnar?

A zigzag this time, left, right.

Would it involve killing him? No. Even she couldn't bring herself to doing that no matter how terribly he'd treated Erik's family.

She hurdled a fallen branch, leaping over it like a deer in trying to keep up with Erik. Was he in such a hurry to get home? Honestly, his pace was making it difficult to follow him, let alone concentrate on devising a plan. Then out of nowhere, Freya felt the warmth building in her chest. This wasn't the warmth of a sweaty workout, this was...

Hiccough.

She covered her mouth and did her best to repress the burst of fire. The flame shot back, smacking her in the face. Luckily a burst of cool air rushed past her at that very moment helping to reduce the effects of the burn. It was a coincidence, she told herself, looking around Walden's Forest and seeing no leaves or branches flap in the breeze. Perhaps she saw no movement because she was running too quickly to notice if it was she who was bouncing or the leaves. And why were they running?

She opened her mouth to call out to Erik but all that came out was another hiccough.

Judging by the heat in her chest, this one would be big. Quickly she cupped her fist before her mouth, creating a narrow tunnel to channel the flame. It shot through her fist and proved too hot to handle. She flung her hand away, which again meant she ran straight through the fire with her face. Her eyes burned and blurred, making them tear up. She couldn't see ahead of her. She tripped on some vines, but caught herself on a branch. There was no going further. She had to stop and rub out the pain in her eyes. As her vision came back into focus, she looked up to find Erik and instead found a spider bug web just opposite the branch, which took her down.

ACHOO!

Freya turned to the right. She knew that sound.

Swooshing noises filled her ears. Without a moment to lose she dove under the largest leaved bush she could find and to her astonishment came face to face with a red-haired girl.

"Grimhild?" she mouthed.

Grimhild smiled widely and whispered back a warm welcome, "Tidings."

Freya opened her mouth to ask what on earth she was doing here, but in true Grimhild fashion, wasn't given the chance. "How wonderful you should find me. Alas, today I am battle geared with nogle and not spear. Lo, Liegeman's joys battle all the same!"

Panic filled Freya. Groggers. There was no way she was about to risk losing her spirit again. Fumbling the side pocket of her backpack, she reached for the nogle Erik had supplied her with.

"Tidings indeed." Grimhild lit up, pleased to see Freya ready for the fight. "This kin is my uncle." She waved a long bone in Freya's face. "Died summers ago in a raid. I would fain see him battle still. Oh! What misadventure do I speak? With his nogle he *does* battle still." She smiled and giggled lightly. "We await the signal."

We? Of course. How could Freya think Grimhild was out here all alone? She glanced around the leaves of the bushes and began to take notice of a hand here, an elbow there. Then Grimhild pointed up. Freya looked and saw a mass of leaves shaped like a man.

"I gooed him in honey. And, albeit he is kind, lo, I find him vile. I beseech you, say nothing—I warmed the honey first." A wicked smile filled her face. "Fire-eyed fury, he tested his Vikinghood not letting others see him wince as I applied it. Foul shame me, lo, I yielded not to the blisters that bubbled about his skin."

Freya couldn't believe what she was listening to, nor the fact that she found herself smiling along to the story.

"Chieftain Ragnar, a foe of my father's, is about. The grogger is of his conjuring. Chieftain Ragnar, not my father that is. So too is a Berserk in the forest. He is called Erik. Take warning, he is most odious. One day I shall like to fell him. Take his bearskin coat, and flee his sight. So slays one a Berserk. It suffocates the beast to have their skin far from their grip."

251

This Freya already knew thanks to Ragnar's actions.

"His own mother fell by his wrath. Foul shame. Honor in death is not for those sent to Helheim."

If only Grimhild knew he wasn't what she made him out to be, but Freya couldn't risk Grimhild knowing they were friends. What if she spied on her as she went to Erik's home, then planned a sneak attack on him? No, best to keep her mouth shut.

"He steals dragon eggs, the Berserk. Father says so to unleash them in the forest. We say hooray! Raise the dragon. Call its mother. Play kubb with it." She laughed at her little joke. "It matters not. Vengeance is ours on the accursed Raedslen race."

Just then a bird cawed from above. But Freya knew it wasn't a bird. The honeyed boy.

"This way, men! Lead the groggers!" A deep voice shouted toward the direction Grimhild and her clan were hiding.

Hiccough.

Freya panicked. She couldn't let Grimhild see her breathe fire, or anyone else for that matter.

"Attack!" commanded the honeyed boy.

In a swift wave as one, the bushes came alive with dozens of Viking raiders, including Grimhild. Axes and nogle were raised ready for battle.

Hiccough.

Unable to control it, a stream of fire shot from Freya's mouth. In her quick thinking, she aimed it for the dirt. No one saw. Thankfully they were too busy advancing on Ragnar's men to have noticed. Metal clashed loudly.

"Fell Harald!" roared the enemy.

"Come and try," Harald answered between the clinking of his axe.

"I shall! Lo, what sight is this? Prepare to take a ride, Harald. The Valkyries have arrived."

The crashing of weapons rang in Freya's ears.

"I am prepared, lo, the ride shall be yours, Askr!"

With only nogle to protect herself, Freya kept low in the bushes. She didn't stand a chance against the brutish forces of a Viking sword.

Between grunts and blows of metal there were sounds of slashing, flesh ripping, and sickening hackings as the warriors tore into each other. There was no need to peek out and check the scene; Freya knew all too well what it looked like. She could smell gut-wrenching sprays of blood and splattered innards, the same as when Ragnar lost three men to Erik's Berserk wrath.

"Why, what Viking do we have here? Harald? You bring maidens to fight your battles?"

It couldn't be! Freya plucked and pulled leaves to let her see. Askr had Grimhild!

He had her pinned, holding her arms against her back.

Another burly man stood before them, his sword drawn and aimed at her chest.

"A fiercer Viking, you have not encountered!" Harald roared back.

Grimhild's shoulders puffed like a cobra's head at her father's high compliment. And like a cobra, she was bent on striking her enemy. Within the blink of an eye she bore backwards against Askr's grip and thrust both legs up. Her high kick caught the burly man under the chin sending him in reverse and allowing her to twist her lower half. Her heel tipped his sword spinning it toward its owner and allowing her knee to jab the blade straight through the man's throat. But the man didn't fall. Instead, a Valkyrie swooped down from the skies on her horse and grabbed at his spirit.

Ragnar's men swarmed toward Grimhild like bees to a honey pot. Outnumbered by Harald's forces, Grimhild was easily freed as Askr made an ill attempt to avenge his clansman's death.

"Away, Valkyrie! He has yet not met his death!" he shouted.

Another man came running at the Valkyrie. "He will be the last of ours to take your flight today!"

But he was wrong. A shriek as shrill as the sirens of the sea blasted from the Valkyrie's lips as she lunged a sword through his side, confirming his lie. Up his spirit rose to the back of her horse and away she flew with the two new claims this battle had awarded her.

"Groggers will return you to us!" Askr yelled out to those he lost, then turned his attention to Harald's advancing men. "Call them forth!" he commanded over his shoulder.

Freya felt the ground shake. The groggers were on the loose, but how many she couldn't gauge.

Harald warned his men, "Shield your eyes!"

On cue they raised shields hidden in the bushes and blocked their faces. Equally taking precaution, Freya shielded her eyes with her hand. With limited vision, Freya could just make out fleeing feet, surely Ragnar's men. Harald's clan, on the other hand readied themselves for an attack by forming a circle, their backs to each other. Their nogle raised, they batted away the enemies' blows of swords and axes with their shields. There were three groggers from what Freya could see, and Harald's men, some twenty still, were waiting for them.

Hiccough.

Ragnar's men retreated slightly as the groggers neared. Their job, Freya knew, was to collect the pouches. Yet as they pulled back, a cape of fishnet fell down upon them. Freya looked up and realized the honeyed boy had dropped it. One of the men must have also looked up for a grogger quickly swooped in and struck him violently atop the head. Swirls of white funneled into the air, and as Freya had witnessed twice before, the grogger pulled open a pouch, but this time not quick enough. A second Valkyrie came out of nowhere and

255

snagged the spirit as her own. The motionless man now lay dead.

Seizing the chance to destroy this grogger, Grimhild leapt out from the circle. With the nogle of her uncle raised high, she whacked the grogger hard against the chest and vanquished the muddied brown conjuring for good. The nogle shattered into a pile of dust triggering a mad response of battle cries from her clansmen. They rushed the remaining two groggers, vanquishing them both with a blow of their kin's nogle.

Ragnar's men hightailed it out of there.

Hiccough.

And so too did Freya.

She ran as quickly as she could, zigzagging to who knew where.

Hiccough.

There was no holding back. She dropped mid-run and blasted the flame at a large stone. The rock sheltered the fire from hitting dry wood and setting the forest on fire. She had to get out of there and find Erik, or a creek, or a bucket of water, or something. But most importantly, away from anything that could burn.

Yet how she longed to just take a rest now that a cooling sensation filled her chest. It would be awhile before the fire could build itself back up. Thinking to enjoy the moment she gazed leisurely at the sky. It was a beautifully clear day, the kind that would inspire her to bike out to the sea. She repositioned her foot and heard a twig snap. She wasn't standing on any twigs as far as she could tell. Quickly, she rolled into a neighboring fern.

"This news pleases me, Askr."

Freya recognized Ragnar's throaty voice.

"Let Harald continue to think he has won. Vengeance is mine. Double our smiths, quadruple our blades and battle gear. We will prepare battle with him. I will raise a legion of groggers, enough to fell each inhabitant of Borg. Take heed, the Valkyries hold no claim over our fallen warriors today or any day hence forth. This ristir will see to that. No Valkyrie has the power to reverse a spell read from it. Harald's men will die in battle, of this I am sure, but Valhalla will not be made their home. The spirits of their dead will raise the bodies of our own. Have the graves been dug up?"

"Aye, uncle."

"Well then," Freya could hear a smile in his voice. "Let us away. Soon will we reunite with our fallen and join their blood thirst with ours. The Norns cannot keep the Nine Realms closed any longer."

Hiccough.

A tickle in her throat forced her to cough. Unable to repress it, she sent a flame soaring toward the two men.

Ragnar took notice of the tree now on fire.

"Sprites," Askr snarled.

"In time, nephew, in time. They too shall bow before me. I will rule this forest just as I will rule the Nine Realms. Come away now."

They trampled and snapped a trail of twigs in their departure. As the noise faded, Freya trusted herself to leave her hideout just in time to notice the fire subsiding. She double-checked herself, swearing her eyes had tricked her into seeing trees fanning their branches to extinguish the flames.

"All right, Walden's Forest," she said to herself. "If your secrets and mysteries can do that, then help me find Erik's home as fast as I can." Stepping aside to locate the nearest tree with exposed roots, Freya didn't see the glistening silken threads of the spider bug web until it was too late.

CHAPTER XIV

A PICTURE WORTH
A THOUSAND WORDS

"Freya."

A jab pierced her shoulder, but the dreamy peacefulness of a good night's sleep lured her from waking fully.

"Freya."

How the voice dared to inflict itself upon her slumber. She rolled onto her side, ignoring it.

"Freya," it said more sternly.

"Ouch." The painful jab came again and though her eyes were shut she instinctively rubbed at her shoulder.

"Freya, waken yourself."

This voice was not going to go away. So against her will

she slowly began to come around.

"Freya, you must away. Flee now."

Upon opening her eyes, the speaker's face gradually came into focus.

"Leif?" Her stomach muscles from gym class pulled her up into a sitting position with one quick swoop. "What on earth is going on?"

"Spider bug web." He pulled a loose fiber of silk from her hair as proof. "Lo, you arrived not alone."

Freya followed where he pointed. Within arm's reach lay a Viking man, no doubt one of Ragnar's. What a fool she was to think he and Askr were alone in the woods. The man, however, was beginning to come to as well; his legs stretched long and his head rolled wobbly from side to side like someone waking from a deep sleep.

"Come away," Leif mouthed, pointing at the man. "You must flee at once!"

But Freya was still a little weak on her feet and stumbled with her first step.

Leif shook wildly, somersaulted into rock form, then sprung into the air and came crashing down upon the man's head. That knocked the man out again and bought Freya a few more minutes to regain her strength.

"Thanks."

"You must steal away quickly. He will waken soon. Let him follow you not into Erik's tree home."

Of course she wouldn't let him follow her. "I'd never do that."

Leif wasn't convinced and pulled once more at the spider bug web silk.

"That was an accident. I had no clue he was following me. And besides, now that he's out cold he won't know which direction I went."

Leif pointed above her head. She looked up and saw a leafless long wispy branch dangling down toward her.

"I'm already there?"

"Now away," he shooed her sternly. Then once more he shook wildly and somersaulted into rock form. His three white stripes and magenta line stared up at her from atop the man's back.

So that's how he gets around, she thought, then took ahold of the branch and pulled it, releasing her grip only when the branch finally met the ground.

The branch sprung back in place and a dull churning noise could be heard coming from the tree's trunk. Freya watched as a side of the trunk rotated outwards, opening a hole large enough to pass through. She entered, ducking her head, and checked for the torch as the door began to close. The torch was gone and she knew that meant Erik would be home. Grabbing her flashlight, she jumped down the ladder and made her way through the earthen tunnel as quickly as she could.

When he pulled back the wooden floor covering, she basically jumped up the rope with excitement at seeing him.

"Have I got a lot of news for you!" she started.

"And I you. Lo, first I ask you keep this near your person." He got up and handed her his bucket, already full with water.

Smiling graciously, she took it. "I see you kept yourself busy while I was left to fend for myself back there. Might I add I was surrounded by Ragnar's men?"

"You battled them? With fire?"

"No, not exactly. But, where to begin?" She cupped her hand and pulled some water to her mouth, then took the pillow from the bench and sat back comfortably on the floor before starting her story. Erik listened attentively as she relayed every last detail of the events.

"Now, I know you said Leif would be my undoing if I shared any secrets with him, but I'm telling you, if it weren't for him just now I wouldn't be here to tell you any of this. That Viking looked like he would have woken up soon. And honestly, I really didn't know he had followed me here. Hey, did you know Leif knows where you live?"

"Aye," he answered with a roll of his eyes. "A sprite of King Walden's is he."

"King Walden is a sprite? Then how can you detest sprites so much but speak so highly of King Walden?"

"For I owe him my respect. He has harbored me when I

262

believe no other sprite would have done so."

"Oh." There was no denying that King Walden was indeed honest and good, but Freya wasn't quite ready to agree the others weren't. "So what happened to you? You said you had news, too."

"Indeed, not as adventuresome as yours. Leif was here to say King Walden has requested my presence."

"Ooooh, that's exciting. When?"

"Tomorrow's first light."

"Did he say why?"

"Nay. He knew not the reason."

"Does King Walden often request your presence?"

Erik shook his head. "Never. We have met more than once, alas, always perchance, never arranged."

"I wonder why he wants to meet you then."

Hiccough.

"The bucket, Freya."

"Calm down. I have it right here." She blew a small flame into the water before the fire had a chance to build inside her. The steam produced reminded her of the groggers and her mind shifted to the task she was called here to do. "Perhaps now's a good time to look at your tapestry."

"Agreed."

Freya stood up and faced it while Erik pulled the torch from the wall near the nogle and lit the torch that hung to the right of the tapestry. The silver thread glistened in the firelight.

The scene made no sense to her. A brown bear, a woman in red, a dragon, and a goblet—there was absolutely no interaction between any of them, no connections, no storyline, and in her mind no reason at all to be in the same tapestry together.

"I don't get it," she said over and over again to herself while shaking her head. "I don't get a single bit of it. Nothing at all."

Erik stayed quiet.

"How about you?" she asked him. "You've had this thing sitting up in here for how long? Have you ever come up with any thoughts about what it could mean?"

He shook his head. "Nay, for I never thought that it *could* mean something."

"Well, that's weird. You're telling me this whole time you just thought it was some gobbledygook?"

Erik gave her an inquisitive look. "I know not of gobbedygook. Is that what you see?"

"No, it's not what I see. Oh, forget it." Half annoyed with the tapestry and half with Erik, she flopped down in the chair, too frustrated to continue. "I wish my father were here. He'd know what to say." Or would he? She glanced at her backpack on the floor and thought of the incomprehensible gift he had left her. An idea hit her and her eyes darted to Erik. "Hey, you're a Viking." In one bound, she leapt up and grabbed her backpack, pulled back its flap, and withdrew the book. "That means you can read runes!" All feelings of annoyance toward him dashed away as she thrust the book in his lap. Opening it she added, "My father hid it for me to find. It's called *The Raedslen,* but more than that, I don't know, I can't read runes."

Erik closed the book and thrust it back her way. "Nor can I."

That wasn't the response she was expecting. "Ugh! Why does this keep happening? Why do I keep running into dead ends?" In a fit of rage, she reached into the side pocket of her backpack and pulled out the picture she'd found in her father's office. "Why'd you leave me this book when no one can read it?" she yelled at her father's image, then dropped the photograph and grabbed the bucket of water. Freya didn't need to hiccough; she needed to explode. And explode she did. A flame roared out of her so forcefully it caused the water to boil. She let go of the bucket and sat defeated. "Now what are we to do?" When she looked at Erik she saw he had picked up the photo and was admiring it.

"You said Volvas do not exist in your time."

There was something about the honesty of his sincerity in knowing nothing of her time that softened her anger. Perhaps it was the same for him. He always answered her questions, and now she could do the same.

"It's a picture, or photograph. It's not magical; it's

technological. There are these things, called cameras, and you capture images with them. Everyone has one, well mostly on their phones. It doesn't make you a Volva to take a picture."

He put his finger on the picture. "This is you."

She swiped it from his hands and looked closely at herself. "Yeah, it's not a very good picture of me though. But Susanne looks really dorky, so I don't mind my face too much." She handed it back to him, pointing out her dorky-looking sister. "And this one's Charlotte, and my mother, father, Mormor, and my grandfather."

Erik was in awe; he didn't want to stop looking at it. He brought it closer to the light, angled it up, and angled it down. He looked at it from every direction possible and even flipped it over.

"Oh, there's only a picture on one side, not both."

But she was wrong. There *was* something on the other side.

In examining what was there Erik said, "I am familiar with these at the top, lo, I was never schooled to read them. I have neither encountered ones so flush with a surface," he added rubbing his fingers across the paper. "Alas, never in my years have I known the runes at the bottom."

Freya took a look at what he was questioning. "Oh, those aren't runes. They're letters in my alphabet. It's my father's handwriting, but the letters don't spell anything."

"Gobbledygook?" he asked of the letters.

Freya laughed. "Yeah, gobbled..." but something caught her eye. "Wait a minute." She took the picture from Erik and looked closer at it. What had caught her eye now made sense. "My father's a genius! He wasn't *writing* something, he was *deciphering* it. Look! Look!" She showed him what she meant. "Here are the runes and here are the letters."

She hurried to open the book. "Now look here. This first rune, right there, that funky chicken foot thing or whatever it is. According to my father's notes that's the letter 'R'! Then, look back at the book. Next comes the downward slanted 'f' thing. Ooh! According to his note that's an 'A'! What's the next rune?" She glanced back at the book where her finger kept her place. "The 'P' looking rune. Ok, that's like 'TH' if I'm reading his chart correctly. Then we have a lightning bolt of a letter n for 'S.' Next comes the half arrow, that's an 'L,' followed by the straight line—ok, an 'I.' And finally the cross, or 'N.' According to this, that spells R-A-TH-S-L-I-N. Phonetically, I'd say 'wrathslin'? Does that mean anything to you?"

"Nay, 'wrathslin' has no meaning to me."

"Hmm, maybe its Viking code for something. Or maybe it's not an exact translation of the runes. I mean, a lot of my alaphabet is missing from this chart."

She looked at him for answers but he gave none.

"Ok, or...what if I have the vowel sounds wrong? What if the 'a' isn't short but long? Like 'raythslin.'"

Erik's eyes lit up. "Raedslen?"

"That's it! Readslen, why didn't I think of that? And the 'th' is more of a 'd' sound. I got this. With my father's notes we can read the runes!" She was grinning ear to ear.

Her enthusasim was addictive, even Erik was grinning. "And the tapestry?" He gave her an encouraging nod to keep reading.

Freya's smile faded. "Oh, I don't think it's that kind of book. I mean, I won't know for sure until I decipher it, but…I think my father left me the book because he knows I ate the egg he gave me."

"Gave?" he was absolutely flabergasted. "Did he not warn you of its powers?"

"Well, no. He couldn't. There was no time. The police were coming to question him and he was scared. He was really scared." She gave a little sigh. "I can understand why now."

"How did you come to eat the egg?"

"My sister."

His face went grave.

"Oh, but it's not like that. She told me to give it to her. But I wouldn't. I didn't know what it was; neither of us did. I didn't want her to have it since it was mine to hide. So…so, I swallowed it."

Expecting some sort of outburst from him telling her off, or how stupid she was, she shrank back. But Erik remained silent. They both did.

There really wasn't anything *to* say, she supposed. The deed was done and that was that. Now it was time to move on. Putting a stop to Ragnar had to come first; his success meant more lives were at stake than just the Raedslen curse, and her family of five. So she closed the book, positioned the chair in front of the tapestry, and racked her brain to see what she was meant to see.

The silver thread stood out to her like a sore thumb. She couldn't get past it. It's curvy and twisty line made as little sense to her as the letters of her alphabet did without the runes.

Freya bolted forward in the chair. "What did you say, Erik?"

"I have said nothing."

"No. Yes, you did—before."

"Before when?"

"You said something about the tapestry—that you never thought it had a meaning. What if that's it?"

"Why—"

"Why would the Norns tell me to look at it? Exactly, my thought too." She turned to him. "Think about it. If my father left me a deciphering tool," she reached into her jeans pocket, "then maybe the Norns did too." She opened her palm and held the forlansk neatly out for him to view.

Erik eyed her empty hand. "I see nothing."

"What do you mean?" She pushed her palm closer to him. He looked again.

Freya could see it. It was neatly curled up in a little pile snuggled between the folds of her skin. "Maybe I really am the only one with the gift of sight. Which means, I guess, I have to figure this all out…on my own."

Erik shifted awkwardly. "I would aid you, please know this Freya. Lo, I know not how."

"Of the two of us, you're the one whose helped the most. I mean without you, I wouldn't have found the Norns, known how to defeat a grogger, let alone have the nogle to do it with, nor would I have your tapestry to view."

"Aye, lo, what I wouldn't give to be the one to bring down Ragnar."

"I'd love that for you too," Freya half laughed. "Then I wouldn't have to do it."

"You will find the way."

"I still think you should go down to his thorpe and just go Berserk on everyone."

"If you think I have not entertained that very thought, then you know me not at all. Lo, until our escort into his thorpe some days ago, I knew not where it lay. Now I understand as to why. Alas, its powers are beyond those of a Berserk's."

"What do you mean?"

"You saw it is hidden. A field, cast of spells, protects it in a way I am not familiar."

"I knew it. I thought there's no way I could have missed

an entire village from up on the hilltop. Yet, great, so now he has groggers *and* a protection field. This just keeps getting better."

"Had the Norns informed you it would be easy?" He cocked his head and threw her a half smirk.

"No," but as she thought about her conversation with them added rather downheartedly, "I'm not really sure the Norns have informed me of *anything*."

"Wrong are you—they created and bestowed you with the forlansk."

"Yeah, but forgot to give me the instruction manual." She met his confused expression with a brush of her shoulder. "Look, I think maybe I just want to be alone with it. You can go to bed or something—I'll take the bench, you can have the sleeping chamber. I have a feeling I'm in for a long night."

He nodded slightly but gave no oral response. His lack of reply gave Freya the feeling she'd hurt his feelings by pushing him away from helping further. He doused the lights near the nogle and behind the colorful glass curtain, then climbed into the sleeping chamber where he kept silent for the rest of the night.

Right, she told herself, let's do this. Looking down at the forlansk in her hand, she tried to imagine how it could be a deciphering tool. Some way or another it could be used in conjunction with the tapestry as the chart had worked with the book. She glanced up at the tapestry. Erik didn't think there was anything to the image, so maybe she shouldn't. Maybe whatever was there would pop out if she stared at it. She was the one with the sight after all.

She stared—with both eyes, then with just the left, then the right, then partially squinting, then for as long as she could without blinkng.

Nothing. No new images, no fewer, not even anything 3D or moving.

Perhaps it was the forlansk. Maybe she shouldn't be holding it. Maybe it needed to be on her eyes to help her see. She gave a quick glance over her shoulder to make sure Erik wasn't watching. If this wasn't going to work, then she didn't need him laughing at her for trying. He could make fun of whatever she was doing *after* her attempts at it were successful. She checked again, still unable to see his face from where she sat; she'd try things out in secret.

Sitting tall, she tilted her head slightly back to ensure the forlansk wouldn't slide off. Then, dangling the silver string above her forehead she lowered it slowly, letting it curl into a pile around her eyes and hairline. She sat for a moment, checking it wouldn't move. Finally, peering down her nose, she looked dead straight at the tapestry viewing every image woven by the threads. There was the bear, the woman in red, the white goblet, and the grey dragon.

Nothing more, nothing less.

Freya hung her head and hunched over, defeated by yet

another idea at trying to figure things out. The forlansk fell, landing on the back of her hand. She would have flicked it to the ground, as was her mood, but as she spied it a thought came to her—the back.

Quickly she grabbed the forlansk and lunged at the tapestry. Turning up its lower right edge, she craned her neck looking for any signs or clues. With the forlansk in the hand she used to pull back the tapestry corners with, she reached over with her other hand and felt all along the edges, borders, and design. Nothing. She dropped that corner, and stood up on the bench to search the upper half as well. When she pulled her hand away from the bottom corner she felt the forlansk tug against it as if caught.

What she saw when assessing the snag was not what she expected. The forlansk had somehow bound itself to the silver thread of the tapestry. She yanked lightly at the forlansk, but it didn't release its hold on the threading. She yanked again, this time a bit rougher, and the forlansk came flying her way, along with the silver thread. Bolting in the direction of her forceful pull, the silver thread unraveled itself from the scene snipping free all woven strands below it.

Freya was horrified. The forlansk was destroying Erik's tapestry. She slapped at the silver thread trying to pin it in place, but it had a mind of its own. Each uncurling of its winding path cut at the woolen threads like scissors to hair. With nothing she could do but watch in mortification as fragments of color fell in its wake, tears blurred her vision. Red, from the woman's woven tunic, dropped in pieces to the floor. Clippings of the bear's fur scattered everywhere as the silver thread twisted across the scene, sending the goblet and dragon into a muted clump of white and grey.

Freya looked at the mess at her feet and let the silent tears fall.

What would Erik think? What would he say? She couldn't wake him. She didn't dare. The tapestry was ruined, his gift, her hope—gone.

She held back any sounds of sobs and fought to regain composure, but it was hard. How she would explain this to him, to herself, she didn't know. The forlansk and silver thread seemed to have tangled themselves up together, on their own. And now they both lay in the pile of clippings.

She wiped her eyes and dabbed her cheeks, then bent down to pick up the forlansk wishing somehow to scold it, if that were possible of an inanimate object. Hunched over, she brushed the wool fragments off her feet and took ahold of the forlansk. Not knowing what to do next, she stepped down from the bench and collapsed onto the chair.

Making situations worse seemed to be what she was good at. At least she hadn't hiccoughed in awhile. And the tears had stopped. But none of this made any difference to the tapestry, which had been halved in two—except—it *wasn't* halved in two.

Freya's jaw dropped. Her eyes widened. She could have kissed the forlansk! The tapestry's image wasn't ruined—it was revealed. There must have been two layers, she realized. Removing the woven wool below the silver thread gave her a perfect view of the layer that had been secretly hidden under the bear, woman, goblet, and dragon. The layer that she could now see was a wild display of reds and oranges. Fire, she guessed immediately. Or rather she hoped, as fire was something she could easily take care of. The other depiction in the tapestry was brown: a box, a rectangle. But what was it? Obviously something that burned—why else the fire? The crate of groggers? Freya wasn't sure. A stick? A tree trunk? The forest—hopefully not. A home? A hut? But why one box?

With her hope renewed in finding the way to put a stop to Ragnar, she found herself once more at a mental block. The solution was staring her in the face, she just knew it was, but interpreting that solution apparently wasn't going to be simple.

Think, think, think. She tried forcing herself to do so. What else can burn?

Books can burn.

Her book.

The Raedslen.

She had to decode it, and now. What if it held the key? What if it burned before she could read it? No, she wouldn't let that happen.

Determined these pages were the answer she was looking

for, Freya dashed over to the table and chair. Seating herself comfortably, she took out her journal and a pencil, opened the book and began.

Already informed of the first word, which she placed her finger on to keep her place, she jotted down "Raedslen" in her journal. Once she had it, she glanced to the first rune of the next word.

Freya did a double-take.

The runes where her finger was placed were dissolving into the page. Her heart raced. Was she too late in translating the book? In a panic, she picked her finger up for fear it was causing the runes to vanish. The word continued to fade from sight, but no others. Then it was gone. She waited for a reaction of some sort, a domino effect perhaps of more words to disappear—but that wasn't the case, luckily. The remainder of the page was still intact.

Freya sat back with a sense of relief. Having avoided that potentially catastrophic event she needed things now to go smoothly and calmly.

She looked down at the next word, not daring to place her finger at it. The first rune there looked like a "P." Consulting her father's key, she wrote down a "th" next to "Raedslen." The work would be tedious, but worth it. Glancing back in the book for the next rune, she saw the "P" had vanished.

"Not possible," she whispered dumbstruck.

Pen in hand, she checked the next rune. A capital looking

"R." Also an "r" according to her father. Freya positioned her pen to her journal page and readied herself to write. But she wouldn't be looking where she wrote. Instead, she was ready to see what would happen to the rune. No sooner did she begin to put ink to paper than the rune began to vanish. Her eyes widened. She tried that trick with the next rune. A letter "a" was what she should write. And she did, just as the downward f-shaped rune disappeared.

Let them vanish; she was relaxed. As long as she could get the runes decoded, she didn't care where they went.

On she went, one by one. And away the runes went, one by one.

As the hours passed, Freya grew tired, dozing periodically to give her brain a rest. She'd wake and stop only to reread what she had deciphered before decoding more, all the while figuring a way to piece everything together: the book and the tapestry. Then, as the last rune came to light, she had it. She knew how to defeat Ragnar.

CHAPTER XV

PREPARING FOR HOME

Light poured down on Freya's face, warming her cheeks and waking her slowly. Stirring gradually, her head rolled stiffly against last night's makeshift pillow constructed of the hardwood tabletop. Her back ached as well, having slept slumped over in the chair.

Smacking her mouth open and closed, she rubbed her sleepy eyes and let the world come into focus. Erik was standing at the table, mashing berries in a bowl.

"Good morning," she said, pulling her head up.

She looked tired, her eyes dark with circles, her hair uncombed, and her face filled with a yawn.

"Is it?" The curiosity to know what she had learned from the book was clear in his voice.

Freya grinned widely. And before she could say, "Yes,

indeed," his eyes lit with life.

"Liegeman's joys! I was right to believe in you, Summoned One. You will fell him...and I by your side will relish the deed. Lo, your sight—what news have you from the tapestry? The book? Have you devised a plan? And more to my interest, how may I assist?" A wicked smile spread across his lips and Freya couldn't help but bask in the glory of his enthusiasm.

She stretched her legs and arms in one final attempt to fully wake, then set forth to explain everything, but first to apologize for the destruction of his tapestry.

With a quick glance wishing to view her description, Erik interrupted her story of the woolen strands. "I see no such destruction or pilings."

"What?" She swung her head around to see if they too had vanished like the runes. They hadn't. "Look there on the bench. They're all toppled on top of each other."

"Nay. A pillow and blanket are all which occupy the bench."

"Nay right back at you." Ready to prove him wrong, she got up and grabbed a handful of the clipped threads. "This one is the forlansk, which I know you can't see," she shoved that one in her pocket, "but these—they are the bear, lady, goblet, and dragon."

Erik disagreed, shaking his head as he also approached the bench. "Here is the bear," he pointed at the tapestry. "The lady," he moved his finger to the left, "goblet, and dragon," each of which in turn he pointed to.

"Are you honestly telling me you don't see all these colors lying in my hand?" She thrust her hand closer to his face.

"I am honestly telling you I see nothing."

Words failed. Could it be this is what it meant to have the gift of sight? "Then I guess you can't see the fire or wood that replaced those four images?"

"Nay. I cannot."

"How strange," she said, pulling her hand back. What an odd feeling it was to her to be able to view things others couldn't. She tipped her palm and let the strands fall, returning them to the pile on the bench. Then with a shrug of her shoulders added, "Let's see if you notice anything different about the book."

Freya saw him eye the book, equally mystified by the occurrences she had witnessed. "The book is also different?"

"Well, it is to me." She walked over to the table and turned back a handful of blank pages. "First, remind me of what you saw last night."

"Runes, same as you."

"Ok, good. And now?"

His brows furrowed as he looked. "Nothing."

With that, she stopped leafing through the pages. "Excellent. Me too."

But her glee wasn't contagious to Erik who picked up the book and began searching for the runes himself. When no sign of them appeared, his confusion grew to agitation. "They are gone."

"Yes and no," she responded with a tap on her journal. "Now don't go asking me how it happened, because I don't know. All I can say is they vanished the minute I decoded them—but decode them I did." A growing smirk across her face told Erik the game was on and they were to be the victors.

His eyes lit up. "Then you know what they say?"

"Yes, I do," she nodded.

"Well, I am all ears." He scooped some berry compote into a bowl, then offered the helping to her.

Freya took the breakfast and began, "Ok, so it took forever for me to make any sense of what I decoded because if you remember some letters are misleading and would give me the wrong sound."

"Aye—wrathslin, Raedslen."

"Right, and so on. So, after finally getting all the letters and sounds right, this is what I got." She picked up her journal to read from it. "I'll spare you the basic blah blah about 'the Raedslen is a dragon and is very dangerous.' Onto the good stuff. Here goes.

Raedslen dragons are the only creature, man or beast, which breeds its offspring in the death Realm of Helheim. Where for other creatures, death ends in this Realm, this is where life for the Raedslen begins. It is in the deep icy fjord waters of Helheim where the Raedslen lay their eggs, using the cold to preserve their unborn young. One moon cycle must pass before the eggs can complete their final stage of incubation. During this crucial final stage, the egg must be removed from the icy waters and removed from Helheim all together. Any remaining egg left in the waters will go unhatched, and so too will the powers of that egg. From here the egg must be buried, receiving the nutrients of the soil it is buried in. It is choice of the dragon which dictates in which Realm the Raedslen will bury their eggs, though the Norns of Yggdrasil keep the Raedslen from making Midgard a choice. The dragon will remain buried for another moon cycle before digging themselves out of their earthen home. These hatched dragons are incapable of flight until full grown, which only takes a manner of days. With adulthood reached, the Raedslen will return back to Helheim to continue the cycle anew.

However, should an egg be discovered and unearthed before the moon cycle is complete, the egg will never hatch. Nesting such eggs together will call a mother dragon to her eggs. If the beast is not destroyed, she will retrieve her eggs and bury them in Helheim where they will then hatch.

To destroy the beastly Raedslen, the magic from the very fire they breathe must be contained within the weapon used to fell them. Fire Giants of Muspellheim are skilled in the art of forging weapons under the heat of Raedslen fire. These weapons become extremely powerful, for like the fire of the Raedslen, they too can destroy magic.

"Ah ha! Did you hear all of that?"

Her explosion of excitement startled Erik and he dropped his spoon of compote back onto his plate. "My ears heard the words which you said, that I can confirm. Lo, their message fails me. Do you desire defeating Ragnar by *burning* him with your fire? Alas, he is not of magic made."

"No, it's not *him* who needs to burn." She glared at him while ever so slightly lifting her eyelids higher and lower as if hinting at the answer. A few moments later his eyes widened and she knew he had it.

"We will need an army."

"Leave it to me, I know where to get one." Already packing her bag to leave, she took one last bite of the compote, then motioned for him to remove the floor covering. "You go to King Walden as planned, but bring him that egg. Tell him he needs to nest it!" She was halfway down the net ladder as she gave the instructions to Erik. "Then meet me on the hilltop above Ragnar's thorpe. Come as quickly as you can!" Now at the bottom of the ladder, she didn't bother to wait for a reply and bolted for the tree trunk door.

Outside, Freya headed straight for Harald's thorpe.

The sun was coming up and the forest was filling with light, making it easy for her to dodge fallen branches, sticky patches of efoi, and glistening spider bug webs. She ran like a deer being chased by hunters, leaping over any hurdle blocking her direct path. In no time she found herself nearing the forest's edge where the open field began to come into view. Freya charged toward that field.

Today it was empty, no Grimhild carrying firewood, no Berserk out to steal an egg, and no ring of looted gold lining the boundary of the thorpe.

It was too early, she supposed, for the villagers to be out and about, and not knowing which hut was Grimhild's and Harald's, she looked up for any signs of smoke in hopes that at least one person would already be awake who could help. The morning was hazy, making the cloudy horizon a perfect backdrop for camouflaging billowing smoke. Scanning the rooftops of the huts, she squinted in search of that smoke. The thorpe was large, housing several dozen small brown homes, but she knew to check the outer skirts of the surrounding huts for what she was looking for. Then, on the opposite side of the thorpe, something caught her eye. Freya could see it; the soft tendrils of curly white wafting toward the sky, the signature mark of the fire rooms. She knew whoever was inside cooking everyone's breakfast would be able to tell her for certain where Chieftain Harald was.

Using the trail of smoke to mark her destination, Freya raced along the edge of the thorpe heading straight for the fire rooms. The clanking of pots and crackling of the cooking fire grew louder as she approached. Those sounds were music to her ears, singing a song whose lyrics told her she was one step closer to defeating Ragnar. She bolted in through the door and without introductions and half out of breath, she ran up to the first person she saw.

"Please, I have to find Chieftain Harald. I know where Ragnar is. I have news of his plans. And I know how to stop him."

There was no need to say more. The mere mention of Ragnar's name was enough for the lady with flour on her face to throw down the dough in her hands and call to the other worker, "Finish the bread and soup." Then she motioned Freya to follow and hurriedly escorted her to a hut near the campfire and tables where she had once hid from a shadowy figure who she now knew was Erik.

"Chieftain," the woman called out. "Chieftain Harald."

The animal hide door drew to a gather on the left of the threshold pulling open like a curtain and revealing the chieftain.

One look at the little girl in jeans and a long-sleeved shirt told Harald the kitchen cook wasn't here for him.

"Freya, what is it?"

But before she could answer, a voice full of spirit called from within the hut, "Is that Freya who has come?"

Harald turned his head. "Aye, Grimmy. Come and greet our friend."

Grimhild popped into the doorway wearing a yellow tunic that was as bright as her personality. "Fire-eyed fury, you are here early. Lo, you have come a good morn, for today I detect the scent of soup and such finer grains and barely has your belly not been made full with. Why, Freya," she tilted her head just slightly, "your face looks plagued. Are you yet again lost?"

"No, nothing of the sort."

"Liegeman's joys for…"

"Please, Grimhild, I don't have time to chat. I need your help—and yours, Chieftain Harald, and all your warriors. Look, I don't know how much either one of you know about what's been going on—about Ragnar or why I'm here," she glanced at Harald whose serious demeanor made her think he was indeed fully aware of Ragnar's intentions and why exactly she was here. "But I know a way to stop Ragnar, how to defeat him and his plans."

Grimhild's eyes filled with wonderment. "A battle," she said dreamily.

"Ragnar keeps like a worm to a hidden thorpe, brewing wickedness of cast spells while conjuring groggers. He lives not ruled by Danelaw, thus accursed is he, unfit for Viking blood. Your plan, Freya: Let us gather our warriors and hear of it. Grimhild, bring forth your uncle and those of the longhouse, I shall assemble the rest. Freya; wait at the tables while we rally ourselves. We will lead out this plan of yours and crush Ragnar once and for all."

It was the reaction she had hoped for. "Thank you, thank you, thank you!" she said, departing for the tables.

"Nay, thank *you!*" Grimhild called back. "For it is to be my first battle!" There was a skip and a jump in her voice as she floated happily toward the longhouse.

Grimhild and Harald must have flown through the thorpe for Freya barely had a chance to sit and think about how to explain her plan, wishing to not eat up hours of detail on how she arrived at it, before the men started taking their places at the tables.

First came a handful of warriors, then another few here and there. Then the numbers arriving began to increase, doubling and tripling those of the original handful. By the time Grimhild returned with her uncle and father, there must have been at least seventy-five in attendance. Freya had seen a turnout of warriors in Ragnar's thorpe, but severely doubted it was as large as this. Outnumbered, she told herself, boosting her confidence that her plan would work. She smiled inwardly and waited for Harald's signal to speak.

"Clansmen," he began, "we have for too long lived in the shadows of an omen ill in nature." Grunts of agreement resonated through the convened warriors. "Prophecies that one day the Nine Realms will unite under a force battle-blood hardened have been told to us since we were wee bairns by those who heard the stories as they were wee bairns."

"The realms cannot and must not be opened," someone yelled out.

"Aye!" came an answer.

"Agreed!" said another.

"Then I counsel you," Harald's voice rose above the crowd, "to look upon the Summoned One and heed her call of action."

Freya quavered under his introduction. So he *did* know who she was. A nervous rush of sweat built up in her palms as the group fell silent and eyed her curiously. Even Grimhild, grinning widely at learning Freya was the Summoned One, was obviously in awe.

"Now," Harald gestured to Freya, "let us learn of your plan."

How she wished she had taken a class on public speaking because standing up in front of this group of Vikings, even if they *were* on her side, was rather daunting.

"Um," she slowly lifted herself from the seat. "Well, my name is Freya…and like Chieftain Harald said," she wiped her palms down the sides of her jeans, "I was summoned…by the Norns…to," a wave of heat burned inside her chest. Freya panicked. She couldn't hiccough. Not here, not now. There was no time to continue dragging out her speech. They had to act. And act sooner rather than later. She swallowed back the warmth in her throat, hoping to cool whatever fire was building, then pulled herself together and said, "Look, I'm obviously not from here, but I have the gift of sight and I know how to stop Ragnar from opening the realms. Though, I need your help to make my plan work." Pausing instinctively for a response, she couldn't believe her ears when no objections were made. She almost leapt for joy; how proud her father would be if he could see her now! "All right, here's what I'm asking. The egg from your thorpe is currently on its way to King Walden. I'm asking that he nest it, thus calling forth the mother Raedslen dragon." A squeal of excitement escaped Grimhild's lips. "But I don't know how much time that buys us."

Harald answered, "Nesting affords us little time. You can anticipate the beast's arrival by this very sun's high rise."

"So noon today, got it. Ok, then that means we have to work fast." The two cooks had come and as quietly as they could were passing around bread and soup to everyone gathered. "When the dragon comes, I need you to wait. Don't slay it. We need it. Ragnar's thorpe is at the other side of the forest, not far from Snobek Creek. There's a hill there and his thorpe lies in the valley below. That's where we need to get the dragon to go. The Raedslen's fire holds magical powers strong enough to break the spell hiding Ragnar's thorpe. Destroy that spell and Ragnar's open for attack. But be careful; he has an army himself made up of groggers." She paused. That was it to her plan. Without anything more to explain she asked, "Are there any questions?" Freya looked around like a teacher surveying her class but no one raised a hand.

Then Harald leaned her way and said rather fatherly, "You have not a sword nor spear. What powers of protection have you in battle?"

"Oh, I won't be up on the hill with you. There's something I must do first. Don't ask why, but Ragnar thinks I'm a Volva—which I'm not. He wants to be in my good graces and I need to use that to my advantage to get into his thorpe. You see, he has a ristir, which I need to destroy."

"Understood. Lo, the groggers? Have you protection?"

"I have one nogle. From Erik. Oh—please don't hurt him. I know he's a Berserk but he's the one who's gone to King Walden with your egg. Erik's been my biggest help. He's not bad or evil or anything like that."

Harald nodded gently. "You speak words my own opinions have already formed. The night he came and stole the egg, he first warned our watchman of his approach before his own form turned Berserk."

"He did that?" It was no surprise to her that Erik could act kindly, but this was the first person she'd met here who shared her view.

"Aye. Lo, I believe not that one nogle of his will suffice you in your journey. I shall offer you nogle of my own kin as well."

Freya was taken aback by his generosity and took the two bones he held out to her. In quick examination of their long thick sizing, she half wondered if this kin was of the same uncle Grimhild carried around. "Thanks." She wedged the bones past the flap of her backpack, leaving them to stick out slightly like arrows in a quiver. Then she looked back up at Harald and said, "I think it's time to get going. We don't want the Raedslen to come too soon and miss our chance at it."

"Agreed." He turned and stood tall, facing the army of men. "Let us don our gear of war with weapons of steel and nogle made. In battle blood we brave together in following the summoned Freya. Karl, remove yourself and half the men to the forest." Grimhild's uncle nodded at his name, then pointed to a group of men farthest from Harald and then to Grimhild. They all nodded in return at Karl. "Once there, await the cries of the approaching Raedslen. You know what to do thereafter to coax it to the hilltop."

"Aye," Karl's voice projected from deep within his belly. He was ready for action.

"Those with me will stand guard atop the hill. Our signal

of attack, both to the skies and to the land, will be the appearance of Ragnar's thorpe." Freya saw Grimhild light up. This was the chance she'd been waiting for, to slay a dragon. And it was Freya's chance too. With the dragon dead she'd be sent home and the curse would be reversed. "Karl and his men will bring down the Raedslen while my men rob Ragnar's thorpe of life."

A loud roar of approval burst through the warriors as if it were a battle cry itself announcing their attack to the enemy.

Harald puffed his chest like a proud peacock at the sound, then shouted with vengeance, "To the forest!"

Hiccough.

Quickly the gathering withdrew, though not silently, as the warriors rallied up their spears, axes, shields, and helmets and fell in line behind either Karl or Harald.

Freya turned her head from the commotion, covered her mouth, full well knowing the pain she was about to inflict upon herself, and coughed. Water welled in her eyes as the fire hit the skin of her palm. She swallowed back screams of agony all the while clapping to pat out the scorching blisters bubbling under the surface of her left hand. The damage was done. Luckily she had thought to cover her mouth with her left hand for surely had it been the other she wouldn't be able to hold a pen for at least a month. It was all worth it, to keep the secret from Harald's men, she thought as she wiped the tears out of her eyes. They were her ticket home, and as dragon slayers they might not take kindly to her Raedslen transformation.

Freya hurried to catch up to Harald's lead.

The group marched through the forest plowing over anything in their way, much in the style of Ragnar's men. Gone went flowers that were stomped and traipsed upon, shrubbery ripped and tore, and stones and rocks skipped in the path of the warriors whose leather shoes kicked them up. Moving an army through Walden's Forest was by no means a way for preserving the delicacy of the landscape. The only things they didn't seem to destroy were the trees.

The forest was vast and after some time, Harald finally motioned to Karl that this is where he should stay. Freya turned and saw thirty or so men fall back and remain at the spot. She continued forward but with a glance over her shoulder suddenly discovered the thirty men had vanished. Perhaps she had traveled farther than she realized and was unable to see them from where she was now. Or perhaps the forest had shifted, helping to hide the warriors from any men Ragnar might have sent into the wood. Freya chose the latter to believe, then focused her attention on following Harald, less because he seemed to know the way to Snobek Creek but more because she believed Ragnar's men could be lurking about.

The forest canopy shaded those under it, making it difficult to pinpoint the position of the sun. And without her watch, Freya wasn't sure how close to noon it was getting. She only hoped her plan was going to work.

It wasn't long before Snobek Creek came into view, with light from the forest's edge flooding the sparse trees lining it.

Harald held up his hand and the men halted. "The valley yonder, is this the one of which you speak, Freya?"

Freya nodded. "That's the one." But she wasn't eyeing the empty gorge as he was doing; she was looking elsewhere. "Erik? Are you here?" She scoured the nearby bushes in an attempt to find him. Harald and his men stood back.

"I am here." His voice unwavering, Erik appeared from behind a neighboring tree.

"Oh, excellent!" She rushed to him, ignoring the uneasiness in the air. Freya had Harald's word of honor that no harm would come to him, but never were there any promises made about the warriors trusting Erik would do the same. She could feel them on their guard but knew in her gut Erik wouldn't turn Berserk on them. "And the egg? Did you find King Walden?"

"Aye." He looked past her as he answered, his mind focused on the number of armed Vikings present. It seemed to Freya that he was calculating his odds against them.

Her brows furrowed. "That's enough!" She turned and slapped the lot of them with her scolding. "We're all on the same side. All of us! I can't have your defenses up against each other when they should be up and against Ragnar. So hug or shake hands or whatever you need to do to get your minds focused on the greater cause that is today. Got it?"

Low rumblings of heavy-voiced "Ayes" told her they got it.

"Now then," she asked Erik, "what did King Walden say?"

"He heeded your request in nesting the egg. Then counseled me its powers were indeed in effect. The Raedslen has been summoned to its unborn young and flies here as we speak."

A glazy haze formed in her sight as she stared, fully aware this was her one shot at succeeding. "Then this is it."

"Be on your way now, Freya," Harald instructed her. "If you are to make your way into the thorpe, go before it is under attack."

Erik grabbed her by the shoulders and turned her to him. "You are going into his thorpe?"

"I have to," she said, pushing away his grip.

"Then I will stand to help you."

"We can't both go. He'll never let me in if you're with me. You said yourself he thinks I'm a Volva. Well, I need to use that to my advantage in order to get the ristir from him. Now let me go; we're losing time."

Erik released his hold reluctantly and Freya wasted no time in departing. Following Snobek Creek's winding path, she led herself away from the warriors, keeping inside the forest for fear her appearance could lead Ragnar's men to Harald's hiding place.

Finally when she deemed herself amply away from them, she stepped out into the sunlight and headed slowly down the hillside.

It was obvious to her she was being watched; not only could she feel the eyes in the forest checking for her safety but she knew any approaching person to Ragnar's thorpe would not go unnoticed. And she was right.

Quickly, she fumbled at her backpack's side pocket. With her eyes on the person coming toward her, she pulled from the pocket her sister's flashlight.

"Freya, we welcome you," greeted the man with blond hair, red sideburns, and a shortened brown beard. He was a younger version of Ragnar, the nephew Askr.

Freya squared her shoulders and puffed her chest full of any and all confidence she could find, which wasn't much. "I knew all too well my welcome would be warm. After confusing me for a friend to that Berserk, you would be a fool to not welcome me here. Now take me to Ragnar; I have news."

Askr's lip curled in what Freya could only assume was a smile, then he gestured her to follow him.

Freya was in. She didn't know what he did or how he did it, nor did she care. She was in. Nor did she look over her shoulder at the hilltop. She knew her friends wouldn't be able to see her anymore and checking if she could see them would only alert the others here that her reasons for stopping by weren't what she said.

He led her to the longhouse and in doing so they passed dozens of large wooden crates. Freya knew what was in those crates but what she didn't know was why Askr zigzagged his way through the thorpe. Was he taking the long route in order to show her the vast numbers of groggers Ragnar had conjured as a means to frighten her? If so, it was working. Or, did he zigzag pass the crates because there were too many other ones blocking a more direct route? She wasn't about to ask. Small talk wasn't on her agenda and neither was doing business with Askr. She was here for Ragnar and Ragnar alone.

In the longhouse they found him seated at his table. Upon his notice of them, he rose. To her his mannerisms were fake. But, then again, she despised everything about him so nothing he could do would ever make her feel he was being genuine. Ragnar took Askr's extended arm and shook it with vigor.

"Nephew, a gift for your uncle? You bestow me with honor worthy of my praise."

"Do you see a bow on my head?" Freya snapped, her confidence growing out of sheer hate for him. "I am not your gift. I have learned you released the Berserk under false belief he is my friend. You failed my test. You thought I yelled out his name to have him saved? I spent nights debating whether or not to give you another chance. Yet the news of your groggers growing in number intrigues me and so I find myself here to view them for myself. Of course, that is, without making eye contact." A sinister smirk crept across her face as if to say she was in on Ragnar's little secret on how to avoid their spirit collection.

"Uncle, she was led past the holding crates."

"No, fool," she spat at Askr. "I didn't come here to see the boxes. I came here to see the groggers." She opened her hand and revealed the flashlight. "If one perchance removes my spirit, you Ragnar, may have my wand." She flipped the flashlight quietly on and pointed the beaming bright light at the wall. "Stand back!" she ordered. Both Ragnar and Askr, mesmerized by the sudden appearance of light, had attempted to touch it. "This is a most powerful wand. Touch its beam and suffer the consequences under the spells it casts." Freya couldn't believe her own ears; lying was either turning out to be quite easy or these two men were simply that gullible.

"A test? And if the grogger fails to snatch your spirit?" Ragnar eyed her with his question or perhaps it was her ulterior motives.

Freya put away the flashlight and took hold of a nogle. "Then I help build the army you've always wanted."

It was the smile she was waiting to see on his face, the one that said she had him hook, line, and sinker. Now all she had to do was destroy the grogger and the ristir would be hers for the destroying too.

"Nephew, bring a grogger."

Askr did as he was told and within moments a group of their men were shuffling one of the crates through the longhouse.

Oh, what had she gotten herself into? Freya's stomach rumbled with fear. If this went south no one here would save her. Without a chance to think this through, the men were already unlatching the crate's lock. Next would come the front panel in its forward fall to the floor. She stepped to the side. Everyone else stayed where they were. She knew, as she had done, that they had all cast their eyes down. Then she saw it: the brown cloak, the cracked muddied hands slightly exposed from under its long sleeves. Freya gripped the nogle tightly and forcefully took one blow at the grogger. The bone shattered right through the conjured beast, falling into a pile of dust at her feet. The grogger in turn vaporized into thin air. She felt a sigh of relief exhale her lungs. Then—

Hiccough.

Ragnar laughed it off. "She-Volvas," he said, mistaking her hiccough for nerves. On the outside Freya laughed too, but inside she was in a total panic.

"I guess that means I'll be keeping my wand."

"Aye. Lo, I recall your mention of my army." His brow raised and his smile faded.

"Indeed I did." She turned and stared at the men with the now empty crate.

Ragnar followed where she looked. "Leave us," he commanded.

Freya watched as they left, then glared at Askr. She needed everyone gone, including Ragnar once she had the ristir.

"And you as well." Ragnar's severe tone severed Askr's chance to stay, his chance to see what it was Freya could do, and the chance for him to play high authority with Ragnar. Freya was no dummy; the removal of his presence was a symbol of loss of power. By leaving, he was stepping down from position of number two and she was stepping up.

Askr hesitated. Then finally, he too slowly made his way out of the longhouse.

Freya was exactly where she wanted to be: alone with Ragnar. Everything was working out according to plan.

She took a step forward, coming nearer to where he stood, and looked him straight on. "Groggers, as you know, are conjured by magic," she began, then pointed at the ristir. "Dark magic."

Ragnar said nothing.

"But to build an army the size you need would take too long if you wish to act quickly. I can help you act quickly. My wand can alter the ristir without changing the spell you read from its runes."

"Ha! Are you now both Volva and Dark Elf?"

"Never you mind what my pedigree is."

Something in her words, or lack thereof, got his attention.

"Continue," he prompted. And she did.

"I can arrange the ristir to conjure ten times the number of groggers you currently create."

Ragnar shifted. It was a good deal and she knew he was interested. "What price must be paid for the bargain you offer?"

Price? Freya faltered. She hadn't thought he'd need to pay for the upgrade. But if she didn't require something in return, then perhaps he'd become suspicious.

A commotion was building up outside the longhouse. Freya broke her concentration and looked at the door. People were passing hurriedly by, each exchanging words with the next but luckily no one was coming in.

"The price, Freya?"

All confused, she turned back to him though not sure what to say.

"RAEDSLEN!" yelled a man's voice into the longhouse.

Without looking, she knew instantly the voice to be "Askr."

"Done."

Freya did a double-take. "Done?" What was done?

Ragnar's eyes narrowed; the deal was as good as sealed for him. "Askr, in exchange for your powers."

"Uncle, did you not hear?" Askr had entered the longhouse and was approaching quickly. "A Raedslen flies above, bringing Harald's dragon slayers in its path."

Ragnar looked up as if he could see beyond the roof. "The protection field."

"Release the groggers, Uncle. We will fell Harald's warriors."

Hiccough.

Freya's eyes widened. Time was not on her side. "The ristir, Ragnar. Give me the ristir and I'll get you more groggers."

Screams and yelling swirled amongst the uproar and chaos taking place outside the door.

"Uncle!"

"Our deal, Ragnar," she hissed at him.

A hot flame shot with fury through the smoke hole in the roof.

The Raedslen had broken the field.

That was the signal. Harald's men knew to go and would be swooping down on the now-visible thorpe. She needed that ristir.

"Come away! Your sword, Uncle. Take it and hide yourself."

Ragnar stared down his nose at Askr. "You would see me go and claim victory to this battle. You would have yourself lead my men to battle!"

Askr shook his head. "Nay, Uncle, you have it wrong."

"Wrong am I, you say?" His eyes widened with anger.

302

"Do with him as you please," he blared at Freya. Then grabbing ahold of his sword he pulled the ristir from his neck and threw it for Freya to catch. "A thousand-fold I seek. You say you will expand my army? Expand them now!" With that he stormed out of the longhouse, his sword gripped ready for battle.

But Askr didn't storm out after him. Instead, he turned and eyed the ristir in Freya's hand.

"Do *what* with me as you please?"

Hiccough.

Sounds of metal striking metal broke through the roars of yelling outside. Harald's men were here. But inside they were nowhere to be found. The door to exit was at the opposite end of the longhouse and too far to get at before Askr could get her.

"Stand back, Askr!" She held the ristir high at arm's length but it didn't intimidate him.

A loud screech from the sky above pierced her ears. She shirked back. The Raedslen had been hit. "Die," she wanted to yell out at the dragon. She could see her family waiting for her with open arms. Her stomach tightened. She didn't need a rescue party; she needed the dragon dead, she needed to be saved by going home.

Hiccough.

Askr raised his own sword, its shiny frame reflecting the fear on her face.

Another ear-piercing screech took them both off guard. Fire shot through the smoke hole catching the thatched roof ablaze.

Freya hurled the ristir up into the flames, then drew a breath so deep she almost knocked herself over. The breath she held, while resisting all itching desires to hiccough, filled her lungs with heat like an engine getting more coal. She counted to three in her head and in one forceful release, blew a mighty flame directly at the ristir. It struck.

"A Raedslen," she heard Askr snarl. "I should have known."

The ash of the ristir and ceiling came falling down on their heads but Freya knew she couldn't stand by and watch; Askr's sword was still raised.

Pulling her eyes from the scene above, she went to catch his next move just as a spear hurled the length of the longhouse rocketed toward the sky. In a moment well calculated she saw the underbelly of the dragon come into view—the spear penetrating the scaly flesh.

A loud screech of pain rang through the clouds.

Into the burning opening came the dragon's hind talon covered in the dripping blood of its belly. It searched for footing on the fragile roof as another spear drilled a deathly blow to its chest. Down fell the beast, slowing its descent with a last beat of its wings. Freya and Askr dashed away, both avoiding its crushing weight. Only Askr ran for the door and

Freya found herself pinned at the back wall.

A burning shot through her side. She was never so grateful for a stomachache in all her life. "I'm going home!" she shouted happily.

"Freya?"

Freya tried peering over the dragon's tail, its body filling the longhouse. "Grimhild? Is that you?"

"Do not you see a felled dragon? Of course it is me! Oh, what wondrous day! Father is robbing life of this thorpe and I have felled my first dragon!"

Beams holding the disintegrating roof came crashing down upon the Raedslen.

"Can you help me get out of here? I can't find a way around."

An arm reached over the meaty tail, followed by a head.

"Erik!" Freya held up her hand and he grabbed it, pulling her up over the tail. "We did it!" she exclaimed, throwing a hug around his neck before she even reached the ground.

"You, Summoned One. It was all you."

"That's not true. Without you I'd..." Freya doubled over in pain. She tried to smile and assure him her leaving was perfect timing, but the pain was too intense.

Erik stood back. All he could do was watch.

"I'm going...home...Erik," she said through clenched teeth.

He nodded. "Aye. Let it be for good."

"It...is...good. I want...to thank..."

All went black. Freya was falling...up. The speed at which she was ascending sent wind stretching her face and pulling her hair. Then suddenly it stopped. Her feet were on solid ground—grassy ground of the National Viking Graveyard.

"I'M HOME!!!!" More excitement couldn't have filled her, not even if her teacher told her she'd never have to take another science class again. She jumped up with happiness and clicked her heels together. Only she missed and came thudding down to the ground. Freya's laughter filled the graveyard. She didn't care that she had missed. She didn't care that she had fallen. She was home. Well, almost. Freya got to her feet and bolted for her house. She had dreamt this day would come. She zipped passed a cluster of old-styled thatch-roofed houses, flew over Salt Creek's wooden bridge, and whizzed by tree-lined fields before eyeing her own home.

The family car wasn't in the drive. No worries; they'd be home soon, she told herself. Freya dashed open the back kitchen door and ran upstairs to her room. She pulled off her backpack and dumped its contents onto her bed. The nogle, which landed on her bed, she decided would be best to hide as she wasn't exactly sure how to answer the questions of what she was doing with some dead uncle's bones. Then she heard the sound of car doors closing.

"Father! Mother! I'm home!" All the yelling, all the

forceful blow of air from her lungs, produced no fire. No hiccoughs. No transformations.

"Freya? Is that you?" Her mother's voice choked back from emotion.

"It is! I'm home for good!"

She turned quickly and grabbed the nogle, which hit the *Raedslen* book which was open to where she had left off transcribing. She tossed the bones under her bed and far away from sight but failed to see the open book lying on her bed full of newly appeared runes.

Grinning from ear to ear in eager excitement to reunite with her family, she called out, "I'm coming!" Then raced downstairs and into the arms of her parents.

about the author

Story time had always been K.W. Penndorf's favorite "subject" in school. But when her second grade teacher opted to read from a tattered old diary, K.W.'s view on books changed forever. Books were now alive, with adventures, dilemmas, faraway locations, heroes, villains, drama, and quite frankly, story. Everything was so real, well, at least in her imagination. She wanted to live in those stories…and she has.

In her senior year of high school, K.W. interned at CBS three days a week, making sure to keep her grades up or the gig would be off. By the sheer nature of the job, stories surrounded her there. In college, she spent a semester abroad living with her sister and brother-in-law in Denmark—where, yes, one can only imagine the crazy stories two sisters conjured up! Then after college, she moved to Germany, and at the age of 25, she opened her own company—a language school, full of (you guessed it) stories. At 29, she moved back to the States, bringing home with her the greatest story and souvenir ever—her husband.

On a train ride into New York City, a vision came to K.W.'s sleepy commuter mind: a girl finding a dragon egg in the middle of a Viking graveyard. Presto! The premise for her debut novel was born—a story that K.W. hopes will change a child's view on books forever.

CPSIA information can be obtained
at www.ICGtesting.com
Printed in the USA
FSOW01n0140210716
22802FS